LYNN RICHARDSON

SCRATCH-OFF

A NOVEL

This is a work of fiction. Names, characters, places, and incidents are the products of the author's imagination or are used fictitiously. Any resemblance to actual events, locales, or persons, living or dead, is entirely coincidental.

Copyright © 2020 Lynn Richardson
All rights reserved.
ISBN-13: 9798649355100

With thanks to Lauren Brewer

1
Just Be a Man

Janet stood at her bathroom mirror dabbing at her puffy eyes with a cold washcloth, but it didn't seem to be doing any good. She tossed the wet cloth into the corner of the vanity and thought about putting on some mascara, but the only tube she could find, in the back of a drawer, was old and dried out. She chunked it into the wastebasket.

"I'm going to be late for school, Lucy," she said to her new puppy. "I'll have to think of a good excuse to tell my students."

The little dachshund looked up and squatted, leaving a small puddle on the floor. Then she padded through it, leaving little wet paw prints.

"I forgot to put you outside. I'm sorry."

They stepped outside together and Janet stood on her patio while the pup sniffed the dewy grass. After making another puddle and leaving a small deposit in the grass, Lucy scrambled awkwardly toward Janet who scooped her up and kissed the top of her little head. As Janet stared across her back yard, puppy in hand, she saw movement. The tarantula was back, slowly making its way across the wooden fence which separated her yard from the woods behind her.

The image was unsettling, especially given her fragile state of mind. *Damn you, Lee. Why couldn't you have stepped up like a man?*

The tarantula's first appearance had been yesterday evening, ultimately causing her breakup with Lee, her boyfriend of fourteen months. The freakishly overgrown spider had emerged from nowhere and scooted aimlessly across her concrete patio where she and Lee were having a beer in the gathering nightfall. Janet spotted it first and grabbed Lee by the arm.

"Holy shit!" she shrieked. "What's that?"

"Looks like a tarantula," he replied, scooting his lawn chair back a bit. "Probably a male, looking for a mate."

"Well, kill it!"

"What? Why?"

"Kill it, Lee! I don't want that thing in my yard!" She grabbed a broom and shoved it at him. "Here. Use this."

Lee sat unmoving. "He's not going to hurt anyone, Janet."

"But…you…what if…" Janet stammered. Irked with Lee's typical passive behavior, she took matters into her own hands and raised the broom to whack the thing but realized that smashing it would leave a big splat of guts on her nice patio. So instead, she held the handle and extended the broom toward the creature, hoping it would hop on and she'd carry it away. The tarantula complied, and Janet walked cautiously toward the fence, but it suddenly got excited and began to scamper up the broom handle. She screamed bloody murder and hurled both the broom and the tarantula over the fence and flailed her hands in disgust, and then charged toward Lee in a fury.

"I can't believe you made me do that! You never even left your chair! What's the matter with you?"

Amused, Lee started to laugh, which was the wrong thing to do. Janet's face grew dark with rage, which proved ineffective in the twilight. She pounded her fists against Lee's chest and ran crying into the house, leaving him bewildered on the patio. When he came inside she continued to bawl and threw his car keys at him.

"Go! Just go! Leave me alone!"

Lee went from perplexed to defensive. "What did I do?"

"It's what you *didn't* do, Lee! I'm tired of you disappointing me! Why can't you just act like a man?"

Lee sputtered, unable to speak.

"Just go, and don't come back. We're done."

"We're done? Because of that spider?"

"It wasn't a *spider*, Lee. It was a grown-ass blood-sucking tarantula and you just sat there, too lazy to help me. What if Lucy had sniffed at it?"

Lee's jaw dropped. "I'm sorry, Janet. I didn't know…"

"That's just it, Lee. You *don't* know. You don't know me at all!" She sucked in a big shaky breath. "We aren't right for each other. I'm sorry, but this is over. Please leave. Now." She wiped her tears with the hem of her tee shirt, baring her tummy.

"You look like you've lost weight," Lee ventured, trying to appease her.

"Shut up! Get out!" Janet gave him a shove. "And don't call me!"

That was just last night, and her emotions were still raw from the upset. And now the creepy arachnoid was back to further torment her. If she were brave enough she'd swat it or spray it with something but she wasn't about to get that close, having heard that tarantulas can jump, and that was enough information to keep her at bay. And anyway, her broom was on the other side of the fence.

She made a mental note to call an exterminator and went back inside, carefully placing Lucy in her crate. "You be a good little girl, okay? I'll come home at lunch to check on you like I always do. You've got food and water, and here's your toy." Janet tossed a red squeaky toy toward the pup as Lucy whined her disapproval at being locked up.

As Janet closed the front door she remembered that today would be the last day to make the obligatory drive home during her lunch break. After today, school was out for the summer.

Her Ford Bronco was low on gas but there was enough in the tank to get her to school. She'd fill up later. She backed out of her driveway, admiring her neat and tidy home, a recent purchase that came with a frightening mortgage.

She looked in the rear-view mirror and flinched at her still red and puffy eyes. She slid on her sunglasses for the drive, which gave her an idea. *I'll take my class outside first thing and let them walk around the track —*

let them use their ear buds and listen to some music. That way, I won't have to explain my sunglasses.

As Janet drove the three mile commute to school her thoughts involuntarily turned back to Lee, and she cringed at the memory of the breakup. It had been sudden, unrehearsed, and harsh. The stunned look on his face and the wetness in his eyes had been painful to see. His voice had cracked as he said goodbye standing on the bottom step of her front porch, his hands in his pockets, looking so dejected.

She had wanted to tell him that it wasn't all about the tarantula, but it was just easier to lay the blame there. There was so much wrong with their relationship; her frustrations had been steadily mounting for months. Still, unraveling the way she had, unleashing her anger so unexpectedly, wasn't her nature and she had broken Lee's heart. She had gone to bed feeling callous and heartless and, as a result, had cried buckets of tears into her pillow.

∼

Fran Goldstein used her backside to push through the double glass doors of Hattie Reed Middle School, where she was greeted with the familiar smell of cafeteria lunches and musty books and sweaty kids. Her purse swung from the crook of her arm, throwing her a little off balance as she carried three large bakery boxes filled with cookies.

Sue Ellen Pack, the school's secretary and Fran's good friend, was already situated at her desk in the front office, peering at her computer screen. Fran paused in the doorway to say good morning and Sue Ellen waved her inside, so Fran set the cookies down and fanned herself with her cotton blouse. "Can you believe the humidity out there? It's not even summer yet, officially."

"What's in the boxes?" Sue Ellen asked.

"Cookies. For my students." Fran paused. "I figure they deserve a treat after putting up with me all year."

"Can I have one?"

"No, you may not. Why'd you wave me in here? What's up?"

"Janet called in. She's going to be late."

"So?"

"So, she didn't sound good. She sounded like she had been crying."

"Hm. Did she say what was wrong? Is she sick or something?"

"No, she said that she just needed a little extra time to get ready. But she is definitely upset about something," Sue Ellen said decisively. "Teachers don't come in late on the last day of school. Or they shouldn't."

"Well, it's none of our business. Janet is a big girl."

"I know. She's like, six feet tall."

"What I mean is, she can take care of herself without you mothering her. If she wants to tell us what's wrong, she will," Fran surmised.

The desk phone buzzed and Sue Ellen picked up the receiver with agitation.

"Hattie Reed Middle School, this is Mrs. Pack," she answered in a fake, sing-song voice. "No, I'm sorry, Mrs. Fischer, the principal isn't in just yet. Can I help you with something?" *Pause.* "I see. I understand that you are upset, but this sounds like something that should have been discussed with Ryan's teacher, weeks ago." *Pause.* "No, it's too late for extra credit. Ryan should have done the class work." *Pause.* Sue Ellen rolled her eyes in frustration. "What are his options? There are no options. Grades are posted."

Fran smiled at her red-faced friend who was doing her best to calm the angry parent.

"Mrs. Fischer, I don't appreciate that kind of language. I'm just telling you what I know. If you'd like to leave a message for Principal Edwards, I'm sure he'd be happy to call you back."

Fran gave Sue Ellen a knowing smile and gathered up her cookies and her purse and mouthed "later" as she backed out the door, continuing down the hallway. *Just one more day*, she told herself. *One more day.* She reveled in the quiet as her sandals slapped against her heels and echoed in the empty hallway. It would be about fifteen minutes before the buses arrived – just enough time for a cup of coffee.

She paused at her classroom door where the plastic sign still hung by one screw despite her many work order requests. *Room 112, Math.* Fran had taught math at Hattie Reed for thirty-six years now, and her retirement loomed before her like a bright and shiny star. She switched on the lights, set her items down, and hurried to the teachers' lounge to make coffee, pleased to find the coffee pot already full. Rustling sounds came from the corner pantry and Aimee Burke stepped out, her hands full of coffee stirrers and sugar packets. Startled by Fran's sudden appearance, Aimee yelped and dropped most everything on the floor.

Fran bent down to help her gather things up. "Sorry to scare you, hon. What are you doing here so early?"

"I couldn't sleep last night. I've been awake since 1:30 so I thought I'd come on in."

Behind Aimee's glasses Fran saw the dark circles under her eyes. Aimee was the school's music teacher and the newest teacher on staff, having been there only a year. She was a timid, jumpy little thing, from Fran's perspective.

Fran poured Aimee a cup of coffee and one for herself. "Janet is going to be a little late today. Would you mind keeping an eye on her first class until she gets here?"

"Sure, I can do that."

"I'd do it, but your room is so much closer." With that, Fran retreated into the hallway. "Coffee's good! Thanks!" she hollered over her shoulder.

Aimee slowly made her way to her own small cubicle in a corner of the band room. She sat down and reached back to gather her long, straight hair into a pony tail, securing it with a rubber band from her desk drawer. She had hoped to talk with Janet early, before the first bell, to see if she might want to plan something for next week. Maybe see a movie or have lunch together. Aimee liked Janet, or "Coach Janet" as her adoring students called her. The good-natured gym teacher with the easy smile had always spoken kindly to Aimee, making her feel like one of the gang.

Aimee's thoughts were interrupted by the first bell. The buses had arrived and the hallways were alive with happy chatter and slamming lockers. Aimee's students filed in with no intention of learning anything, their minds on summer vacation. Some had deliberately disregarded the dress code. She left her room to peek on Janet's class in the gymnasium and was surprised to see Janet already there, herding her students outside. She returned to the band room feeling restless, just like her students. She went through the motions of taking inventory of the band instruments while the kids helped to clean up the room and, when there was nothing left to do, she allowed them to talk quietly among themselves, listening to music and playing board games.

Aimee tidied up her desk and thought sadly about the long summer that lay ahead, with nothing fun planned.

I hate my life, she mused. *I'm pathetic.*

~

During lunch break, as her tank filled with gasoline, Janet sat in the driver's seat of her Bronco with the door open and her face aligned with the cold air blowing from the air conditioner vent. She grabbed a handful of her thick, dark hair and twisted it into a knot, securing it with a pencil from the console.

"Gonna be a hot summer, ain't it?" a voice spoke out.

Janet looked up to see a grinning young man with bad teeth and a ragged truck on the other side of the gas pumps. He couldn't have been more than twenty, with sun-baked, sinewy arms.

"Yeah, I'm afraid it will be," Janet replied. "Wish it would rain."

"Not me. I'm a roofer. C'aint work in the rain, and I need to work."

"Wow," she commented. "I can't imagine being on a roof all day in this heat. How do you do it?"

"It's all I ever done. Ever since I's sixteen."

"I guess you're used to it, then, but it must be hard work," Janet said as her gas pump clicked off.

"Yes, ma'am."

Janet flinched. Twice this week she'd been "yes, ma'amed" by someone other than her students.

"Well, you have a good day and be careful out there," she said cheerfully. "Drink lots of water."

"Yes, ma'am. Gatorade. You have a good day, too."

Craving a Coke Icee, Janet counted her blessings as she headed inside the station. Compared to that young man, she had it easy - a job she loved in air-conditioned surroundings, reliable transportation, and now a new house. She'd worked hard for those things, but that young man had worked hard, too. Maybe she took too much for granted. Maybe she should spend more time being thankful for her cushy life and less time wishing for more, namely, someone to share it with. But was it so wrong to long for that?

As Janet stood in line with her Icee she watched a wiry little woman pay for a bag of Skittles and two Arkansas Scholarship Lottery tickets, leaving her to wonder why someone would throw away their hard-earned money on the unlikely chance of striking it rich. What were the chances that those tickets would pay off? If anything, that little woman would be lucky to break even.

Janet stepped up to the clerk with her drink, trying not to stare at the three silver studs lanced through one of his eyebrows, making him look like an edgy Gomer Pyle.

"Will that be all?" asked the clerk.

"Yes, that's all," Janet replied. "Actually, that's not all," she blurted, surprising herself. "I'll take one of those tickets like that lady just bought."

"Over there." He pointed to a countertop display showcasing no less than twenty different scratch-off tickets to choose from, in bright colors with names like "Pot of Gold" and "Ultimate Cash," each crying out for attention.

"Which one?" the clerk wanted to know.

"I'm not sure. I've never bought one before."

The man in line behind Janet cleared his throat, prompting her to hurry up.

"I'll take that one," Janet said. "Number fifteen."

Number fifteen was a bright green card with brassy yellow lettering boasting a top prize cash payout of $100,000 to a lucky winner with the right numbers. He tore one off for Janet.

"That'll be $10.00. $11.72, with the Icee."

Janet paid with exact change and Gomer muttered a perfunctory, "Good luck."

"Thanks, I'll need it," Janet replied as she pushed through the door. "I never win anything."

The humidity smacked her in the face and the roofer was gone. She sat in her hot car fanning herself with the ticket, and felt a brief rush of excitement at the thought of winning some cash. But just as quickly, buyer's remorse set in and she wished she had her ten dollars back. Now that she had a mortgage, she'd have to be more frugal with her money.

She dropped the lottery ticket into her purse and involuntarily checked her phone to see if Lee had texted. He had not. She hoped he was okay. As she drove, Janet allowed herself the memories.

In their early days of dating she had thought Lee might be "the one." She had seen him for the first time at a girls' soccer match which she was coaching. He sat on the sidelines in a folding chair, seemingly by himself, his long legs stretched out in front of him. He looked to be Janet's age, lanky with a boyish face. She noticed that he was cheering for the opposing team.

After the match he stayed long after the other parents had drifted back to their cars, busying himself with picking up bits of trash and dropping them into a trash receptacle. Janet, toting her gym bag and two soccer balls, called out to him. "Thanks for helping out!"

He looked up and smiled, then came walking toward her. He shyly introduced himself. "I'm Lee. Lee Harris. My niece is the goalie for the other team," he said, almost apologetically.

"I'm Janet Kayler. Nice game. And your niece played like a beast. Her team deserved to win. But don't tell her I said so."

Lee smiled again, just a flicker. He seemed unsure of himself but his face was kind. Janet saw reddish hair poking out from beneath his ball cap. They walked together to the parking lot, their two vehicles the last ones there. As she threw her gear into her trunk space, Janet noticed that Lee towered over her by several inches, which was a pleasant surprise. She closed the door to the cargo area, fiddling with her car keys to stall a bit.

Lee cleared his throat. "I was just wondering…would you like to meet up sometime? For coffee or something?" His eyes never met hers; they looked to some far-off, important place on the other side of the soccer field.

Janet smiled at the memory. She had found his shyness endearing. "That would be nice," she had answered. "What do you have in mind?"

"Whatever you want," he replied.

And while Janet would have preferred that he suggest a place, she took the lead and said, "Do you drink beer?"

"Yeah. Sure."

"I could use a beer right now," she added, feeling flirty. "You wanna' meet me at The Bottleneck? It's close."

"Sounds good. I'll see you there in a few minutes."

"Wait," Janet hesitated. "How old are you, Lee?"

"I'm twenty-six."

"Oh. I'm almost thirty."

"Okay." He seemed unfazed.

That was last spring. They'd had a good run. But now it was over.

~

The final bell rang at the end of the day, officially turning the students loose for the summer. They bolted to the waiting cars and buses, some hopping on bicycles, pedaling like their lives depended on it.

"Have a good summer, y'all!" Janet called out. She gathered up the gifts and cards on her desk and placed them in the cardboard box which held her other personal items. She hoisted the box, grabbed her purse with one finger, turned out the lights with her shoulder and pulled the door shut. She was a mix of emotions as she approached her vehicle in the parking lot.

Fran stood waiting, leaning against her Honda Accord, flicking ashes from her cigarette.

"Hey, Fran," Janet said, without enthusiasm.

"Why the face?"

"I don't know," Janet whined. "I always feel a little sad when school ends."

"What say we celebrate?"

"Celebrate? What do you have in mind?"

"You have a swimming pool at your new house, right?"

"Yes, an above ground pool," Janet replied cautiously.

"Would you be up to some uninvited company?"

"What, today? You want to come over and swim?"

"I was thinking you and me and Sue Ellen and Aimee."

"Aimee?"

"Sure, why not? She seems nice and she doesn't seem to have any friends."

"Do they know about this?"

"No, I just thought of it, but it's a damn good idea. I'd love to see your new house."

"It's small. Nothing fancy."

"Yeah, but you've got a pool. And a new puppy."

Janet scratched her arm with her car keys, considering Fran's suggestion. "Do you think they'll want to come?" she asked, referring to Sue Ellen and Aimee.

Fran blew smoke straight up into the air. "Why wouldn't they?"

As if on cue, Sue Ellen exited the school huffing and puffing with a big box in her arms, followed by Aimee with her own box.

Fran met them head-on. "Janet is having a swim party at her house. 5:00. Be there."

Aimee's face transformed into a big smile. Sue Ellen's, too. Janet seemed a little caught off guard but played along. "I can grill some burgers and hot dogs."

"I'll bring potato salad," Fran said. "And I've got half of a cheesecake in my refrigerator."

"I'll bring chips and drinks," Aimee said.

"And I'll bring cookies," Sue Ellen set her box down to clap. "Oh, this will be fun! We can talk trash about the other teachers."

2
Maybe You're Too Picky

Two hours later the women relaxed on Janet's patio, savoring the aroma of grilled hamburgers and hot dogs. Aimee sat cross-legged on a recliner.

"What kind of cookies are these? They're really good."

"Cherry Winks," Sue Ellen called out from the pool, her large bosom bobbing in front of her. "The grandkids love them. They ask me to make them all the time."

"They are tasty," Janet agreed. "And your potato salad is good, too, Fran."

"That's not *her* potato salad," Sue Ellen scoffed. "She picked it up at Handy's Market and put it in a bowl. Didn't you, Fran? I'll bet the empty container is in your car."

"Did not," Fran retorted from her recliner where she lay in a navy blue and white striped one piece, her salt and pepper hair glistening in the sun. Smoke curled from a half-smoked cigarette in one hand while the other hand held a clear plastic glass of bourbon and Coke.

"Sure you did. Handy's makes their potato salad with extra big chunks of egg, and they use dill pickles instead of sweet. Everyone knows you don't put dill pickles in potato salad. It came from Handy's, I guarantee it," Sue Ellen insisted.

"No one cares, Sue Ellen," Fran replied without opening her eyes. "Did I tell you guys that I signed up with an on-line dating service?"

"No! How is that going?" Janet wanted to know.

"It's been a waste of money. There's nobody out there who meets my qualifications."

"Which are?"

"No older than sixty-five. No beer gut. Must be a good kisser and must like to cook. No ear or nose hair. Preferably Jewish."

"Maybe you are being a little too picky," Aimee suggested meekly.

"Well, if I can't be picky, then what's the point of paying for a dating service? I can go to a hardware store and find at least three almost suitable men on any given day."

"Is that what you do on weekends? Hang out in hardware stores?" Sue Ellen teased.

"No, dummy. Well, sometimes," Fran admitted. "Other times I just wait for the phone call."

Sue Ellen looked puzzled. "What phone call?"

"You know, the scammers. The unlisted numbers. I hang up if it's a woman, of course, but the last one I got was from a gentleman named Kabir, calling to talk about my extended warranty. We hit it off right away."

"How do you mean?" Aimee asked.

"You know, there was some flirting. I gave him a compliment, he gave me a compliment." Fran tapped her cigarette ashes into her empty glass.

Janet shook her head. "Fran, you shouldn't…"

"What happened then?" Sue Ellen prodded.

"He hung up. They almost always do. But I feel good about Kabir." Fran lay back in her chair and smiled contentedly. "He'll call back."

"Geez, Fran," Sue Ellen stated, glancing worriedly at the others. "He might live on your block, right down the street. He might be a serial killer. Have you thought about that?"

Fran only shrugged.

Janet changed the subject. "Does anyone want another hot dog or burger? There's plenty left." She was wearing a worn gray sports bra with red nylon gym shorts, her strong shoulders tinged with sunburn.

"I'll eat another hot dog," Sue Ellen called out. "Is there a charred one?"

"Here's one," Janet said, handing it to Sue Ellen on a paper plate with a dollop of mustard.

"Ooh, that's perfect!" Sue Ellen reached for the plate while clinging to the side of the pool.

"Born to be wild," Fran muttered.

"This is fun!" Sue Ellen exclaimed. She wore a polka-dot one piece with a skirt over her ample body. "I haven't been in a pool in years! Dillard used to take me to Branson and we'd get a motel with a swimming pool, and we'd jump in together holding hands."

"That's really sweet, Sue. If you're seven." Fran never missed an opportunity to needle her friend. She turned to Janet. "Are you going to tell us why you were late to school today and why your eyes were red?"

"What?" Janet asked.

"You're not a crier. Does it have to do with that boyfriend of yours? What's his name?"

"His name is Lee. And he's not my boyfriend. At least, not anymore."

"Oh, I'm sorry, Janet. What happened?" Sue Ellen asked between bites.

"I broke up with him. Last night." The others waited. "I don't know… I mean, the longer we were together, the more I realized that Lee is just not a good match for me."

"I could have told you that," Fran declared. "I met him that one time, at Office Depot. Remember?"

Janet sighed. "Yes, I remember."

Fran went on to tell the story. "So I go to Office Depot to get a new printer and I see Janet talking with this tall guy wearing a red and black shirt and I think, *Hey, there's Janet! I wonder what she's doing here!* And she introduces me to this guy as her boyfriend, Lee."

"So he works there, at Office Depot?" Aimee asked.

"He does," Janet nodded.

"So anyway," Fran went on, "I ask him to show me a cheap printer and by the time he explains all of the features - and I mean *all* of them - and reads the complete warranty out loud, my eyes are glazed over."

Aimee giggled.

"He's really smart, though," Janet said defensively. "He's got a college degree. He's just kind of nerdy when it comes to electronics. He takes his job seriously."

"So you broke up with him because he's a nerd?" Sue Ellen wanted to know.

"No, I broke up with him because he's boring. And he's kind of a wimp. He never wanted to do anything fun or adventurous!"

"How do you mean?" Aimee asked.

"Golf is the only sport he likes, and he doesn't even play the game! He just likes watching it on TV. Can you imagine anything more tedious?"

"No," they all replied in unison.

Janet turned thoughtful. "We didn't have anything in common. When we first started dating I asked him if he liked to run and he said, 'What do you mean?' and I said, 'You know, do you like jogging in your neighborhood?' And he said, 'Sure, I run all the time.' I was so happy to hear that. Finally, a running partner! But he was lying. He didn't like to run at all. He always had an excuse not to go with me. He didn't even own any jogging shoes!" Janet sighed loudly. "I can't get him out of the house. Just last weekend I asked him to go with me to the garden center to pick out some plants for my flowerbeds, and he said, 'Your flowerbeds look fine just like they are.' My flowerbeds are bare. There's only mulch."

"He sounds lazy," Fran frowned as she shook a cigarette from her pack.

"No kidding. I mean, Lee treated me well, as boyfriends go. And he was a good kisser, too. But he just didn't have any ambition. No passion about anything. I don't think we ever once had a fight, and I *really* wanted to have a fight!" Janet nibbled on a Cherry Wink. "But he was considerate, and he was polite, and he liked my parents, although they weren't crazy about him. My dad called Lee an underachiever; my mom thought he was dull and asked me if he was anemic. But he did bring me little gifts from the store," Janet added, as if that negated everything else.

"What kind of gifts?"

"Like, you know, packages of Post-it notes where the cellophane was torn, or scissors from the clearance bin. He was really thoughtful like that."

Fran snorted into her second bourbon and Coke.

"He sounds nice," Aimee stated. "What kind of things did you want to do, that he didn't want to do?"

"Besides jogging? Well, you know how I love being outside, how I love a good challenge or a competition, but Lee, he'd rather be inside working a jigsaw puzzle or watching golf or folding my towels. Can you believe that? As long as he was with me, he was happy, which is sweet, but that doesn't necessarily make for a good boyfriend. I mean, is it too much to ask to want to get out of the house? Take me to watch a ball game! Take me fishing! Take me *somewhere*!"

"Did you ever try to talk with him about it? About being more outgoing?"

"Sure I did! Day before yesterday I told him that he needed to step things up, to be more spontaneous and add some spice to our relationship, and you know what he did?"

"What did he do?" All eyes were on Janet.

"Well, I had to drop him off at work because his car was in the shop, and when I pulled up to the front of the store he turned and lunged for me and started trying to make out and paw at me, right there in the Office Depot parking lot at 7:40 in the morning."

Fran cackled. Aimee giggled again.

"That must have felt awkward," Sue Ellen surmised, frowning.

"No shit. It was ridiculous. That's when I decided that Lee is emotionally immature. I knew that I couldn't be with him any longer." Having said that, Janet decided not to tell about the tarantula scenario. It was too embarrassing.

"So are you happy that you dumped him?"

"I don't feel good about it, but I don't regret it. I'd rather stay single for the rest of my life than be with someone who bores me to death."

"So then why were you crying, honey?" Sue Ellen wanted to know.

"Because I think I broke his heart!" Janet exclaimed. "And it's not my nature to hurt other people. Lee is a good guy. He never mistreated me. He was kind. What if I never meet anyone who loves me like he did?"

"Don't sell yourself short, Janet," Fran said. "You deserve better and you'll find it."

"But how do you know that?"

"We are not meant to live our lives for others. Your soulmate is out there. You just haven't met him yet."

"That's exactly what my mother said!" Janet declared, her eyes wide.

"Your mother was right," Fran said. "And if it will make you feel better, you can always have another talk with Lee when you're not so emotional. Explain to him why you don't want to be a couple anymore."

Janet pressed her lips together and nodded. "Yeah, I probably should do that. Well. Enough about me. Let's get in the pool!"

She climbed the short pool ladder and did a cannon ball, sending a wall of water over Fran, who yelped and jumped in, as well. Aimee executed a dainty hop from the ladder, barely making a splash in the water. The foursome whooped and sputtered and formed a circle, treading water together. Aimee's long hair lay plastered against her face and shoulders. She tried to wipe the lenses of her glasses and smooth her billowing tank top while reaching for a raft. The others grappled for the rafts and inner tubes while Lucy barked and wagged her tail with excitement.

"So what is everyone doing this summer?" Janet asked, tossing her thick, dark hair away from her face.

Sue Ellen spoke first. "Dillard and I are taking the grandkids to Dollywood in July. We go every summer."

"Don't you think they're getting too old for Dollywood?" Fran questioned her. "Hell, they were too old *last* summer. Why don't you take them somewhere different?"

While Sue Ellen thought about that, Fran outlined her summer plans. "I'm going to sleep in every morning and then I'm going to watch 'The View' and drink my coffee, and I'll tend to my vegetable garden and do some flea marketing, and after my nap I'll watch

'Judge Judy' and have a cocktail." She nodded. "And maybe I'll go visit my sister in Bella Vista."

"What kind of vegetables do you grow in your garden?" Aimee asked.

Sue Ellen snorted. "Fran doesn't have a vegetable garden! She doesn't know the first thing about gardening. Do you, Fran?"

Fran stuck her tongue out.

"She only said that to sound interesting. What about you, Aimee?"

Aimee bashfully ticked off her summer agenda. "Well, there are several books that I want to read. I started one last night. And I've never been to the Clinton Library, so I might go there, and in July I'll be helping my church with Vacation Bible School."

The others nodded slowly, uninspired. Then it was Janet's turn.

"Well, I guess I will use the *alone* time to unpack some more boxes and hang pictures. I need to shop my car insurance. And I have to get some dental work done before school starts back." She made a face. "*Damn!* Now that I've said those things out loud, my summer sounds like crap."

The group turned somber. There was silence except for the splashing of feet and Lucy's barking; she had found a worm on the concrete near the grass. One by one they exited the pool except for Sue Ellen, who tried valiantly to straddle a raft. Janet wrapped a towel around her midsection and closed the grill. Suddenly, she turned around, hands on her hips.

"Hey, guys, you know what? We should go on a trip – the four of us!" she grinned. "Somewhere fun. Somewhere far away."

Fran lit a cigarette. "Yeah, that'll happen," she spoke through clenched teeth, the cigarette bobbing up and down. "None of us have money for a fancy vacation. At least I don't," she noted, looking around at the others.

Heads wagged slowly back and forth as they all considered their lack of extra money. Janet sighed and shrugged her shoulders. "Oh, well. Never mind. Truth is, it took everything I had to buy this house and now I'm broke."

Sue Ellen perked up. "Wait a minute! Not so fast! How about we go to Branson for the weekend!"

There were groans all around. "It's so crowded there, Sue," Janet said. "This time of year it's a lot of walking on hot concrete and standing in lines. I meant somewhere exotic; somewhere we've never been. Somewhere with a beach."

"That does sound nice," Aimee agreed. "I've never seen the ocean."

"I haven't, either," Fran said. "It's been seven years since Joel died and I've only been out of state once, and that was to Texas for a class reunion. I always thought I'd retire early and see the world, but that'll never happen. Not now."

Janet and Sue Ellen exchanged knowing glances. Fran's husband had not been a believer in life insurance, and his passing left her without a pot to pee in, so to speak.

"Anyhoo," Fran sighed, "I doubt we can afford to go anywhere with a beach." She removed her sun visor and ran a hand through her short, spiky hair. "Teachers don't get paid what we're worth."

Heads nodded in agreement.

"We spend our lives teaching the little sum-bitches and then they grow up and become corporate assholes and entrepreneurs, making triple the money that we make," she went on, her voice dripping with sarcasm, "and we get the satisfaction of knowing that we were a positive influence in their lives. That's our reward."

"Do you not enjoy teaching anymore, Fran?" Aimee asked.

"Oh, don't get me wrong. I enjoy teaching. It's the kids I don't like. Ungrateful little turds. Every year they get more smart-mouthed and know-it-all, arguing with me, stealing my cigarettes. They all want to know why they need math. They think a smart phone with a calculator is all they need to get them through life." She squinted as she took a long pull and blew smoke upwards into the air. "Hell. Maybe it is."

"I know what you mean," Aimee agreed. "My class would rather I yank out their fingernails than make them read sheet music. But most of them are good kids."

Fran grunted and things got quiet again. Aimee removed Lucy from her lap and began to gather up empty paper plates and cups. Sue Ellen rested against the side of the pool, staring thoughtfully at the worm that Lucy brought her. Even Fran looked wistful.

Janet sensed that her friends' minds were far, far away on sandy beaches and swaying palm trees, and she felt bad for bringing up the idea. She covered the platters of leftover burgers and hot dogs with foil. "Anyone want to take some of this home?" she asked, breaking off a bite of hamburger meat for Lucy.

"Can I take a plate to Dillard?" Sue Ellen asked as she tried to hoist herself from the pool, to no avail. Janet offered a hand and pulled her up the narrow ladder which barely cleared the woman's wide girth.

"Will someone take a selfie of me? Dillard likes me in a swimsuit."

Aimee picked up Sue Ellen's phone and took a half dozen photos while the woman turned this way and that, her freshly permed hair hanging in tiny wet ringlets.

"Okay! I think I got some good ones," Aimee said, handing the phone back.

They finished cleaning up around the pool, carrying the leftover food inside and placing it in the refrigerator.

"That was fun, Janet!" Sue Ellen exclaimed. "We should do this more often."

"I agree," Aimee nodded.

"Nice of you to have us over, Janet," Fran added. "I love your new house. Bye, Lucy!"

Janet stood at the end of the driveway, waving them off as their cars pulled away, one by one. She checked her mail box, which was empty, and said, "Come on, Lucy, let's go inside. Party's over."

∼

That evening, Janet lay curled up on her couch with her second glass of red wine. She flipped through the TV channels, stopping on the evening news where dozens of U. S. soldiers were shown filing down the steps of an airplane. A large crowd of people stood cheering and waving, holding up signs and cell phones. Janet turned up the volume as the excited newscaster described the event.

... a homecoming of more than three hundred troops from the Wisconsin Army National Guard, arriving late this afternoon in Milwaukee, after a nine-

month deployment in the Middle East and Afghanistan. The 1ˢᵗ Battalion 121ˢᵗ Field Artillery had been deployed to conduct support missions in the region...

Janet watched the emotional reunions as family members and friends welcomed their soldiers home. The camera zoomed in on one soldier who cried as he held his infant daughter for the first time. Teary-eyed, Janet wondered what it must be like to put one's own life at risk for the safety of others, with no promise of ever returning home to loved ones. The thought was overwhelming.

The camera zoomed in on the troops as they continued to make their way down the stairs of the plane, each one clad in camo and shouldering a backpack, their expressions joyful and relieved. Some searched the crowd for familiar faces while others kept their eyes on the tarmac. Janet wished that she could give each soldier a hug and tell them how much she admired them.

She reached for Lucy and turned her over on her back, stroking the pup's soft, fat tummy with her fingers. "It's just you and me, Lucy, but one of these days I'll meet a good man and get married and we'll be a family. You'll have a daddy."

The dog's little black feet began to churn as she ran in her sleep. Janet gently massaged her tiny pink foot pads.

"We just have to be patient."

~

The next morning Janet stood at her kitchen window in her bathrobe, her hair wet from showering. The drone of a lawnmower down the street reminded her that she would soon have to buy one for her own yard. She groaned at the thought. *I don't know anything about lawn mowers. I wonder how much they cost.*

The thought of money – or the lack of it - reminded her of the lottery ticket. She remembered taking it from her purse last night but then Lucy had tinkled on the floor and distracted her. Janet returned to her bedroom and spotted the lottery ticket on the corner of her dresser.

"Look what I've got, Lucy!" she said, waving the ticket. "A chance to win some big money!"

The little dog wagged her tail at the sound of her name. Returning to the kitchen, Janet fished for her glasses in the decorative bowl at the center of the kitchen table and then dug around some more until she found a nickel. She examined the glossy ticket. *Arkansas Scholarship Lottery*, it read. *$100,000 top prize cash payout!* Then she turned it over and glanced at the rules and regulations on the back.

"Are you feeling lucky, Lucy? Okay, here goes nothing."

Using the nickel, Janet scratched away to reveal the five winning numbers across the top, then sat back and contemplated what to do next. The remaining scratch-offs, of which there were fifteen, could change her whole future. But not likely. She would be very happy to win twenty dollars, she decided.

Starting with the middle one, Janet slowly scratched away at the dollar sign which concealed the number underneath, and blew away the shavings. It was not a match. Next she tackled the four corner ones. No match. She continued in a methodical fashion until only two remained.

She stood, needing a break. Maybe if she walked around a bit and said a prayer, her luck would improve. She did so, then poured a Diet Coke over ice and sat back down, staring at the card. *Stop being ridiculous,* she chided herself. She picked up Lucy and got her settled on her lap. "Come on, girl. You can be my good luck charm."

Debating over which of the last two she should scrape first, Janet sucked in her breath and started with the right one, hesitated, went to the left one, then went back to the right one. Flustered, she viciously scraped both at once, revealing numbers 23 and 14.

Her eyes traveled upwards to the row of winning numbers. 2, 11, 19, 23, and 27. Her heart jumped.

"Hey! How about that! We've got a match, Lucy!"

She squinted at the tiny print, hoping for a cash prize of twenty bucks, but what she saw sent her blood rushing through her veins. *Ten thousand dollars,* it read. She stopped breathing for a moment and stared out the window, accidentally squeezing Lucy until the little dog whimpered.

It's a mistake. I'm reading it wrong.

She dared to look again and there it was in tiny black numbers. *Ten thousand dollars.*

Janet sat very still for a full minute with her eyes closed. When she opened them she expected to see something different, but nothing had changed. She very gently placed Lucy on the floor, afraid that she might jinx something if she moved too quickly. *I need someone else to look at this.* She rose from the table and found her phone by the kitchen sink and scrolled shakily through her contact list.

"Fran? Hey, it's Janet. Yeah, I'm good. There's something I need you to look at. I'm about to send you a photo."

~

Janet lay in bed that night, having a hard time absorbing the fact that she had actually won some serious money. She could do a lot with ten thousand dollars. She could hire a crew to fill her front flowerbeds with shrubs and azaleas and purple fountain grass. She could buy a lawnmower or, better yet, she could pay someone to come and mow twice a month. What if she replaced her electric stove with a gas one and bought a new, larger refrigerator to match? Or, maybe she should sell her Ford Bronco and pay cash for a reliable used car, thus eliminating a car payment. She could pay off the gas grill which she had charged on her only credit card and buy new patio furniture. Or, she could invest her winnings, wait ten years, and turn it into a lot more money.

The possibilities were endless. Gutters! The realtor had told her that her new house had no gutters, an attempt at cutting corners by the builder, and that the installation of gutters would reduce erosion of her yard during heavy downpours. Janet had been given someone's business card with the suggestion to call for an estimate.

She tossed and turned, suddenly feeling stressed about the easy money and how to spend it. Her whole life she had been taught to manage her money wisely, but she had never been in charge of a windfall.

She thought about inviting her dad to come over tomorrow, to sit with her at the kitchen table and advise her. But wait! Much as she admired and trusted her father, she was a grown woman and should be able to figure this out for herself. That's what she told herself, anyway. As her ceiling fan whirred above her she thought of Fran and Sue Ellen and Aimee, wondering what they would do with ten thousand dollars. Suddenly, she jumped out of bed, switched on the light, and opened her laptop. In the search bar she typed, "Caribbean cruises."

3
Riding Shotgun

On a sunny Saturday morning Sue Ellen and Dillard pulled into Janet's driveway with a honk, and Aimee pulled up right behind them, parking against the curb. Dillard left the motor running while he hoisted his wife's large suitcase and a smaller one from the trunk of the car, depositing them next to Janet's vehicle. He turned to gather Sue Ellen into a hug and said, "Have fun, sugar. I'll miss you. You girls try to stay out of trouble, now," he teased.

"I'll call you when we get to New Orleans," Sue Ellen promised, giving him a peck on the cheek. As Dillard prepared to leave she hollered after him, "I'll get presents for you and the grandkids! And don't forget to take your stool softener!"

Janet shoved Sue's luggage into her cargo area and then turned to dust off her hands. "We've got a pretty day for the drive, don't we?"

"I was so excited last night that I could barely sleep!" Aimee said. "This is like a dream come true!"

"There's a box of donuts over there on the porch, if anyone wants any. But I already rinsed out my coffee pot."

"Frannie's not here yet?" Sue Ellen asked.

"I guess she's running late," Janet replied, glancing at her phone. At that moment it rang and she saw that it was Fran. "We're waiting on you," she deadpanned. *Pause.* "No, I never said I was picking you up. We decided that everyone would meet here at 8:00." *Pause.* "No, I never said that." *Pause.* "Okay. Hurry."

"Fran thought we were picking her up," Janet explained. "She's on her way."

Ten minutes later Fran pulled into the driveway, parking beside Janet's Bronco. She locked her Honda with a chirp and dragged a small piece of luggage on wheels. "Y'all should have told me you changed the plan. I could have already been here."

"Nobody changed the plan. This was always the plan," Janet mumbled.

"Is that all you brought?" Sue Ellen asked, incredulously.

"I like to pack light. What else could I possibly need besides pajamas, a couple changes of clothes, my swimsuit and a toothbrush? What did y'all bring?" Fran wanted to know, looking around at the others.

"You didn't mention shoes," Janet noted.

"I'm wearing them," Fran replied.

"You should have packed more shoes," Janet stated.

"Why? How many did you bring?"

"Three pair, besides what I'm wearing."

"I brought four pair," Aimee said.

"I brought eight pair," Sue Ellen boasted. "Dillard said I should be prepared for anything. Did you at least remember your formal wear, Frannie?"

Fran considered the question without expression as she tapped a new package of Marlboros against her palm. "My formal wear. Hmm. You mean like a ball gown and a tiara? And some little glass slippers?"

"I'm talking about for 'Dinner with the Captain' night! Didn't you read about it on the website? It's dress-up! I packed the dress that I wore to our son's wedding and a new handbag to match. And earrings."

Fran exhaled upwards and squinted through the smoke. "Sue Ellen, Eugene got married ten years ago. Did you try the dress on?"

"Well, no, but I also brought my funeral dress, just in case."

"Your funeral dress."

"Sure. Every woman has a funeral dress, or pantsuit. Don't you?"

"I do not."

"Well, you should. Don't you want to look your best when you're lying in your coffin?"

"At that point I won't care, you nincompoop."

"You two need to hush and get in the car," Janet scolded, tossing her duffel bag into the cargo section. "Aimee, you ride shotgun."

"I hate to tell you," Fran persisted as they climbed in and fastened their seatbelts, "but it's a fat chance that we'll even see the captain. There'll be hundreds of people there and I can't imagine that he would choose to sit down with us."

Janet made one final adjustment to the heap of luggage. "Okay. We're leaving, and I'm not stopping until we get to Vicksburg. And you can't smoke in my car, Fran. Sorry."

"I can't have a cigarette until we get to Vicksburg? But that's in Mississippi!"

"Consider it motivation to quit."

"What about Lucy?" asked Aimee, looking around for the little dog.

"I dropped her off last night at my parents' house. She'll be fine. They love her. Okay, everyone ready?"

"Ready!" they called out in unison.

"This is gonna be so fun! Seven days on a Caribbean cruise!"

"Thank you, Janet! You're the best friend ever!"

"My first trip without Dillard!" Sue Ellen did a little dance in the back seat.

Janet smiled into the rear view mirror and backed into the street. It felt satisfying, knowing that she was able to make this vacation possible, thanks to a random stroke of luck. She had done something impulsive and whimsical - had chosen adventure over practicality - and it sure felt good.

~

Once on the interstate, Sue Ellen remembered about her motion sickness and dug around in her purse for her Dramamine. Within twenty minutes she was sound asleep, leaning into Fran who was flipping through a magazine she'd brought along.

Aimee sat up front with Janet. As Janet drove, she studied Aimee in her peripheral vision. Long-legged and thin as a rail, Aimee looked younger than her twenty-eight years, pretty in a fresh, natural sort of way. Her long blonde hair was pulled back into a simple ponytail and a scattering of freckles danced across her nose.

"Something is different about you today," Janet commented.

"I'm not wearing my glasses. I got contacts."

"Oh! Cool. I wear contacts. You like them?"

"I do. So far."

"So, I guess I really don't know that much about you," Janet said, making friendly conversation. "You're so quiet. You're from Bentonville, right?"

"Right."

"How'd you end up teaching in Conway? I heard Bentonville schools are booming."

Aimee looked out the window. "Yeah," she paused, "I just needed to move away from that area. Bad memories."

Janet waited for more. Fran, too, was listening from the back seat, but Aimee offered nothing else on the subject. She gazed peacefully out the window and sang along with a Justin Timberlake song on the radio.

"You have a nice voice," Janet said.

"Thanks. I like to sing. My parents were musicians, so I guess I was destined to become a music teacher." Aimee chuckled rather sadistically. She turned to face Janet. "What about you? How long have you taught physical education?"

"Five years now. I like the middle schoolers. It's a good age."

"I think so, too," Aimee agreed.

"They're still young enough to be outgoing and fun, you know? And they still maintain a small degree of innocence."

"I know what you mean. I can tell when they have crushes on each other, can't you? It's so cute how they go about it." Aimee hesitated. "Have you ever been married?"

"Me? No. Just the one serious boyfriend, Lee. I dated some in college but nothing to write home about."

"Oh."

"I plan to keep an open mind about dating but, to be honest, my standards are probably too high. I want someone just like my dad."

"That's nice," Aimee said. "My advice is, don't lower the bar. You're an attractive woman, Janet. You'll find the right guy in time."

Janet looked at herself in the mirror, frowning. "I think 'attractive' is a stretch. I think I'm kind of plain."

"No, you're not!" Aimee argued. "Your beauty is unpretentious, the kind that sneaks up on a person, with your blue eyes and dark hair. Kind of a 'girl next door' look."

"Well, if you say so. My nose is kind of cute, and I do like my blue eyes," Janet admitted.

"You should wear a little mascara; you'd be surprised at the difference it makes."

They barreled along I-30 approaching the Arkansas River Bridge. "There's Verizon Arena," Janet pointed out. "They're doing Monster Jam there this weekend. I went last year with my dad. It was awesome."

Fran spoke from the back seat. "Did you hear that Cher is touring again? How old do you figure that woman is? She's got to be in her seventies by now."

"And still doing sell-out concerts," Aimee pointed out.

Soon they left Little Rock behind and followed the signs toward Pine Bluff and then to US-65 South. Sue Ellen snored in the back seat and Fran nodded off, as well, resting against a neck pillow. Aimee whispered to Janet, "Why do Sue Ellen and Fran behave the way they do with each other? Why do they quarrel and bicker so much?"

"Ahh," Janet replied, as if settling in for a long story. "I used to wonder the same thing, but they are just playing with each other. It's all in good fun."

"But Fran is kind of mean to Sue Ellen. She calls her names."

"Yes, she does," Janet agreed, keeping her voice low. "Fran doesn't sugarcoat, with anyone. But with Sue it's like water off a duck's back. It's like she doesn't even notice. And anyway, Sue Ellen can dish it out, as well, when she wants to."

"I just don't understand how they can talk to each other like they do and still be friends. I would never hold up under such insults," Aimee admitted.

Janet considered how to answer. "It's what they do, and it works for them. They seem to thrive in a contentious relationship. Maybe it's just to get attention. But I assure you, underneath that crusty exterior, Fran has a soft spot for Sue Ellen."

"Hmm," Aimee murmured, unconvinced. "I don't see it."

"There's a story behind those two," Janet whispered. "I'll tell you sometime."

After a long stretch of highway driving, Janet circled back to the subject of Aimee's parents being musicians. "I'm curious about your parents. Were they singers? Were they in a band?"

"They were a guitar-playing duo and I don't remember much about them. My brother and I mostly grew up in the foster care system."

"Oh, I didn't know that, and I didn't know you had a brother," Janet said, thrown off by this revelation.

"Yeah. His name's Chris. He's four years younger than me. He and I grew up with different families."

"That must have been really hard. I'm sorry. So, where does your brother live now? What does he do?"

"Oh, it's not a happy story, Janet. I'm sure there are more upbeat things to talk about."

Janet gripped the steering wheel. The women in the back seat were sleeping soundly. "I'd like to know more about you, so if you want to tell me, I'm a good listener."

Aimee crossed her legs, and then uncrossed them, and then crossed them again, bouncing her leg. "Well, our parents abandoned us when Chris was eight and I was twelve. They were free spirits, those two. They took off in the summer, headed to some indigent country to do missionary work through their music, leaving me in charge. They never came back."

Janet threw a troubled look at Aimee.

"My foster families were decent to me. I still keep in touch. But when I turned eighteen I had to make some decisions. I had a partial scholarship to the U of A in Fayetteville, but I didn't have a car or any money of my own, so I put my college plans on hold. It was more important to me to find my brother and take care of him; at least, to see him through high school. A state service helped me to locate Chris, living with a family in the same county. I petitioned the court for guardianship and it took a while but they eventually granted it."

"Oh, Aimee, that's wonderful! So, how did things turn out? With you and Chris?"

"Not great. I mean, at first things were working out. I found subsidized housing and Chris and I shared an apartment. But he was a messed up kid. He had some serious abandonment issues. Then he got in with the wrong crowd and began doing drugs and had some scrapes with the law." Aimee took in a deep breath and let it out. "And then he got arrested and spent seventeen months in a juvenile correction facility."

Janet reached over and patted Aimee's hand, not knowing what else to say or do.

"When he got out, he kept his nose to the grindstone for a while, but he just couldn't stay with it. I guess I wasn't enough. He needed a father figure." Aimee paused. "Now he's in prison."

"In prison?"

"Yeah. He's at the Wrightsville Unit serving a four year sentence for breaking and entering."

"Oh, my gosh, Aimee…I don't know what to say. I'm so sorry," Janet stammered. "Do you see him?"

"Occasionally. Not in a while."

"But, so, how did you manage college?"

Aimee chuckled. "Not very well! I took out student loans and worked two jobs to put myself through, and I didn't graduate until I was twenty-seven. Last year. Hattie Reed is my first teaching job."

Janet sank low in her seat and they drove in silence until Aimee spoke again. "I have a problem with anxiety. I take pills for it. And sometimes I can't sleep at night, for worrying about Chris."

"I don't know how you do it," Janet uttered, shaking her head.

"I give it to God. I turn all my problems over to the Lord," Aimee responded. "That's how."

Fran was stirring in the back seat. "I need to use the bathroom pretty soon. How much further to Vicksburg?"

"We're almost there. Next exit." Janet switched into the right lane.

"Hallelujah. I'm having nicotine withdrawals," Fran declared. She shook Sue Ellen's shoulder. "Wake up, Sue, we're here! We're boarding the ship. Where's your passport?"

Sue Ellen sat up, eyes frantic, a thread of drool from her bottom lip to her chin. "What? Already? Why'd you let me doze off? Where's my passport, Frannie?"

"Just kidding, you idiot. We're making a bathroom stop. We're in Mississippi."

Sue Ellen sat back, relieved, but cranky. She cast a dirty look at Fran. "You need to work on your people skills, Fran. That wasn't funny."

Janet talked over them. "Y'all go use the restroom and get yourselves a soda or whatever while I gas up. Last stop 'til New Orleans."

"We're not stopping for lunch?" they asked in unison.

"I haven't seen anywhere to stop for lunch except for that Cracker Barrel back there, but I missed the exit. Let's just snack 'til we get there."

"I would have loved some chicken and dumplings at Cracker Barrel," Sue Ellen muttered under her breath.

Aimee scampered inside the gas station with Fran on her heels. Sue Ellen took her time, still fuzzy-headed from her nap. Once they had taken care of business and were all settled back in the car, they tore into their Snickers bars and Funyuns and Little Debbie snacks while Sue Ellen looked on, wounded.

"I don't know why y'all are eating that junk. I told you I brought healthy snacks for us. I guess no one appreciates my efforts." With that, she reached into a small cooler and snatched a Ziploc bag filled with a dozen boiled eggs and raw carrots.

"No, you're not," Fran warned her.

Sue Ellen took a large bite of egg and it was only moments before its sulfuric odor permeated the vehicle. She chewed slowly and took another bite, all the while eyeing Fran's Snickers bar.

"That smells vile. You're stinking up Janet's car," Fran complained as she licked chocolate from her fingers.

"You'll be sorry, all of you," Sue Ellen scolded the group. "Don't you want to look good in your swimsuits?"

From the front seat Janet took a noisy slurp of her grape Icee and said, "It's a little late for that, don't you think? We're on vacation! Why not just enjoy yourself and eat what you want?" Her phone dinged and she looked down to see a text from Lee. "Ha! Check this out. Lee says he just ran four miles. Like hell he did!"

Fran let loose with a throaty chuckle. "He's hoping to impress you and get you back. He probably ran around the block."

Janet sighed. "Too little, too late. He had his chance."

"That's right. He had his chance," Aimee concurred with a little nod of her head.

Sue Ellen polished off her boiled egg and stubbornly pulled out another one. Windows came down in unison and Fran fanned the air in front of her face. "Chutzpah," she muttered.

~

They reached the outskirts of New Orleans late in the afternoon. Sue Ellen had managed to stay awake after Vicksburg and was in a jovial mood. She called Dillard to let him know that they had almost reached their destination. Fran rolled her eyes as their conversation ensued.

"No, Dillard, the enchiladas are for tonight. The chicken tetrazzini is for tomorrow night. Just go by the list on the counter. What? No, leave the foil on for fifty minutes, then take it off for the last ten minutes. I wrote it all down for you." She frowned. "I guess you could have the tetrazzini tonight, if that's what you want, but it's not what I had planned. Do you see the button that says 'bake'? Just push it and then set the temperature for 350 degrees, like my note says. No, not now, unless you're getting hungry already. Didn't you eat the salad I made for your lunch? Why not? How could you not see it?"

"Say goodbye, Sue," Fran said, loud enough for Dillard to hear.

"No, honey," Sue continued, "we haven't seen the boat yet. First we're going to a hotel to spend the night, remember?"

"It's not a boat, it's a gigantic cruise ship," Janet muttered from the front seat, and Aimee snickered. Fran tried to swipe Sue Ellen's phone from her hand.

"Okay, honey, I'll call you before I go to bed. I hope you like the chicken tetrazzini. I put a little sour cream in this time to …"

Fran grabbed Sue Ellen's phone and ended the call. "Don't force the rest of us to listen to your nonsense, Sue. Be respectful. We're on vacation, thanks to Janet."

"Yeah, and I'm trying to listen to the GPS," Janet frowned.

Sue Ellen hunkered down, her feelings hurt, but only for a fleeting moment. For the next twenty minutes they skirted New Orleans, admiring the churches and the above-ground cemeteries while the GPS directed Janet to their hotel.

In four hundred feet, turn right on Oleander Boulevard. Now turn right. Proceed for one half mile.

"Almost there, guys!" Janet smiled into the mirror.

Your destination is on the left.

All heads turned. On the left stood a flower shop, a CPA office, and a dumpster.

"Well, this can't be it," Sue Ellen remarked.

Janet was typing into her phone. "Y'all hush, I'm trying to concentrate. Oh, okay, I see what happened. There's an Oleander Street and an Oleander Boulevard. I made a wrong turn back there." She whipped the car around as the generic voice declared, *Recalculating! Recalculating!*

Five minutes later they pulled up to the hotel. "Here we are, girls! This is where we spend the night."

"It looks nice," Aimee said, rolling down the window.

"Where's the ocean?" Sue Ellen asked.

"We won't see the ocean until tomorrow," Janet reminded her. "C'mon, let's get checked in. I'm beat."

4
Champagne and Towel Animals

The next morning four phone alarms went off simultaneously at 8:30 am. Janet jumped out of bed first and headed to one of the two bathrooms in the suite. "When I get done showering, y'all three had better be up. And I'm not kidding."

"Geez, aren't you a pleasure in the morning," Fran griped, scooting further under her covers.

"We're supposed to be at the port by noon. That's when they start the boarding process. But I want to allow us plenty of time to get there in case I make a wrong turn or something. I've never driven in a big city like this before." She pulled the bathroom door to with a click, and when she emerged five minutes later she was pleased to see that two of the three were out of bed.

"C'mon, Frannie. Up and at 'em!"

"Just let me snooze for five more minutes," Fran mumbled. Janet grabbed her covers and gave them a yank, leaving Fran lying there in the nude. Everyone shrieked and turned their backs as she slowly climbed out of bed and took her time getting dressed.

"What?" she asked irritably, meeting their embarrassed stares. "Sleeping with Sue Ellen is like sleeping with a baked potato. I got hot."

"Well, warn us next time, would you please?" Janet suggested.

Fran shrugged. "I'm going outside to smoke. I'll meet y'all in the breakfast area."

The foursome assembled around a table in the downstairs lobby for a quick continental breakfast. Sue Ellen, though, was bent on making two waffles for herself while the others nibbled on cereal and muffins. Janet paced, trying to hurry her along, and then Fran disappeared for another smoke. Despite the delays, they were able to check out and leave the parking lot by 10:00, seat belts snapping.

"Okay, ladies! Here we go! Our ship awaits us!"

Sue Ellen held in her lap a large Styrofoam cup full of packets of grape jelly from the breakfast bar. Fran watched as she dumped them all into her purse.

"Excuse my asking, but what in God's name are those for?"

"They're for the grandkids. Whenever Dillard takes me out to breakfast I always bring some home."

"But why?"

"I use them for stocking stuffers. They're just the right size, don't you think?"

"Every kid's dream," Fran said cynically.

"You're just jealous because you didn't think of it."

"I don't have grandchildren. And you're forgetting that I'm Jewish. We don't hang Christmas stockings."

"But you do eat toast, right? Here. Have some."

Fran swatted the jelly packets away. "Just look out the window, Sue Ellen. You're getting on my nerves."

"Fine. I'm going to call Dillard," she announced, and from the front seat Janet said, "Make it short. Please."

Sue Ellen dug around in her tote bag for her phone, pulling out all sorts of random items and laying them on the seat beside her as she rummaged.

"Glitter? Why in the world do you have glitter?" Fran wanted to know.

"Oh, this?" Sue Ellen asked, holding up a rather large plastic bottle of ultra-fine pink glitter. I don't know. I guess one of the grandkids dropped it in here. Probably Lydia. She loves to make glitter pictures."

She found her phone and called her husband. "Hi, honey! Yes, I'm fine! We're on our way now, to where they keep the boats. How are you? Did you have a bowel movement?"

Everyone groaned.

"What do you hear from the grandkids? Really? Oh, good for them. Tell Lydia that I have her glitter. Are you enjoying your meals? What's that? You loved the tetrazzini?" Sue Ellen glanced proudly around at her friends. "I knew you would! Don't forget, today is trash day. Okay. Okay. I'd better go now, sugar. The girls are looking at me. I love you, too." She heaved a big sigh as she ended the call and settled into her seat.

Fifteen minutes later they arrived at the Port of New Orleans to a rather chaotic scene. Vehicles were lined up bumper to bumper while security staff used flashlights to wave them this way and that through the unloading area. Horns honked and a loudspeaker system barked unintelligible announcements. Families stood huddled on curbs with their luggage, trying to contain their children.

Janet squinted to read the signs and changed lanes, only to have a female officer glare at her and blow her whistle, directing her back to the original lane.

"Geez! Relax, why don't you?" Janet grumbled.

"What will you do with your car?" Aimee asked.

Janet's expression suddenly turned panicky. "I haven't thought about it!" She glanced around, looking for a long-term parking sign.

"There!" Aimee pointed. "Straight ahead!"

Relieved, Janet followed the arrow pointing to the right and joined a long line of cars, snaking their way up the ramp into an enormous parking deck. Parking spaces were few and far between and, when they reached the highest level, Janet prepared to start back down the ramp.

"Look!" Aimee cried. "They're leaving! Just back up a bit."

They waited while a family of six piled into their car and slowly backed out of their space. Janet pulled in smoothly and four seat belts unsnapped.

"Dammit!" she cursed. "I think we were supposed to offload our luggage back there, when we first arrived. I panicked about the parking. Now we'll have to carry it all down the elevator."

"It's fine, Janet," Aimee soothed, patting Janet's arm. "We have plenty of time. You've done a great job getting us here and anyway, this is just a tiny glitch."

Janet's anxiety subsided. Aimee's calm and reassuring attitude was refreshing compared to the two troublemakers in the back seat.

"I'm rooming with Aimee!" Janet announced. "And that's that."

∼

Their cruise liner was gargantuan. There she sat, gleaming white and spectacular in the morning sun, secured to the dock with massive ropes. The ladies leaned against the port railing, craning their necks to take in the sheer height of the vessel. Sea gulls flew in circles around a flag which flapped in the breeze at the very top. Janet felt proud to have made this happen for herself and for her friends. It felt like a dream come true.

"Can you believe that something so enormous can float in the water?" Fran pointed out. "It doesn't make sense."

"I can't even imagine what's going on inside," Aimee wondered out loud. "They must be cleaning all of those cabins where thousands of passengers just stayed, getting them ready for thousands of new passengers, including us."

"Look down there," Janet pointed out. "See all those forklifts on the loading docks? There must be a dozen of them, all loading pallets of food. What an operation!"

Sue Ellen asked, "Which deck are we staying on, Janet? I've forgotten what you told us."

"We'll be on deck ten. It's called the Lido Deck, where all the action is."

"What kind of action?" Sue Ellen asked.

"It's where the swimming pools are, and the food buffets and the outdoor bars. It's where everyone goes to party."

"There's even a big movie screen where they show movies at night," Aimee stated.

"But won't it be loud?" Sue Ellen wondered. "What if we can't sleep?"

"You can sleep when you get home, Sue. We're here to have fun."

"What's on all of those other levels?"

"Well, I think every level has staterooms, for the passengers. But there are also restaurants, lounges, a fitness center, a casino, spas, art galleries, gift shops. We'll be walking our legs off."

Sue Ellen was like a little kid. "Oooh, I can hardly wait! How much longer until we board, Janet?"

"Should be soon. Why don't we make our way over there?"

"Wait! Let's get a group picture with the ship behind us," Aimee suggested. They looked around for someone to take the photo.

"I just remembered!" Sue Ellen exclaimed. "The grandkids got this for me." She reached into her large tote bag and pulled out a selfie stick. She snapped her phone into the mount and said, "Okay, everyone scrunch together and say cheese!"

They took turns getting group photos on their phones and then began to stroll along the port, admiring the line of ships with their colorful flags and their fancy names. Suddenly a man's voice boomed over a loudspeaker, urging all boarding passengers to report to their designated area within the port facility. After much confusion and bumping into each other the girls managed to find their assigned area which was already filling up quickly.

Janet waved her friends into a cluster where they put their heads together. "Okay, we should have done this at the hotel, but does everyone have their drivers' license and their passport? And I don't mean in your luggage which is already on the ship. I mean do you have it on you?"

One by one they held up their documents.

"Okay, good. *Do not lose them.*"

"Got it, coach!"

"You jumped through hoops to get all of us expedited passports and I don't intend to lose mine," Fran declared. "Besides, it's a good picture of me."

"So, here's the deal," Janet continued in a hushed tone, "Watch your purses. Keep them zipped or snapped shut so that a pickpocket can't grab your wallet. That's why I wore a fanny pack," she noted, patting hers. "Good luck to the creep who tries to get my fanny pack off of me."

Sue Ellen's eyes grew wide.

"Don't give out your room number," Janet continued. "And later on, if you're at a bar, don't let anyone drop anything into your drink. You've heard about that, right?"

Before Sue Ellen could question Janet about that, there was a sudden surge toward the door and they found themselves following a long hallway with signs pointing to 'Security Checkpoint.' Sue Ellen kept grabbing for Fran's hand and Fran kept swatting it away.

"This is where we have to show our documents. They won't let us on without them," Janet reiterated. "And it looks like they are scanning purses and tote bags up ahead." Her height advantage sometimes came in handy. Once through the scanning process they found themselves in an enormous room with roped-off lines of people waiting their turn to be checked in.

"I need a cigarette," Fran muttered.

"Can't have one," Janet shot back.

It took twenty minutes to reach the front of their line where a woman wearing a badge waved Aimee forward. She nervously produced her documents and posed for a picture, and in return was given a cruise card, a schedule of events, and a map of the ship. She turned to the others with a celebratory fist pump and stepped aside while they followed suit. Once they were all checked in, more signs led them to the gangway, the long ramp which connected them to the ship.

"Is this the gang plank, Janet?" Sue Ellen wanted to know.

"It is, and be glad it is walled in on both sides or else Fran would have already pushed you off." Janet winked at Fran.

Excitedly they bustled along the gangway until, suddenly, they found themselves in the cavernous atrium of the vessel. Like country bumpkins, they stared upwards at the gigantic crystal chandeliers and the glass elevators ascending and descending along the towering walls. Exquisite flower arrangements, plush velvet loveseats, and classical piano music lured them closer in, where they were greeted by a female server dressed in black and holding a linen-covered tray with flutes of champagne.

"Hello, ladies! Welcome aboard!"

"Thank you!" Fran helped herself to a flute and went in search of a place to smoke. "I'll be back in a minute," she promised the others. "Don't go anywhere without me."

Sue Ellen accepted a flute of champagne and sat down on one of the loveseats. Janet and Aimee did the same. As they sat there feeling very special, an attractive dark-skinned woman holding the hand of a little boy came walking swiftly in their direction. She was dressed in a tunic with splashes of orange, yellow and red over some flowing black pants and gold sandals with heels. She looked to be about fifty, her hair stylishly untamed and streaked with gray, her long earrings swaying. The boy was dressed as if for church, complete with suspenders and a little bow tie. The woman returned their stares with a dazzling smile as she swept on past.

"I'll bet she's somebody important," Sue Ellen whispered. "She looks like a movie star or something."

Fran reappeared, looking much more relaxed. She set her empty glass down and said, "What say we go find our rooms, girls?"

Janet and Aimee pulled Sue Ellen to her feet and the foursome headed to one of the glass elevators. Fran pushed the button for the Lido Deck and, as the elevator lifted them high above the atrium, Sue Ellen did a little dance.

Aimee smiled. "Look who's feeling sassy!"

"Stop it! People can see you!" Fran scolded.

Janet took a deep, exhilarated breath. They were here. They were really here.

As promised, their luggage awaited them outside their stateroom doors. Fran used the card key on cabin 10283 and found the room to be just as described on the website. Two single beds separated by a night stand. Two closets, a dresser, and a bathroom with a small shower.

"Cute!" she commented. She unzipped her bag and began putting her things away, choosing the smaller closet for her hang-ups.

Sue Ellen, though, seemed disappointed. "This room is for both of us? She turned in a full circle. My goodness, it's so tiny. Look at that little commode!"

"We talked about this, Sue," Fran reminded her.

"But there's no bathtub. I like my bubble baths."

"Sue Ellen, we all agreed to get inside rooms. The balcony rooms cost more and remember, you said you might get seasick looking at the ocean from your bed."

"I said *might*," Sue Ellen recalled.

Fran's glare told her to zip it. "Don't you dare say a word to Janet about the size of this room. We wouldn't even be here if it weren't for her."

Ashamed of herself, Sue Ellen changed course. "Which bed do you want, Frannie? You pick."

"I'll take the one with the crab." On her pillow sat an adorable creature fashioned from a white bath towel. On Sue Ellen's bed sat a towel frog. She took out her phone and took a photo of each.

"Let's go see what their room looks like," Sue Ellen said, hurrying across the hall to cabin 10284 where the door was open. Aimee was lining up her hair products on the dresser top.

"Aren't these just the sweetest little cabins?" she gushed. "Look at the monkey on my bed!"

"I got a little frog," Sue Ellen smiled. "Fran's is a crab."

"How appropriate!" Janet remarked. "Mine is a rabbit."

"I wonder who made these?"

"I'm guessing our steward," Janet replied.

"When will we see the ocean?" Sue Ellen asked.

"We're docked on the Mississippi River for now. We won't leave the port for another couple of hours. Want to do some exploring?"

"I'm starving," Fran frowned. "Can we eat first?"

"I'm hungry, too," Aimee admitted.

"Okay, then let's get something to eat. The announcer said some of the buffet lines are open. Let's go!"

∼

The fragrant smell of fresh pizza was impossible to ignore. They filled their plates with hot slices and found a shaded table.

"Mmm, so good!" murmured Aimee with her mouth full. "I was famished."

"Me, too," Fran said, stabbing at her side salad.

Sue Ellen took a picture of her pepperoni pizza slice.

"Really, Sue Ellen?"

"I just want to remember my first meal on the ship. Mind your own business, Fran."

Janet's phone buzzed and she peeked at it. "It's Lee, wanting to know where I am." She said her words out loud as she typed her reply. *I'm on a ship headed to Honduras.*

"That should throw him for a loop," Fran predicted.

Janet swallowed a bite of pizza and wiped her mouth. "Did you guys remember to buy a cruise ship plan for your cell phone?"

Everyone nodded but one. "What are you talking about?" Sue Ellen asked.

"Remember, Sue? We discussed it when we made our reservations."

"I don't remember that."

"It's called an international plan. It saves you a lot of money on phone calls and texting and such. Without it you have to pay roaming charges once the ship sails."

"Roaming charges?"

"Just go call Dillard and he can call your provider to set it up."

"Provider?"

"Just go call him, Sue," Fran dismissed her with a wave of her hand.

Sue Ellen ambled away to call her husband and soon returned all smiles. "I'm all set! Dillard is going to set it up just as soon as 'Judge Judy' goes off."

"Oh, so Dillard is a fan, too!" Fran exclaimed. "I love it when she shouts, 'You're an idiot!'"

A broadcast over the P. A. system interrupted their discussion.

Ladies and gentlemen, welcome aboard! My name is Travis Rand, your Cruise Director! I'll be your go-to person for all questions related to entertainment and activities. You'll see me all over the ship and at most of the events, and you'll recognize me by my white, short-sleeved shirt and my name tag. We will sail at approximately 3:30 pm at the very capable hands of Captain Mike Anderson. We'll be making three ports of call to Mahogany Bay, Belize, and Cozumel, in that order. Please know that your safety is of utmost importance to us so please notify me or any crew member with any questions or concerns. My job, folks, is to make sure that each and every one of you has the time of your life on your cruise, and I'm about to get things going and keep things moving! Join me right now on the Lido Deck where we're going to dance and party until the sun goes down! Thank you for sailing with us and I hope to see you on the dance floor!

Aimee stood excitedly. "Well, what are we waiting for? Let's go get ready!"

5
Cold Turkey

Fifteen minutes later the foursome gathered in the hallway, dressed casually for an evening of fun in the open air. They looked each other up and down and Sue Ellen's eyes stopped on Janet. "Is that what you're wearing, Janet?"

"What's wrong with what I'm wearing?"

Sue Ellen faltered. "Well, it's what you wear at school every day. Gym shorts. Polo shirt. Didn't you bring anything, you know, flirty?"

Janet laughed. "Flirty? Me? I buy most of my clothes at Academy Sports and, last time I checked, they don't have a flirty department."

A throaty chuckle came from Fran. "You'd better hush up, Sue, or she might put her whistle on."

Sue Ellen pressed her lips together disapprovingly but changed the subject. "Girls, I'm missing a piece of luggage. My smallest bag isn't here."

"Don't worry," Aimee assured her. "I'm sure they will deliver it soon. You can check with Guest Services if it doesn't show up."

"Okay. Does my new top look okay? Dillard bought it for me," Sue Ellen went on, smoothing the front of it.

"It looks nice, other than the price tag hanging under your arm," Fran noted.

"Oops!" Sue Ellen giggled and held up her arm. "Cut it for me, will you, Fran?"

"Do I look like Edward Scissorhands?"

With exasperation, Janet cut the tag with her toenail clippers and waved her friends along. "Come on, let's go!" She took off in long strides, leading the pack, while the others scrambled to catch up.

The Lido Deck was already crowded with people of all ages and a live band was performing. They stood together at the railing, surprised to see that the ship was moving and the New Orleans skyline was passing by. Captain Anderson was navigating them down the river to the point where it would spill into the Gulf of Mexico.

"Look! I'll bet that's our cruise director!" Fran exclaimed, pointing.

Travis stood on a platform wearing his white shirt and tan cargo shorts, shouting into a microphone and revving up the crowd. He was pointing and directing everyone to form a conga line while the band launched into a lively Cuban number. Several hundred guests, adults and children alike, swarmed the dance floor and formed a long line, holding on to the shoulders of the person ahead of them. The line snaked this way and that, the dancers festive as they kicked their legs to the music.

Janet jumped in, followed by her friends, and once they got the hang of it they couldn't be stopped. Sue Ellen struggled to keep up, though, and stepped on the heels of Fran's sandals, sending Fran cart-wheeling to the floor. With nothing to hang onto, Sue Ellen then stumbled and landed in a heap. The conga line snaked around both of them. Afraid of being trampled, Fran groaned and slowly pushed herself from the floor. She grabbed Sue Ellen's hand and pulled her to a sitting position before skulking away in embarrassment.

Sue Ellen, dazed, looked around for a familiar face but Janet and Aimee had long since danced away. She was surrounded by a sea of legs.

"Hey, lady, get out of the way," said a teenage boy with rings in his nose.

A strong, tanned arm reached out and helped her to her feet. "You okay, ma'am?" Travis asked. "Do you need to go to the infirmary?"

"What? Oh, no, no, I'm fine. Just a bit bruised, I think," she stammered, totally humiliated. Travis was quite handsome up close.

"Are you sure? Because you look like you could use some help."

"Well, on second thought, maybe if you could just help me to a chair," she whimpered, gripping his elbow and faking a limp. Travis led her to an empty chair and waited as she sat carefully down.

"So, Travis, tell me what's it like being..." she began, but he had already jumped back onto his platform. Aimee and Janet danced by, waving and kicking.

After a while the rowdy passengers were gasping for breath and the conga line began to break up. Travis signaled for the band to wind down and they transitioned into a country-western song.

"Alright, people, who wants to learn to line dance?" The crowd erupted in applause. "Line up in rows, please. If you already know the Electric Slide, get in the front couple of rows. The rest of you can learn the steps by watching the ones in the front." With that, he hooked his thumbs into his pockets, cowboy style, turned his back and started dancing, sliding and toe touching the platform.

Aimee watched from the sidelines. "He's so cute," she declared, to no one in particular. Suddenly feeling brave, she joined the ranks of dancers, taking a place three rows back. It wasn't long before she had memorized the steps and was dancing in perfect unison, smiling happily with her long hair swaying.

Fran returned from hiding and found Janet, and the two of them watched their friend dance.

"Would you just look at her," Janet said. "Who knew she could dance like that."

"Who knew she had legs like that."

Janet and Fran located Sue Ellen and the three stood near the tiki bar where they watched for an empty table. They finally snagged one and sat down, saving a chair for Aimee who eventually joined them, breathless and happy with flushed cheeks.

After much deliberating they ordered exotic frozen beverages. Sue Ellen got a Bahama Mama which arrived with a paper umbrella and a plastic monkey. Janet and Fran chose frozen pineapple Margaritas, and Aimee a Pina Colada. Janet watched Sue Ellen as she slowly stirred her drink with her straw, peering into the glass with concern.

"What's the matter, Sue?"

"I'm just checking to make sure there's nothing fishy in my drink."

"Like what?"

"You just this morning warned us about it, Janet. You said not to let anyone drop anything in our drinks!"

Fran scoffed. "She was referring to perverts who prey on unsuspecting women. By drugging them. For sex."

Sue Ellen whipped her head around the table, horrified.

"Drink up, sister," Fran assured her. "I doubt you have anything to worry about in that regard. Anyway, if a man dropped something in your drink it wouldn't be just floating around on top like a dead fly."

Sue Ellen drew herself up. "And why wouldn't I have anything to worry about? There are plenty of men out there who would love to have their way with me."

"Enjoy your Bahama Mama, Sue Ellen. I'll be on the lookout for sex predators," Janet assured her.

Sue Ellen took a baby sip, and then another, and soon she forgot all about tainted drinks. "I wonder what Dillard is doing."

"No one cares, Sue Ellen," Fran said. "Oh, but he did call earlier."

Sue Ellen's head jerked up. "He did?"

"Yes. Said you weren't answering your phone. Said to tell you that he was going to Applebee's for dinner, to try the baby back ribs."

Sue Ellen was crushed. "But, what about the casserole I made him? I had his meals all planned out."

Fran patted her knee. "I'm just kidding. I'm sure he's trying to turn the oven on as we speak." She reached for her cigarettes and realized she was out. "Crap. Where can I buy some cigarettes around here?" she asked, looking around.

"This would be a good time to quit, Frannie," Sue Ellen suggested.

"Why would I do that?"

"For your health, silly. I want you to live a long life. Grow old with me!"

Fran scoffed loudly.

"I mean it. Let's make a deal. If you promise to quit smoking, I'll give up sweets."

"Right. You'll give up sweets."

Emboldened by the alcohol, Sue Ellen insisted, "No, I mean it! If you will quit smoking cold turkey, starting now, I promise I'll give up desserts."

Fran sat back in her chair, considering her friend's deal. "Nah, Sue Ellen, I have the willpower to do that, but you don't."

"Sure, I do!"

"No, you don't."

"Yes, I do!"

Fran thought about the money she would save, not buying cigarettes, and Sue Ellen would surely lose some weight. It was a tempting proposition. Fran's eyes narrowed as she stared at her friend.

"Fine! You're on. Starting now." She crumpled the empty pack and tossed it in the trash can.

Sue Ellen beamed, as did the others. "Deal! And remember, Frannie, we have witnesses. So no cheating."

"This should make for a very interesting week," Aimee commented.

They were finishing up their second round of drinks when Janet suddenly stood. "There it is, Sue Ellen! There's your ocean!"

The ship was surrounded by water on all sides. They had reached the Gulf of Mexico. The women scrambled excitedly to the railing to gaze out over the sparkling gulf waters. The sun was just beginning to set, casting a pinkish-orange glow on the endless horizon. Sea gulls squawked above them.

"It seems too good to be true," Fran said wistfully, leaning into Janet's shoulder.

"I know, right?"

Their cameras clicked away as they captured their first sighting of the mighty ocean. Sue Ellen tugged on Aimee's sleeve. "Aimee, take a picture of me, will you?" She handed her phone to Aimee and leaned back against the railing, both arms outstretched, her chest bulging.

"Um, why don't you just drop one arm and turn a little, like you're looking at the ocean?" Aimee suggested.

Sue Ellen complied. "Okay. How's this?"

"Perfect." Aimee took several photos and handed the phone back. "How about we finish our drinks and go get some dinner? I'm starved."

The tipsy group made their way to the bustling buffet area where they split up to check out the endless bins of mouth-watering selections, just as the website had promised. Boiled shrimp, juicy roast beef, grilled salmon, and steaming lasagna. Baked chicken, steak kabobs over rice, savory ham, prime rib. Asian, Mexican, and Greek cuisine. Soups and salads of every variety and an impressive array of desserts.

Fran filled her tray and, trying her best to walk in a straight line, slid into a booth by a window. One by one the others joined her with heaping plates and smiling faces. For a few moments they traded salt and pepper shakers and tubs of butter and then they dug in. It did not go unnoticed that Aimee ducked her head for a brief prayer.

"Oh, my stars!" Sue Ellen exclaimed around a mouthful of lasagna. "This tastes even better than mine."

Janet sawed off a bite of her prime rib and savored it with her eyes closed. Suddenly she stood. "I forgot to get a baked potato. Anyone else need anything?"

"I'll take a baked potato," Fran replied.

Aimee smiled. "I'm good, thanks. Y'all, this shrimp alfredo is so delicious."

"Did you see the chocolate mousse? That's what I want," Sue Ellen said, "after I finish my lasagna." She stuffed half of a buttered hot roll into her mouth.

"Um, aren't you forgetting something, my fat little friend?" Fran asked with raised eyebrows.

"What?" Sue Ellen asked.

"Have you already forgotten about our deal?"

Sue Ellen sat back against the booth and groaned in dismay. "But Fran, it's our first night! Can't you make an exception?"

"Only if you'll go buy me a pack of cigarettes."

Sue Ellen hesitated. "How about we start tomorrow? At least let me have one dessert," Sue Ellen whined.

"Okay, you can eat it while I blow cigarette smoke in your face."

The two glared at each other contentiously. Janet returned with two potatoes and a bowl of shrimp cocktail. "I do love a good baked potato," she remarked as she sat back down, and then she noticed the tension. "What are y'all talking about?"

"Nothing," Fran declared, and went back to her meal. Sue Ellen chewed a bite of roast beef, looking like she might cry. Three children chased each other past the booth, shrieking with laughter.

"No running!" Fran hollered after them, too loudly, in her best teacher voice.

Janet elbowed her good-naturedly. "They're just kids having fun, Fran."

"I know," she snapped. "I'm just feeling grouchy all of a sudden. I'm sorry."

It was clear to Janet that her well-meaning friends would suffer from the pact that they had made. Gently, she asked, "Are you guys sure you want to do this? Give up your favorite thing while you're on vacation?"

Fran lifted her chin defiantly and Sue Ellen did the same, both wanting out but neither willing to concede.

"I mean, you were both drinking when you made the deal. It was a drunken deal."

The women continued to stare each other down.

"Okay, then!" Janet proclaimed. "Good luck to both of you. And I mean that."

"Yes, good luck to both of you," Aimee chimed in. Then, rather timidly, she said, "I'd really like to get some pie or something," and she slipped away from the table.

"I'll go with you," Fran said. "Did you see those raspberry tarts?"

Janet got up, too, with a look of pity for Sue Ellen.

"Just go!" Sue Ellen dismissed Janet with a wave of her hand.

Aimee returned with banana pudding, a cherry turnover, and a dish of crème brulee. Janet chose pecan pie. Fran carried a cup of coffee and a raspberry tart for herself and a dish of sugar-free orange Jell-O for Sue Ellen, who gave her a grateful look.

"Thank you, Frannie."

Janet turned to Aimee. "How do you stay so thin, Aimee? You eat like a lumberjack!"

Aimee giggled. They finished their desserts in contented silence. It had been a long, full day and fatigue was starting to set in.

"It seems like ages ago that we were jockeying for a parking space at the port, doesn't it?" Janet remarked. "I'm wiped out."

"Me, too," Sue Ellen agreed, scooting her way out of the booth.

Aimee scraped the last of her crème brulee and licked the back of the spoon. "This has absolutely been the best day of my life!"

They left the food area and skirted around the pool which was now lit up with lights. A few people still splashed and played in the water but the partying and dancing had subsided, for the most part, after the band shut down. Janet yawned widely and carried her shoes as they headed for the carpeted, air conditioned hallway that would take them back to their cabins.

Aimee showered first and emerged from the bathroom in her pajamas, her hair twisted into a knot on top of her head. She hummed as she bent over her suitcase, digging for her slippers. "Thank you for including me, Janet. I'm having the time of my life."

Across the hall, Sue Ellen phoned Dillard while Fran prepared for her shower. Even with the bathroom door closed, Fran could hear her fussing.

"Look at my list, Dillard. The pasta salad was meant to be a lunch item. Now you've eaten tomorrow's lunch as an after-dinner snack. Huh? Well, what time is it there? Oh. I forgot about the time change. *Pause.* I understand that you were hungry, honey, but now you won't have anything for your lunch tomorrow. I had everything all lined out for you."

Fran shook her head and smiled. As much as Sue Ellen got on her nerves, Fran admired how much she loved her family and how well she took care of them. Her constant mothering was irritating, yet endearing. She and Joel had not been so fortunate as to have children, and Sue Ellen's large and growing family was enviable.

She stood under the hot water of the tiny shower with her eyes closed, thinking of Joel. They would have just celebrated their fortieth anniversary, had he not run his car off the road and down an embankment. Hot tears welled up in Fran's eyes. She turned her face up to the showerhead, remembering, until the emotions subsided and she regained her composure. She turned the water off and stepped onto the bath mat and plucked a towel from the metal rack. The little bathroom had filled with steam, rivulets running down the mirror.

Fran dried off quickly, rubbing her short hair briskly and combing it back with her fingers. She craved a cigarette badly and cursed herself for making that pact with Sue Ellen. Her first and last cigarettes of the day were the ones she cherished the most.

She wrapped herself in a robe, took a deep breath, and stepped from the bathroom.

"Your turn, Sue. I'm going to bed."

"I just talked to Dillard. I hope he remembers my birthday. You know it's coming up soon," Sue Ellen said casually, cutting her eyes at Fran.

"Mmm, hmm," Fran murmured, sliding between her sheets.

"I told him I'd like to have a pretty pajama set. Something luxurious."

"What the hell for?"

"Lots of reasons!"

"Give me one."

"Well, what if there was a tornado back home, during the night, and I got blown into a tree? I'd like to be wearing some nice pajamas when they find me."

Fran snorted. "Go take your shower, you knot head, before I drop my robe and flash you."

Sue Ellen retreated into the tiny bathroom and twenty minutes later emerged to find the room dark and Fran sleeping. She tiptoed around, stubbing her toe on a suitcase, and cursed. She fumbled with the small bedside lamp and turned it on, disturbing Fran.

"What the hell, Sue," Fran grumbled, wincing at the light.

"I just need to find my pills, honey, then I'll turn the light back off. I didn't know you were going to sleep already."

Fran scooted further under her covers.

Sue Ellen took her pills, swallowing them with what was left of a warm bottle of water on the dresser. She smacked her lips, climbed into her bed, and turned out the light. The women lay in the pitch darkness of their room, the only sound the far-away laughter of children in the hallway. Sue Ellen took in a deep breath and exhaled loudly, hoping to wake up her friend.

"Fran? Pssst! Frannie, are you awake?"

"Oh for God's sake, Sue. Yes! I'm awake. Thank you for waking me. Again."

"Did I ever tell you that Dillard and I had to get married?"

"Do what now?"

"I was only seventeen. He was a linebacker on the high school football team and I was on the pom-pom squad. We conceived Eugene under the bleachers one night, after the Homecoming game."

In a put-upon voice Fran replied, "And you are telling me this because…?"

"Because I never got to finish high school! I lied on my employment application. I lied to you and to the Principal and even to the Superintendent. I was hired under false pretenses."

Fran lay silent for a moment, staring into the dark. "It doesn't matter, Sue, not now. You've done a great job and you've been an asset to administration, for all these years."

"But I lied," Sue Ellen whined.

"Who cares now. Water under the bridge. I still love you and I won't tell."

Sue Ellen's voice was muffled under the covers. "I was hoping you'd say that, Frannie. I love you, too."

6
Search Us if You Must

At 7:30 am the P. A. system crackled. *Good morning, everyone! Travis Rand here. Hope you slept well! It's going to be a sunny, fun-filled day as we cross the beautiful Gulf of Mexico. Destination: Honduras! Just outside your stateroom door you'll find a schedule of activities for adults and children alike, or you can just lay by the pool and soak up the sun. Our mission is to show you the time of your life, so get out there and have fun!*

From beneath her covers Aimee mumbled a good morning to Janet. When Janet didn't respond, Aimee lay very still and listened to her roommate's breathing, wishing she could sleep so soundly. She slipped out of bed and tiptoed to the small bathroom, emerging minutes later in a swimsuit and cover-up. She stepped into her sandals, donned her sunglasses, grabbed her journal and headed for the pool area, craving a hot cup of coffee and some quiet time.

On the Lido Deck a number of sun worshipers had already claimed their spots. Women were lounging in skimpy bikinis and men in rumpled swim trunks, all lathered with sun screen or tanning lotion, wearing stylish sunglasses and ear buds in their ears. For a few minutes, coffee in hand, Aimee stood at the railing gazing out over the ocean, a warm breeze tossing her hair across her face. She closed her eyes and prayed, as she did every morning. Then she sat down and began to write.

Janet arrived about thirty minutes later, her eyes puffy from sleep. She sat across from Aimee, blowing on a steaming cup of coffee. "Hey, early bird! Whatcha doing?" she asked.

"I'm just writing. Journaling."

"Like, poetry?"

"No. Just random thoughts."

Janet took a sip of her coffee and gazed out across the ocean which sparkled like diamonds in the morning sun. "Would you just look at all that water? It's like being in a whole different world."

"It really is magnificent. Thank you again, Janet. This cruise is just what I needed."

"Me, too. And you're welcome." She stretched out her legs and put her hands behind her head. "I heard the other two bickering in their room. I guess they'll be along soon. Have you had breakfast?"

"Not yet. I'll eat something soon, though." She reached down to scratch her leg and disturbed a delicate spider web beneath the table with drops of dew clinging to it. She came up out of her chair with a yelp, spilling her coffee. Heads turned to see what was going on.

Embarrassed, Aimee moved to a different table, checking beneath it before sitting down.

Janet was amused. "I take it you're afraid of spiders."

"Yes, I am. Deathly afraid. Big or small, harmless or not. I can't tolerate a spider."

Sue Ellen arrived, followed by a scowling Fran.

"Don't mind her," Sue Ellen explained. "She's in nicotine withdrawal. She tried to bite me. Hey, look at all the people at the pool already! Should we go for a swim?"

"I'm not doing anything until I have some breakfast," Janet said. "Anyone want to join me?"

They all filed into the dining area, overwhelmed once again with the never-ending array of selections.

"I don't know where to start!" Aimee exclaimed.

Fran trailed behind Janet to the omelet station. Aimee went another direction for pecan waffles and fruit salad. Sue Ellen hovered dangerously near a tray of chocolate croissants but opted for scrambled eggs, biscuits, and bacon.

They ate with gusto, the fresh ocean air having fueled their appetites. Janet finally spoke. "So, what shall we do today? Did anyone bring the schedule of activities?"

"I did. Look at this," Fran said, tapping the flyer. "Bingo at 11:00 in the auditorium. I love Bingo. I'm going."

"I'll go with you!" Sue Ellen said.

"Does anyone want to just lay by the pool? Because that's what I'm going to do," Aimee said. "I'm already in my swim suit."

"Let us see it!" Sue Ellen pleaded.

"No," Aimee giggled, modestly. "It's nothing special. I don't even have a tan yet."

Janet spoke up. "There's a nice jogging track. I'm going to go for a run, but I'll find you at the pool later," she said to Aimee.

"Okay! Why don't we all meet up for lunch? Say, 1:00?"

"Sounds good!"

The handsome cruise director strode past and smiled. "Hello, ladies! Enjoying the cruise so far?"

They all nodded and smiled sweetly. Sue Ellen playfully saluted him. "Yes, sir!"

"Great! It's a beautiful day!"

As he hurried away Fran elbowed her. "You don't need to salute him, you birdbrain. He's not the captain."

"I was just playing," Sue Ellen said, indignantly. "I think he's cute."

"What's his name again?" Janet asked.

"His name is Travis," Aimee said, rather dreamily. "Travis Rand."

~

Aimee lay stretched out in her turquoise two-piece, drifting in and out of sleep and occasionally reaching for her bottle of water. The warm tropical sun felt therapeutic. Janet eventually joined her wearing a black one-piece cut low in the back.

"So, you do own a swimsuit," Aimee teased.

"My mother insisted on buying this for me."

"You look good. You're very toned."

"Thanks," Janet replied modestly. "It comes with being a physical education teacher."

Janet got settled and they lay quietly with their eyes closed, lost in their own thoughts. Aimee tapped her foot to the piped in music and hummed along. "Hey," she remembered, "you were going to tell me about Sue Ellen and Fran. You said there was a story behind them."

"Oh, yeah, I did, didn't I? Okay, but you didn't hear this from me, okay?"

"Of course!" Aimee replied. "My lips are sealed."

"Well, years ago, before I started teaching at Hattie Reed, there was a job opening for school secretary. Somebody got fired mid-year, I heard. Anyway, Fran was one of the teachers asked to sit in on the interviews. Word is, Sue Ellen applied for the job and showed up for her interview with a plate of cookies. Cherry Winks, to be exact."

Aimee giggled. "No!"

"She was overdressed, she had only a high school diploma, and her resume was short and unimpressive. But Fran liked her, better than the other candidates."

"Why is that?"

"Well, the conference room had a glass door and Sue Ellen kept waving at the students in the hallway." Janet smiled as she went on. "It was annoying to Fran, of course, but it also spoke volumes about Sue Ellen's personality, and how much she obviously loved kids. The other candidates were not nearly as enthusiastic about the position."

Janet took a long pull from her water bottle. "Sue Ellen never once asked about the salary, but she did say that having health insurance would be a wonderful thing. Apparently, Dillard was out of work at the time."

"So they hired her?" Aimee presumed.

"No, not right away. The principal was prepared to offer the position to someone else, a younger girl, fresh out of college. But Fran pushed hard for Sue Ellen, who seemed a better fit for the position. Despite her lack of work experience, Fran saw an eager, bubbly, down-to-earth grandmother, desperate to land the job. Fran was able to convince the principal to give Sue Ellen a chance, and eleven years later, she's still there."

"Aw, that's a really nice story," Aimee commented.

Janet raised herself up on one elbow. "That's not all. Sue Ellen was about three weeks into her new job when she started having sharp pains in her side. She never told anyone, not even her husband, because she was still within the waiting period for family health insurance. Anyway, Fran saw her crying one day, doubled over at her desk from the pain, and she called an ambulance, despite Sue Ellen's objections. Fran even called in a substitute teacher for her own classroom so that she could follow the ambulance to the emergency room, and along the way she called Dillard."

"So how did it turn out?"

"Sue Ellen's appendix burst in the ambulance but, thankfully, she made a complete recovery in the hospital. Meanwhile, Fran slipped down to the Business Office of the hospital and paid the bill in full, even the ambulance charge."

Aimee was astonished. "Did she really?"

"She sure did. And she insisted that Sue Ellen not pay her back."

"That's cool. I'm glad you told me that story. But those two – they crack me up."

"Yeah, they are a barrel of laughs."

∼

While Janet and Aimee soaked up the morning sun, Fran and Sue Ellen were on the Mezzanine Level, admiring the merchandise in a high-end boutique. Sue Ellen tried on a straw beach hat with a big bow in the back.

"What do you think of this one?" she asked Fran.

"You already have a beach hat," Fran replied.

"I know, but I just wanted to see how this one looks on me." She pursed her lips and playfully tossed her head back and took a selfie. Then she did it again, and again.

"Stop it!" Fran insisted. "You look like you're being goosed."

"I'm trying to look sexy like those models in the magazines. Do you know how they get that pouty look? They say the word 'prune.' Like this." Sue Ellen tried to imitate the pose again.

"Stop doing that! You look ridiculous." Fran snatched the hat from Sue Ellen's head. "Come over here and look at this."

Sue Ellen followed Fran to the purse section where Fran removed a soft leather clutch bag from the display rack and pressed it against her face. "Feel how soft the leather is."

"Ooh, that is beautiful!" Sue Ellen gushed. "Let me see it. Made in Italy! Are you going to get it?"

Fran peeked at the price tag. "Ha! I don't think so. It's $279.00." She pressed the clutch against her chest and closed her eyes. "Joel bought me one like this, for our tenth anniversary. I don't know what ever happened to it." She returned the clutch to its place on the display and moved on to the perfume counter where she sampled a tester.

"You about ready to go, Sue?" Fran asked, sniffing her wrist.

"Not quite. Give me another minute," Sue Ellen replied, leaning over the jewelry case.

The store clerk smiled and asked, "May I help you with something?"

Sue Ellen pointed to a piece. "I'm sure I can't afford it but could you show me that necklace? That one, right there."

Fran drifted back over to the purses and again stared at the fawn-colored clutch with a blank look on her face. Suddenly her expression changed to one of joy. "Well, there you are!" she whispered. "Is that where you've been hiding all these years?" She reached for the clutch and kissed it and placed it in her tote bag.

Fran idled up beside Sue Ellen at the jewelry counter and said, "You can't afford anything in this case and you know it. Let's go."

"Thank you," Sue Ellen nodded to the clerk, a stern looking woman with a jet black beehive, stiff from too much hairspray.

"Can we peek in the candle shop next door?" Sue Ellen asked.

"Sure. Why not?"

As they left the boutique the security alarm blared, stopping both women in their tracks. They looked quizzically at each other, embarrassed by the stares of other shoppers. Much to their relief the alarm subsided as a second clerk appeared out of nowhere.

"Just let me check your purchases, ladies," she said importantly. "Perhaps we failed to remove a security tag."

"We don't have any purchases. We didn't buy anything. Sue Ellen, did you buy anything?"

"No, I did not."

"I'm terribly sorry for the inconvenience. Please come with me," the clerk beckoned.

They followed her to a back room next to the employee restroom. A squirrelly looking man dressed in a suit and sporting a goatee greeted them. His badge indicated that he was store manager.

"Ladies," he nodded at Fran and Sue Ellen. "Is there a problem, Judith?"

"They activated the alarm, yet they claim that they didn't buy anything."

"I see," the manager said, clearing his throat. "Is it possible that either of you might have put some merchandise in your pocket or your purse? Unintentionally, of course."

Fran bristled up at the very idea. "Yes," she replied sarcastically. "My friend here tucked a pair of Jimmy Choo heels into her giant bosom. Was that wrong?"

"Whaaat?" Sue Ellen turned to Fran, her face flushing deeply.

But the store manager found no humor in Fran's cynicism.

"I'm *kidding*," Fran relented. "Search us if you must, but we haven't stolen anything. We may be a lot of things, but we're not thieves."

A security guard suddenly appeared.

"Seriously?" Fran asked.

"Good afternoon!" he greeted everyone cheerfully. "I'm Officer Turley. Let's see if we can clear this up. May I have your names, please?"

"I'm Fran Goldstein."

"And I'm Sue Ellen Pack."

"Thank you," he said, quite pleasantly, writing on his pad. "Would you mind emptying your hand bags on this table top? One at a time, please."

Sue Ellen dumped the contents of her purse and things rolled every which way. She deftly caught a miniature bottle of Cracker Barrel pancake syrup as it rolled off the table. The two men poked around in the messy pile until they were satisfied that nothing had been stolen. Fran then dumped her tote bag rather indignantly and stepped back, her jaw set. All eyes turned to the leather clutch bag with its exorbitant price tag dangling.

"Wait," Fran said, turning white. "Wait just a doggone minute. I was looking at that little purse, I admit, but I never put it in my tote bag."

"Yet there it is," the store manager remarked, his fingers tented.

"I'm telling you the truth! I put it back on the shelf!"

"Then how did it get," he directed his eyes to the table, "there?"

"I – I really don't know. But I assure you that I didn't steal it. I've never stolen anything in my life."

There was a long period of silence during which they all took turns clearing their throats. The two men retreated to a corner and spoke in low tones.

When they returned, the store manager said to Fran, "This is a troubling situation."

"No shit," Fran retorted.

"She's Jewish! She can't control what she says!" Sue Ellen blurted out, as if to justify Fran's insolence.

The men stared intently at Fran for a bit and then the store manager came to a decision. "You are free to go, Miss Goldstein. However, you and your friend are not to return to this store for the remainder of the cruise."

"Yes, sir," Fran said, swallowing her pride. "Thank you."

"Yes, sir," Sue Ellen echoed.

Once they were outside the store in the throes of the other shoppers, they found a bench and sat down together.

"Well, that was awkward," Sue Ellen muttered.

Fran looked shaken. "I distinctly remember putting that purse back in its place on the display. Sue Ellen, did you…?"

"I swear I didn't, Frannie. I wouldn't dare set you up to be, you know, arrested or something."

"I didn't think you would. But somebody did."

"Maybe it fell off the shelf and into your bag."

"Not likely."

"You know ships have jails, don't you?" Sue Ellen whispered. "They're called brigs. You could have been thrown into the brig and become somebody's bitch."

"Shut up, you dimwit. You're not helping."

"C'mon, Frannie, let's go. It's almost 1:00," Sue Ellen said. "I'm hungry."

Fran followed along behind her friend, trying to make sense of what had just happened.

7
Brad and Angelina

The shrill sound of Sue Ellen's voice jolted Aimee and Janet from their poolside naps. She waved from the other side of the pool. "Yoo-hoo!"

Aimee and Janet slowly stood to gather up their things. Aimee wrapped herself in her swimsuit cover-up but not before the older women had seen her willowy frame.

"That child needs some meat on her bones," Sue Ellen muttered.

"No kidding," Fran agreed.

"I'm starving!" Aimee called out. "Let's eat!"

As they entered the buffet area the aroma of Mexican food wafted through the air. "That smells wonderful," Fran said.

"Oh my goodness! Look at that ham!" Sue Ellen watched as a member of the kitchen staff carved thin slices from a large, juicy shank. He wore a white apron, a tall white cap and gloves. "Madam? May I serve you?"

"Yes, please." Sue Ellen accepted a savory slice of ham on a plate and placed it on her tray. She added a baked potato with all the trimmings and then wandered around to see what else might strike her fancy. She opted for macaroni and cheese, a Caesar salad, and a shrimp cocktail. Carefully she made her way to a table and set her full tray down.

Fran appeared with enchiladas, fresh fruit, and a large slice of chocolate cake. Aimee went for the shrimp quesadillas, seasoned rice, and a dish of peach cobbler. Janet was last to sit down, having chosen grilled salmon, scalloped potatoes, and three deviled eggs. The table got quiet as the women dove into their meals.

"Frannie, tell them what happened in the boutique." Sue Ellen turned to the others. "It's a really funny story!"

Fran glowered at Sue Ellen. "I told you not to say anything."

Puzzled, Sue Ellen said, "No, you didn't."

"Yes, I did."

"No, you didn't. Why can't I tell them?"

"*Because I'm asking you not to! It was embarrassing.*"

Based on Fran's tone of voice, Janet and Aimee knew better than to press the issue. Sue Ellen looked a little hurt, disappointed that Fran had squashed a perfectly good story, but she merely lifted her shoulders in resignation and sliced off another bite of ham.

Once they'd reached their fill the women stood, groaning, and walked single file toward the pool area. The sky had darkened during lunch and a blowing wind felt damp. "We're about to get some rain," Fran predicted.

They passed a group of excited kids in wet swimsuits hovered around an ice cream cone machine.

"Oh, look! They're making ice cream cones!" Sue Ellen cried. "Hi, kids! Are you all having fun? Does anyone need help?" One child couldn't reach the cones and another dropped her ice cream, but Sue Ellen was right in the middle of it all, wiping up their messes and doing what she did best.

Then the ladies ran shrieking and laughing through the driving sheets of rain, arriving at their cabins soaked and breathless. Their beds were made, towels and toiletries replenished, and floor items tidied up. A new towel animal sat on each bed along with chocolates on the pillows.

According to the business card that he left behind, their steward's name was Wayan. As if on cue, a slight knock on Janet and Aimee's door announced his arrival. They opened the door to a small, smiling man, obviously not of American descent. He struggled with his

English as he introduced himself. "Hello. My name is Wayan. I am your steward."

"It's very nice to meet you, Wayan. I'm Janet, and this is my roommate, Aimee."

The door across the hallway opened and Sue Ellen and Fran peeked out.

"And these ladies are our friends, Sue Ellen and Fran," Janet continued. "We're all from Arkansas."

Wayan nodded and smiled pleasantly but offered no response, leaving them to wonder if he had understood a single word. Aimee quickly pulled up a map of the United States on her phone and pointed to the state of Arkansas.

"Ah, yes," he said.

Sue Ellen was curious. "Where are you from, Waylon?"

"It's Wayan, Sue Ellen. Not Waylon," Fran corrected her.

"I live here. On the ship."

"But where did you grow up?"

"Sorry?"

Aimee stepped in. "Your home? Where were you born?" she asked sweetly, speaking her words slowly and clearly.

"Bali is my home," Wayan beamed.

"Bali! How interesting! You are a long way from home."

He nodded. "You like these?" He motioned to the towel animals.

"Yes!" they all replied in unison.

"Did you make them?" Aimee asked.

"I make them."

"Our cabin is so clean and comfortable. Thank you," Aimee said.

"Yes, thank you," the others joined in.

"Wayan, I'm missing a small suitcase." Sue Ellen enunciated the words slowly and loudly. "I need my Mary Kay."

He smiled politely. "I will check for you."

"And Wayan," Fran spoke up. "See if you can get someone to fix the sign on our door. It's been hanging like that for months."

Wayan stepped outside the door and studied the room number sign, puzzled because the sign was as it should be. "Okay. Have a good day!" He waved as he left.

"Are we supposed to tip him, Janet?" Aimee asked.

"No, we signed up for automatic tipping on our final bills, remember?"

"I wonder what it's like to live and work on a cruise ship. I wonder if he has a family," Aimee speculated. "I'm going to ask him next time."

Sue Ellen retreated to her room. "It's nap time for me, girls. Bye-bye."

Fran followed her and curled up with a romance novel, longing for a cigarette and not at all sure that she could keep her end of the deal. The cravings were brutal.

Aimee scribbled in her journal while Janet called her parents to check on Lucy. The rain continued throughout the afternoon but no one cared, cozy as they were.

~

In celebration of their first full day at sea, the girls met for evening drinks at the same tiki bar where they had gathered yesterday. The rain had subsided and the sun had broken through gloriously.

"Just think," Janet proclaimed, "Another day of sailing tomorrow and then we'll be in Honduras. Can you believe it?"

Sue Ellen was working on her second Bahama Mama and was loose as a goose. "No, I can't. This is fantastic! I'm so glad you won that money."

Janet winked at her.

"But my makeup case still hasn't turned up. All of my Mary Kay is in there. And my panties."

"Your panties?"

"Yes. My panties."

"So," ventured Fran, "does this mean you're not wearing any?"

"I'm going commando. It's a thing."

Janet involuntarily spit her drink across the table and Aimee laughed out loud.

"Well, whatever it's called, it's indecent. What's the matter with you?" Fran scolded her.

"It's not indecent," Sue Ellen objected, "but it does feel strange. I will be glad to get my suitcase back because it's got a brand new package of special panties in it."

"Why so special? Victoria's Secret?" Aimee guessed.

"No, JC Penney. Big Girls' Cotton Hipsters, they're called, designed to control muffin tops."

"Okay," Aimee nodded without expression, "but why are you going without underwear? Why aren't you wearing the ones you had on when we boarded yesterday? You could have washed them."

"Because."

"Because why?"

"Yeah, because why?" Janet wanted to know.

"Because I threw them away!" Sue Ellen snapped.

Fran groaned and closed her eyes. "I don't like where this is going."

"It's not what you think. I was just so busy packing and freezing casseroles for Dillard that I forgot to do laundry, so when it came time to leave the house I couldn't find any clean undies. So I wore some of Dillard's."

"You wore your husband's underwear in my car?" Janet glared.

"I didn't see any harm in it. They were boxer briefs, with the comfort flex waistband. But I knew that Fran here wouldn't approve so I tossed them in the trash in the ladies' room as soon as we boarded. How was I supposed to know that my luggage would get lost?"

Aimee wasn't satisfied and needed clarification. "So…before you left your house, when you couldn't find any clean undies, why didn't you open up the brand new panties?"

"Because I wanted to save them for the cruise! You know how it is. You buy something new for a special occasion, you *save* it for that special occasion. Otherwise, it's not new anymore and you have to buy something else new. Am I right?" Sue Ellen looked around for validation but got only blank stares.

"I didn't want to open the package, *okay?*" she huffed. "They weren't for riding in the car. They were for cruising."

"Can I smoke a cigarette?" Fran asked. "Because this vision of her in Dillard's boxers is killing me. I might as well die happy with a cigarette."

"Look!" Janet pointed. "There he goes again!" All heads turned as their cruise director sprinted past them and up a flight of stairs.

"He seems to be everywhere," Fran remarked.

"I talked with him earlier," Aimee said. "He stopped to say hello while I was sunbathing. Before you got there, Janet."

"Lucky you," Janet said.

"He's very personable. But he's married, so that's that."

"How do you know he's married?" Sue Ellen wanted to know.

"Because he had a wedding band on his ring finger. That's the universal clue."

"Oh."

"Anyway, I'm done with men for a while. Done."

The others raised their eyebrows at each other.

"Do you want to talk about it?" Sue Ellen asked, hoping for some juicy girl talk.

"Nope."

Sue Ellen cast her eyes down, feeling rebuked.

"Wait. I'm sorry. That sounded rude. It's just that I'm really down on men right now. They can't be trusted."

"Was it a bad break-up? I didn't know you were seeing anyone," Janet remarked.

"No, nothing like that. It was…well, if you really want to hear the story, I guess I can tell you, but it's ugly."

The girls settled in, all ears, and Aimee heaved a big sigh.

"So, you all probably figured out that I'm poor. I'm having a hard time making ends meet, right? My apartment is expensive and my car needs work. I teach piano lessons twice a week and still I can barely pay my bills. So anyway, I saw an ad where this couple was looking for a house-sitter for a few days. I seemed to meet the qualifications – responsible single person, over twenty-one, dependable transportation, no pet allergies. $500 for three days and nights. I called right away and the wife hired me over the phone. She sounded desperate. Apparently somebody had died and they had to attend an out-of-state funeral."

"So what happened?" Fran asked.

"Well, it turned out to be a disastrous experience. I'm going to need another drink to tell the rest."

"My treat," Janet said, jumping up. "Hold that thought."

Janet returned quickly with another cocktail for Aimee and took her seat. "Go on."

"They seemed nice, in their early thirties, I'd say. Mr. and Mrs. Bennett. He was a building contractor and she owned a boutique. Their house was really nice - a beautiful brick two-story. The wife thanked me and went to sit in the car while her husband gave me a quick tour of the house. He was very good looking and kind of flirtatious. After the tour he gave me a house key and their contact information and told me that I could help myself to the wine in the kitchen. Then I said, 'Your ad mentioned a pet.' And he said, 'Oh, yeah, my wife has two cockatoos in a cage in the front dining room. They were an anniversary gift from me. Which I now regret.'" He smiled and winked at me when he said that.

"Hm, I'm not sure I like this guy," Fran mumbled.

Sue Ellen was itching to hear more. "Go on, then what happened?"

"He showed me the birds, Brad and Angelina. They were in a big fancy cage and they were really pretty, with big plumes on their heads. Mrs. Bennett had left a note clipped to their cage with instructions on how to care for them - how much to feed them, and how often. She said they wouldn't be any trouble at all, but she added a P. S. that they were very expensive exotic birds, which of course made me nervous."

"Uh-oh," Janet whispered, gulping her drink.

"Did they get out?" Sue Ellen wondered.

Aimee scoffed. "Ha! If only it were that simple. So, after the Bennetts left, I went out to my car to get my things and ..."

"You killed them, didn't you?" Fran surmised. "The cockatoos."

"I didn't mean to! It was an accident!" Aimee cried.

Janet shook her head slowly, "Oh, my Lord."

"Did you strangle them, honey?" Sue Ellen asked, patting Aimee's knee.

"*No!* I didn't *strangle* them! Why would I strangle them? Geez, what kind of a person do you think I am?" Flustered, Aimee shook her head and said, "Now I can't even remember what I was saying."

"You were saying how you went out to the car to get your things."

Aimee cleared her throat and took a deep breath. "Right. So, I had brought a small bag and some clothes on hangers. I left my things in the foyer because I wanted to check out the back yard before I went upstairs. I remembered what Mr. Bennett had said about the wine so I poured myself a glass and stepped outside on the patio. I felt like a queen, getting to stay in such a lovely house and getting paid for it."

"Skip all that nonsense and get to the good stuff," Fran insisted.

"Oh, sorry. So I ended up having a second glass of wine. It was a very good Cabernet. But then it started to rain so I went inside. I couldn't remember when I was supposed to feed the birds so I looked at the instructions and that's when I saw the spider crawling along the windowsill. I'm pretty sure it was a brown recluse. And I screamed, which scared the birds and they started flapping their wings and screaming, too. I didn't know birds could scream."

"What did you do then?"

"I ran through the house looking for bug spray and I found a big aerosol can in the pantry. I got after that spider pretty good. I sprayed and sprayed and sprayed, chasing it all around that window until it finally curled up into a crinkled wad and fell onto the floor. I crushed it with the foot of a dining room chair." She tossed back her drink. "I imagine it's still there." She shuddered.

"I was so upset about the spider that I forgot about the birds. I poured another glass of wine and grabbed my things and headed upstairs to unpack and have a nice bubble bath." Aimee paused. "Did I mention that the carpeting was white? What kind of people have white carpet in their house?"

"People who don't have kids, that's who," Sue Ellen said.

"So with the wine in my right hand and my clothing draped across my left arm, I start up the stairs and a clothes hanger hooks itself on the newel post and it yanks me backwards, and wine sloshes everywhere. All over the white stair runner and the dove grey walls. It was a big glass of wine, too. What a waste."

Fran snorted and bourbon came out of her nose. Janet clapped her hand over her mouth and Sue Ellen dissolved into giggles.

"It wasn't funny, y'all!" Aimee cried, smiling as she said so. "I found some rags and started sopping up the wine and then I ran to the pantry to look for bleach and of course there wasn't any. I sat down on a step and cried for a long time because I knew I couldn't fix it."

"Then what did you do?"

"I was afraid to have more wine so I had my bubble bath and got ready for bed, and then I remembered about feeding the birds. So I went back downstairs, stepping over the carpet stains, and I find both cockatoos lying on their backs with their feet in the air, dead as doornails."

"Ohh, Aimee!"

"Holy crap!"

"At first I wasn't sure they were dead. Their eyes were closed but I thought maybe that's just how they slept. But I poked them with a straw and they didn't budge. I guess I killed them with the bug spray."

Janet pressed her lips together, trying not to laugh, and instead she wet her pants a little bit.

"Keep going, Aimee," Fran prodded her. "You have to tell us the rest. What happened then?"

"Oof. Well, I decided I should tell them about the wine stains and the dead birds before they got home, to give them time to vent some of their anger. So I sent them an e-mail apology with pictures and I told them they didn't have to pay me for the house-sitting, and that I would stay for free until they got home. I got a scathing reply from Beverly, who insisted that I replace the cockatoos and the stair runner immediately. I didn't hear anything from Robert. I was so scared."

"What happened when they got home?"

"They got back late in the evening on Sunday and I was all packed and ready to go, expecting to be raked over the coals. Beverly was apparently so upset with me that she marched straight upstairs without looking at me, but Robert didn't seem too upset about the birds or the carpet. I told him that I knew that giving up my house-sitting fee wouldn't begin to reimburse them for the damages but that I would do my best to repay them."

"And what did he say?"

"He said, 'Don't worry about it. I'm sure we can think of some way to make this right.' So I asked him, 'How?' and he said, 'Have dinner with me this week and we'll use our imaginations.'"

"Whaaat?" Sue Ellen's eyes were big and round. "He said that? You know what that means, don't you?"

"Of course she knows what that means, Sue Ellen!" Fran snapped. "She's not a child! What did you say to him, Aimee?"

"I was shocked. I said, 'Wait. What?' And he looked me up and down and said, 'I'm sure we can figure out a way to smooth this over.'"

Fran was disgusted. "What a schmuck."

"I didn't know what to do, but I said something like, 'You're a married man and I doubt your wife would appreciate that sort of arrangement.' And he said, 'Who cares?' and I said, 'I care. I'd rather owe you money for the rest of my life than to do something like that.'"

"That was the right thing to say, Aimee," Janet assured her.

"He just smirked and said, 'Look who's getting all self-righteous! How about I just send you a bill, then.' But he never did."

"Shame on him!" Sue Ellen frowned. "That skunk!"

"Yeah. It was the worst weekend of my life. And for Brad and Angelina, too."

The table fell silent for a long moment until Sue Ellen stood and announced, "I'm going to the ladies' room." As she walked away a nearby table of teenagers pointed at her and made insulting cat calls.

"Yo! Mama! You need to cover up!"

"Where do you buy your bras? At the feed store?"

Sue Ellen lifted her chin, a sure sign that she had heard them, but she kept going. Fran's eyes narrowed as the insults continued.

"Hey, lady, you're blocking the sun!"

"I'll bet she's headed to the buffet."

Fran stood with clenched fists and addressed the table with fury in her eyes. "Y'all need to shut the fuck up! Where are your manners? Didn't your parents teach you anything? Like mind your own business? Respect your elders?" Her fiery eyes traveled from one kid to the next. "Don't make me come over here again. Better yet, just get the hell out of here – all of you - you disrespectful little shits!"

Fran's wrath sent the kids wide-eyed and running. She sat back down, shaking, avoiding the astonished looks on her friends' faces. "I need a cigarette," she muttered.

"Geez, Fran. Remind me to never get on your bad side," Janet said timidly.

But Aimee was clearly in awe. "Fran! That was awesome! I've never seen you like that!"

Fran had surprised even herself with her outrage, and the incident left her feeling a bit embarrassed. "Friends take care of friends," was all she had to say.

Sue Ellen ambled toward them, relieved to see that the rude kids were gone. "I'm going to sit on the side of the pool and splash my feet. The water looks so nice and cool."

"You've had a lot to drink, so be careful," Fran advised her.

"I will, Frannie!" Sue Ellen wiggled her fingers at her friends and wandered away, finding a spot at the shallow end of the pool.

Fran slowly folded a piece of gum into her mouth and chewed thoughtfully. She turned to face Janet and Aimee. "There's more to that woman than meets the eye," she declared. "She's got a good heart."

Janet and Aimee waited, expecting Fran to say more, but she didn't.

"Only a true friend would come to her defense the way you did," Aimee remarked.

"It's the least I can do. She helped me out once, in a much bigger way, and I'll never forget it."

"Are you going to tell us a story?" Janet asked. "Please?"

Fran snapped her gum and said, "Why not? Let's give credit where credit is due."

Aimee and Janet both pulled their chairs in closer.

"You both know I lost my husband seven years ago."

"Right. A car accident. I'm so sorry, Fran," Janet said quietly.

"Thank you. But you may not know that Joel was unfaithful to me. He had a mistress during the last years of our marriage."

Janet was shocked. She had no idea. "Fran, you don't have to talk about this…"

"But I want to. He was a college professor - a brilliant man. His car went off the road and down an embankment one night, and he was killed."

Aimee's face softened. "I'm so sorry, Fran! I didn't know."

"The woman was with him, and she survived the accident. The newspapers were kind enough to withhold any information about her."

Aimee and Janet exchanged looks, not sure what to say.

"It's not like I didn't know about her. I did. It had been going on for quite some time." Fran paused to take a gulp of bourbon. "I kept hoping that Joel would tire of her."

Sue Ellen hollered from the pool and they waved back at her.

"He wasn't a believer in life insurance. He left me with nothing except our mortgaged home and two vehicles. I was struggling with the funeral arrangements, and that's when Sue Ellen offered to help. She went with me to the funeral home and she made a lot of the decisions that I couldn't make. I was barely functioning."

Fran's eyes glistened with tears, remembering. "Sue Ellen knew about Joel's mistress. She had seen them together, more than once. It was humiliating."

Janet sank a little lower in her chair, but Fran went on. "On the day of Joel's funeral, I was seated on the front row with Sue Ellen and Dillard, waiting for the service to begin, when all of a sudden Sue Ellen stood up and marched to the back of the church. I turned around to see where she had gone." Fran's eyes dropped to her lap.

"And?" Aimee urged her.

"And, wouldn't you know it, she had spotted that *woman*, standing at the back of the church, looking for a seat. Sue Ellen wasn't having it. She pulled her into the foyer and got right in her face and told her that she was not welcome, and that she needed to leave."

"Oh, wow! And did she? Did she leave?" Janet was wide-eyed.

"Damn straight she did. Sue Ellen took her by the arm and escorted her out of the church and all the way to her car! And from that moment on, I've had nothing but respect for Sue Ellen Pack."

Fran waited for her friends to absorb that information before she went on. "I know I don't show it, but she and I decided a long time ago that neither of us wants to feel indebted to the other. That puts too much pressure on a friendship. We prefer to call it even and keep squabbling."

Janet sat back in her chair. "Gosh, this has been a very enlightening evening. I've learned so much about both of you. I don't even know what to say."

"There's nothing to say. It's just life. Life happens," Fran said matter-of-factly. "Now let's go get that bimbo out of the pool so we can call it a day."

8
I Have Nothing to Wear

The morning crackling sound from the P. A. system was becoming familiar, signaling another announcement from the cruise director.

Good morning, everyone! Today will be another full day of sailing. You'll find today's activity schedule on your door, and I hope you'll take advantage of the many fun things to do on the ship. And in case you need reminding, tonight is Dinner with the Captain in the Blue Fin Restaurant on Deck Three. There are two seating times, so please check in at the time you selected when you made your cruise reservation. And remember, folks, this is a dressy affair so no blue jeans, please!

Janet listened carefully and sat up in bed. "Aimee, I'm gonna need your help," she said sheepishly.

"With what?"

"I have absolutely nothing appropriate to wear tonight. Can we go shopping?"

Aimee's face broke into a wide grin. "Yes! Of course! Shopping is my thing. I'd love to help you find something."

"Thank you. I wonder what time the stores open."

"Probably nine. Maybe ten."

"Okay, then we have plenty of time."

Sue Ellen and Fran could be heard in the hallway. "You're such a dang know-it-all," Sue Ellen was saying as they barged in, oblivious to the occupants still lounging in their beds.

"I'm just trying to explain to you that you can't keep calling Dillard two and three times a day, Sue! Your bill is going to be sky-high! I'd bet my bottom dollar that he never got you an international plan."

"Well, you're the math teacher. Tell me how many times I can call him."

"I don't know! It's not my job to manage your expenses. Anyway, Dillard is a grown-ass man. You don't need to babysit him about those casseroles."

Sue Ellen pouted, her mouth a straight line.

"Stop it. You look like an Emoji."

"I liked you better before you gave up cigarettes, Fran. Let me go buy you a pack."

"You just want an excuse to go make an ice cream cone."

"Shut up. Both of you," Janet snapped.

"What are y'all doing today?" Fran asked sweetly as she sat down on Aimee's bed.

"We're going clothes shopping. Janet wants something new to wear to dinner tonight," Aimee explained. "Want to go with us?"

"Ugh," Fran said, reminded of yesterday's near arrest at the boutique. "No, thanks. Sue Ellen and I are going to see if we can win some bingo money. She's gonna need it for her phone bill."

~

Aimee hit the ground running as soon as the stores opened. She rifled through racks and studied mannequins while sizing up her tall, long-waisted roommate.

"What are you, about an eight? A ten?"

Janet shrugged. "I have no idea. I know I'm a men's large, extra-long, in tee shirts."

Aimee laughed, but Janet didn't, so Aimee cleared her throat and said in a perky voice, "Well, then, we'll just have to see!" She herded Janet into a dressing room with three garments in her arms.

Janet pulled her polo shirt over her head and stood in her gray sports bra – the one with the little balls of fuzz clinging to it. Aimee made a mental note to take Janet to the lingerie section.

"Try this on first." Aimee handed her friend a pale yellow tank top with a long, lightweight jacket to go over it. The jacket was a splashy, beachy pattern of turquoise, orange and yellow. Janet wriggled into the colorful duo with some white pants and studied herself.

"Nah, that's not me," Janet said. "I look like a kaleidoscope."

"It's pretty on you, though."

Janet frowned and shook her head.

"Okay, let's try something else, then," Aimee said cheerfully, and hung the outfit on the door.

Next was a pale blue sundress which zipped up the back. "This will show off your tan," Aimee said, "and your eyes."

Janet frowned. "I really don't wear dresses. I can't remember the last time I put on a dress."

Not to be discouraged, Aimee reached for the third item, a black tunic in a soft knit fabric, sleeveless with gold trim around the neckline and hem. "This is classy, don't you think? This will look good on you," she promised.

Janet tugged it over her head and it fell beautifully around her torso and her narrow hips. Her eyes lit up as she gazed at herself in the wall mirror.

"Oh!" Aimee exclaimed, pointing at the mirror. "That's it. That's the one. Stay right there and I'll be right back with some slacks."

"Make sure they're long enough!" Janet called after her.

Aimee returned moments later with black dress slacks, long and lightweight. They, too, were a great fit.

"Perfect! Are your ears pierced, Janet? Because I have some gold earrings you can borrow that will really set this off. Did you bring any dress sandals?"

"No, but I brought a new pair of Crocs. They're brown, though."

Aimee made a face. "Well, you're not wearing brown crocs with this outfit, so prepare to spend more money. But I promise you, you're going to look like a million bucks."

Meanwhile, Fran and Sue Ellen were returning from bingo, arguing, as always. "It's really not that complicated, Sue," Fran was saying. "Let me explain it to you this way. Let's say a baby is being born right now, in the state of California. Let's say it's noon there."

"Okay."

"So the baby is only a few seconds old. Brand new. Right?"

"Right."

"What time is it in Georgia?"

Sue Ellen counted on her fingers. "It would be, hmm, 3:00 pm in Georgia. So that means the baby is already three hours old. In Georgia," she reasoned.

"No, *the baby is what it is*, only a few seconds old. It's the time of day that changes, depending on where you are."

"But you said…"

Fran changed tactics. "Try to see it this way, Sue. You and Dillard are about to watch the Super Bowl at your house. Kick-off time is at 5:30 pm in Arkansas."

"Okay."

"But if you're watching in Colorado, kick-off is at 4:30."

"Right!" Sue Ellen bristled. "That's what I'm saying! They're already an hour into the game! They'll know the final score way before us! How can that be fair?"

"Wait. What? No, no, no, Sue Ellen, you've got it all wrong." Flustered, Fran stopped abruptly and yanked her key card from around her neck. She jabbed it several times into the card slot on the door, but nothing happened. No green light. She turned the card around and tried again. Nothing.

"What are you doing, Fran?"

"Well, duh! I'm trying to get into the room so I can lie down and take a nap. You're giving me a headache."

"But this isn't our room, honey."

Fran jerked her chin at Sue Ellen. "Of course this is our room. See?" She held the card up.

"The numbers don't match the door. Our room is on up the hall."

Embarrassed, Fran stepped back from the door and made a big to-do of sweeping her arms for Sue Ellen to take the lead. "Fine, Miss Smarty Pants, lead the way to our room. Be my guest. But don't talk to me when we get there. You make me tired."

Sue Ellen kept her mouth shut but couldn't help but wonder why Fran had suddenly lost her clarity.

∼

As evening approached Aimee used her styling wand to put loose waves in her friend's shoulder-length hair, raking her fingers through to separate the waves, and then sprayed it with something that smelled like coconut.

"Do you like it, Janet?"

"I do. I really do. Wow."

Aimee rummaged through her makeup bag and Janet said, "Go easy on the makeup, kiddo. Don't make me look like a clown." She had never been one to wear more than mascara and lip gloss.

After applying primer, foundation and a light dusting of powder, Aimee concentrated on Janet's blue eyes. Her eyebrows were naturally dark and well-shaped so Aimee left them alone. She used a soft brush to cover Janet's eyelids with an iridescent shade of peach, and then accented the crease with a peachy-bronze color. Janet applied the mascara and liner herself. The result was a fresh, natural look, with just enough color to draw out the blue in her eyes.

Janet bent to look at her reflection in the dresser mirror. "Oh! Well! I should wear makeup more often, shouldn't I? I look a lot better."

"You look beautiful, if I do say so myself. But your eyes are so pretty to begin with, so I didn't have to do much."

Janet reached for her roommate and hugged her. "Thank you so much."

"Are you wearing the new lingerie?"

"Yes, if you must know! I can't believe I let you talk me into it. Who's gonna see it, anyway?"

"You never know!" Aimee giggled. She glanced at the time and shouted, "Yikes! I'd better get myself ready! We're supposed to be there at 6:30."

∼

The foursome gathered in the hallway and complimented each other on their appearances. Much to Sue Ellen's delight her missing suitcase had arrived and everyone felt better knowing that she was fully clothed. She wore the funeral dress, and her face glowed with Mary Kay Cosmetics and false eyelashes.

Fran was dressed in white pants with a multi-colored top and a beautiful necklace. Aimee looked dazzling in a tight-fitting, off-the-shoulder emerald green cocktail dress.

Wayan suddenly rounded the corner. "Ah. Lovely ladies. Shall I take your photo?"

Thrilled at his offer, they cozied up together in the hallway in a number of sassy poses. Then Wayan walked with them to the elevators.

"Wayan, do you have family back in Bali?" Aimee asked him.

"Yes, my mother and father, two brothers, one sister. I see them once a year."

"Once a year?"

"August. I see my family in August."

"And the rest of the year you are on the ship?"

"Yes. Save my money to go to Bali. Very expensive to go."

Then Wayan nodded politely and backed away. "Enjoy!"

Once he was out of earshot Sue Ellen exclaimed, "Imagine being away from your loved ones for so long!"

"Do you think he's happy?" Janet wondered.

"I'm sure he's got lots of friends on the ship. Other crew members. They all stay together, you know, in bunks. They eat together and everything," Aimee explained. "At least that's what I've heard."

Several large groups were already waiting for an elevator, including three men with short military haircuts. The tallest one with dark hair turned casually and smiled approvingly at Janet before he looked away. She felt herself flush.

The elevators were busy and the waiting became awkward so the three men headed for the stairs. As they did so, the same tall fellow made eye contact with Janet and nodded politely.

"Did you see that?" Fran whispered. "That good-looking hunk was giving you the eye!"

"No, he wasn't."

"Oh, yes he was, Janet! I saw it, too," Aimee said.

"I've never seen you look so pretty, Janet. A little makeup is becoming on you," Sue Ellen noted.

"Thanks," Janet smiled. "Point taken. I'll start fixing up more. What say we take the stairs, too?"

After descending eight flights of stairs they found the Blue Fin Restaurant where two lines of guests had formed. The lines moved quickly as young hostesses directed each couple or group to their assigned table. Janet caught herself looking around for the handsome guy who had given her the eye but then remembered, with disappointment, that he and his buddies were not dressed for dinner; they were wearing athletic clothing.

"I wonder who we will be sitting with," Aimee speculated. "I hope they're interesting."

"I hope they don't have kids," Fran grumbled. Now on day three without a cigarette, she was struggling to keep her irritability in check.

After signing in they were given card 38-J and the hostess pointed in the general direction of their table. "Some of the others are already there," she smiled.

Sue Ellen was giddy. "This is so exciting," she whispered, barely able to contain herself. As they approached their table for eight they could see that two seats were occupied by a dark-skinned, mature woman and a little boy. The woman was dressed in a red halter dress with a striking silver pendant around her long neck, her flamboyant hair held back from her face with a colorful scarf.

Sue Ellen gasped and nudged Aimee. "Isn't that the woman we saw in the atrium?"

Aimee nodded discreetly. "That's her."

Janet checked the table number and smiled at the woman and boy. "Hello!" she greeted them.

The lovely woman returned a broad smile with perfect teeth. "Hello, ladies! Please, come and join us!"

The boy rose and stood politely until everyone took a seat. He wore a navy blue suit with a white shirt, his bow tie yellow with navy stripes. The woman touched him on the arm. "Jamal, would you like to introduce us?"

"Sure. I'm Jamal Clarke and this is my grandmother, Birdie."

His eyes were large and dark, his black hair shorn close to his head. When he smiled, a dimple appeared in his left cheek.

"I'm Janet. It's very nice to meet you both."

"And I'm Fran. I like your tie, Jamal."

"I'm Aimee. You have very nice manners, Jamal. How old are you?"

"I'm six but I'll be seven in August."

Sue Ellen beamed at the little boy. "My name is Sue Ellen. Aren't you handsome in your Sunday suit! Did you say this beautiful lady is your grandmother?"

"Yes, ma'am. Birdie is her name. I had a mama but she fell out of a tree and died. Now she lives in Heaven."

Birdie lifted her eyebrows at her grandson. "Jamal, I never said that your mother fell out of a tree. Where in the world did you get that idea?"

Jamal frowned at his grandmother in confusion. "But you said she went out on a limb, for the cause."

An awkward pause followed and Fran chuckled uncertainly. Birdie laughed out loud.

"Please excuse my grandson. He takes everything so literally, I have to be careful what I say. And I should warn you that he has no filters," she added, hugging the little boy's shoulder. "Jamal, we'll talk again before bed about your mother. She was a brave and fearless woman who put herself in danger, but she didn't fall out of a tree."

Janet wanted to giggle but instead said, "I'm sorry for your loss, both of you. And we're schoolteachers, so we're used to unfiltered comments."

"Thank you. I appreciate that. I'm sure you ladies know that drinks are complimentary tonight," Birdie stated. "I've just ordered a Cosmopolitan." Even as she spoke, a female server appeared and placed Birdie's cocktail in front of her, and a Shirley Temple in front of Jamal.

"Thank you," he said, and then grinned at his grandmother, who winked in return.

"I'm Liz," said their server. "Welcome to the Blue Fin. What can I get for you ladies? Have you seen the wine list? Or perhaps you'd prefer a cocktail?"

Aimee ordered a glass of Cabernet, as did Janet. Fran ordered a Jack Daniels with Coke. Sue Ellen was unable to make up her mind. "What is that you're drinking?" she asked Birdie.

"It's a Cosmopolitan, and it's delicious. Want a sip?"

"Okay, I'll try a sip." As she swallowed she smacked her lips a couple of times and proclaimed, "Yes! That's what I want."

Liz smiled and said, "I'll be right back, ladies."

"So, where are you schoolteachers from?" Birdie wanted to know.

"We're from Arkansas," Sue Ellen responded. "I'm not a teacher, though. I work in the front office."

"Arkansas. Home of the Razorbacks, right? Woo pig sooie?" She wiggled her hands in the air, much to their delight, and everyone laughed.

"Jamal, tell the ladies where we are from."

"Florida."

"I mean, originally."

"Jamaica. I'm Jamaican. So is Birdie," he said proudly. "But we live in Tallahassee now. I'll be in second grade when school starts back."

"Jamaica!" Aimee exclaimed. "I've never been there, but I'd like to see it. Is it beautiful?" She directed her question to Jamal.

"I don't know," he shrugged and looked at his grandmother.

"Jamal doesn't remember Jamaica because we've been in Tallahassee since he was two. After we lost his mother – my daughter - I felt he would have a better life in America. Jamaica has a high rate of crime and violence, and the economic situation is, well, suffering. It was quite a culture shock – the move to the States – but we are happy."

"Do you work?" Aimee asked.

"I do! I work as a guidance counselor at Tallahassee Community College. So in a sense, we are all in the business of education, aren't we?"

Liz returned and began to place their beverages around the table. "Anything else, ladies?"

"I'd like another Cosmopolitan," Birdie smiled. "No hurry."

"And you, sir? Another Shirley Temple?" Jamal nodded after glancing at Birdie for approval. He popped the cherry into his mouth before Liz took his glass.

"This is fun!" Sue Ellen exclaimed. "We don't get a chance to get dressed up very often, do we, girls?"

Birdie tapped her glass with a spoon. "I propose a toast. To new friends!" Six glasses clinked together.

Aimee motioned to the two empty chairs at the end of the table. "I wonder where the other guests are. They're running late."

"Maybe Captain Anderson plans to sit there," Sue Ellen said, hopefully. Her eyes traveled around the expansive dining room. "I wonder what he looks like."

A jazz band played on a small stage and the atmosphere was festive. Sue Ellen jiggled her shoulders and drained her glass. "Just look at all the glamorous people! Isn't this wonderful?" She waved at Liz. "Honey, could you bring me another pleash, drink?"

Liz smiled at her slurred words. "Sure, I'll be right back."

Birdie, Fran and Janet had their heads together, discussing the pros and cons of testing for college admission. Aimee chatted with Jamal while Sue Ellen took photos of herself until her second Cosmopolitan arrived, and soon she was flying high. One of her false eyelashes popped loose at the inside corner and twisted up and out. Fran noticed and started to tell her but then decided not to, instead smiling wickedly into her bourbon and Coke.

Jamal stared at Aimee and declared, "You're pretty."

"Well, thank you! And you look very handsome! What is your favorite thing to do, Jamal?"

"I like to play with my friends, and ride my bike, and I like to dance. But mostly I just like to be with Birdie. She's my best friend. We do lots of fun stuff together."

"Like what?"

"Well, today we went to the water park. Have you been? Birdie put me on her lap and we went down the biggest slide of all, and I wasn't even scared."

"That sounds fun." Aimee was in awe of this little boy being raised by his grandmother. What a remarkable bond they seemed to have. As Jamal excitedly told her about their plans for tomorrow, her eyes drifted over to a couple making their way through the dining room, headed in their general direction. She sucked in her breath and suddenly felt wracked with nausea, her heart pounding.

Aimee bent her head to Jamal and whispered, "I feel sick, honey. I have to go."

She picked up her purse, put her head down and hurried to an exit door at the back of the room. So quickly did she slip away that the others didn't even notice.

~

Aimee ended up in a "staff only" area and got some questioning looks. "I'm sorry," she apologized, "I'm looking for the ladies' room."

"That way, miss. Right around that corner."

Aimee made it into a stall just in time to vomit. She steadied herself, her legs shaking, and wiped at her mouth with a handful of toilet paper. When she felt like her stomach had settled she went to a sink and rinsed her mouth.

I can't believe this is happening.

She took a deep breath and, clutching her purse, found a stairway and started climbing, putting distance between her and the restaurant. *I can't go back.* When she tired of climbing stairs she wandered through the crowded casino, but the smell of cigarette smoke made her stomach churn again. She was desperate for fresh air but didn't know how to get outside.

Suddenly she pushed through some glass doors and found herself on the running track. She stopped short and gulped in some air. As she did so, an evening jogger almost ran her over.

"Hey, lady, watch where you're going!"

Frightened, Aimee ducked back inside and began to follow a hallway, trailing her hand along the wall, her heart palpitating. She descended some stairs and followed another hallway, going nowhere in particular but needing to be alone. She took note of the cabin numbers. 663, 665, 667. *I'll feel better soon. I just need to lie down.* She noticed that the carpet beneath her feet was the same as that in her dentist's office, a festive swirl of coral, blue, and beige. *How funny that I would notice that. I'll have to remember to tell Dr. Downs.*

She turned a corner and saw what looked to be a small meeting room, its door standing ajar. It was a library, she realized, with a couple of small couches and an armchair. Making sure no one else was in the room, Aimee turned off the light and closed the door. Then she shut her phone off and collapsed into the armchair. *I'll just rest here for a little while and then I'll call Janet.*

As she nodded off in the darkness, the library door slowly swung back open.

9
Pineapple Up-down Side Cake

The newcomers stood at the end of the table. "Hello. Sorry we're late. I'm Robert. This is my wife, Beverly. What have we missed?"

Janet spoke first. "Hi! We're just having cocktails. I'm Janet Kayler," she said, extending her hand.

Jamal studied Robert as the others introduced themselves. "He's got jeans on, Birdie! That's against the rules!"

"Shhh, Jamal!" Birdie scolded, shaking her head.

Beverly was an attractive woman with dark, glossy hair pulled up into a twist with long, wispy bangs framing her face. Robert was attractive, as well, with shaggy blonde hair and boyish features.

Beverly asked, "What are we drinking tonight?"

"You should get a Shirley Temple! Mine is really good! You want a taste?" Jamal offered.

Before Beverly could respond, a dark-complected man with his hair in a bun appeared at their table. "Good evening," he greeted them. "I'm Enrico, and I'll be your server tonight. Everyone having a good time?"

Sue Ellen nudged Fran. "See his hair? That's the style," she whispered. She took a photo of him when he wasn't looking.

Enrico handed out fancy menus and even gave one to Jamal. "You're looking sharp tonight, young man," he remarked.

Jamal sat up straight and grinned. "Thank you. I'm wearing a bow tie. It sticks on."

"Very clever," Enrico responded. "I think…"

Robert interrupted, "My wife will have an apple martini and I'll have a Scotch and water. No ice."

Enrico nodded politely. "Of course, sir. I will ask Liz to come and take your order."

"I just gave you my order," Robert said, dismissively.

"Yes, sir, as you wish. And now I'll give you a few minutes to look over the appetizer selections." Enrico backed away and disappeared.

For a few moments the ladies sat in silence and perused the menu, contemplating Robert's rudeness. Fran gave him the stink-eye.

Birdie broke the stony silence. "Jamal, why don't you order a fruit medley? You like fruit and I'll bet it will be really special."

"Okay," he nodded.

"What is bisque?" Sue Ellen asked, pronouncing it *bis-cue*, which prompted a snicker from Beverly.

"First of all," Beverly replied, too loudly, "it's pronounced *bisque*, and second of all, you probably wouldn't like it."

Fran's head jerked up. "How would you know what she likes?"

"Well, I figure since she can't pronounce it, she'd probably be happier with something more common."

"You figured wrong. Sue Ellen, let's you and I both get the strawberry bisque. I hear it's wonderful."

Beverly shrugged her shoulders and shared a look with her husband. "Okay. Suit yourself."

When Enrico brought the appetizers they watched in great anticipation as he distributed their selections - shrimp cocktail, vegetarian gumbo, grilled mushrooms, escargot, and chilled strawberry bisque. Jamal's eyes grew wide as his glorious dish of fresh fruit was set before him.

"Put your napkin in your lap, honey," Birdie whispered.

The girls took turns sampling each other's appetizers and Liz returned to take more drink orders. Sue Ellen was curious about the small brown shells on Beverly's plate at the end of the table.

"Eshcushe me, honey, are you cracking pecans down there?" she asked, referring to the little tongs in Beverly's hand.

Fran elbowed Sue Ellen, but it was too late.

"No, I'm simply removing the escargot from their shells. Have you never had escargot?" Knowing the answer, Beverly winked at her husband.

"No, I never had a scargo. I've never had a scargo, have I, Frannie?"

"It's a French delicacy," Beverly continued, clearly enjoying the mockery. "Here, try one. I've removed one from its shell." She passed it to Sue Ellen on a butter plate.

Fran, now angry, spoke up. "Stop, Sue Ellen. It's a garden snail. Don't eat it."

Sue Ellen giggled, thinking that Fran was joking, and popped the buttery, chewy nugget in her mouth. Thankfully, Enrico arrived with the salads and distracted Sue Ellen before she could express an opinion about the snail. He placed salads around the table, a variety of garden, Caesar, and spinach creations. Birdie had ordered French onion soup in lieu of a salad, and its aroma was divine.

In an effort to be cordial to the unpleasant couple at the end of the table, Birdie asked, "Where are you two from?"

"We're from Arkansas," Beverly replied.

"What a coincidence! My friends here are from Arkansas, too! But my grandson and I live in Florida."

Beverly smiled indulgingly but Robert showed no interest whatsoever.

"We work together," Janet explained. "We teach middle schoolers."

"Ahh, teachers," Beverly responded. "I hear it's a noble profession. I thought about being a teacher when I was younger but realized I wanted something more challenging, so I went into business for myself. I'm an entrepreneur."

Her husband gave her a look but kept stabbing at his salad.

Fran's eyes flashed. "You don't think teaching is challenging?"

"I'm just saying it doesn't interest me, that's all."

Before Fran could offer a rebuttal, Sue Ellen's phone rang loudly to the tune of "Achy Breaky Heart," a ringtone of which they had all grown weary.

"For the love of God, Sue Ellen, when are you going to change that?" Janet grumbled.

"Hi, honey!" Sue Ellen answered, ecstatic to hear from her husband. "Did you get my selfie?" There was a pause. "I can't hear you. What?" Her expression quickly changed from delight to aggravation. "No, Dillard, I dunno where your b-brown, where your brown belt is."

The others looked away, a little embarrassed for her.

Sue Ellen was garbling her words. "Di' ju not get my shelfie, Dillard? I'm all dressed up here." There was another long pause as she frowned and drummed her nails on the table top, presumably waiting for Dillard to find the photo. Suddenly her face lit up again. "So whatcha think?" *Pause.* "Huh? My eye?" She reached up and found the errant eyelash strip, plucked it from her lid and tossed it aside, where it landed in Birdie's empty soup bowl.

Enrico returned to gather up the salad plates and Sue Ellen abruptly ended the call, not about to miss the next course.

"Chef is offering three superb entrees tonight. Please allow me a moment to tell you about each one." He cleared his throat importantly and began. "We have a nine ounce broiled filet mignon, our most tender cut of meat, prepared to your liking and served with buttery sautéed mushrooms and wasabi horseradish mashed potatoes. We also have a broiled Maine lobster tail served with drawn butter, creamed spinach, and a baked potato. And finally, we have veal parmesan with our popular macaroni and cheese and a steamed vegetable medley. By the way, you may select one, two, or all three entrees. Any questions?"

There were none.

"Very well, then. I'll be back for your orders when your friend returns."

The girls looked around and realized that Aimee's chair was empty. Jamal explained. "She got sick. I think she went to throw up."

Janet frowned. "How long has she been gone?"

"I don't know. She left before those new people got here."

"Really? But that was..." Janet felt completely ashamed that she hadn't noticed her roommate's absence. Yet, to be fair, Aimee was a quiet presence in any situation. Still, how could she not have missed her?

"Fran, I'm going to go check on Aimee. Please tell the others to go ahead and order. Order the filet for me, please. Medium rare."

She went directly to the ladies' room in the restaurant but did not find Aimee there, nor did she find her in the ladies' room in the outside lobby. Puzzled, Janet waited for an elevator and returned to their room but found it empty, as well. She checked her cell phone. No messages.

Bewildered, she returned to the Blue Fin and took her seat. "I can't find her," she whispered to Fran.

"She's not in the room?"

"No, and she's not in the ladies' rooms."

"Try not to worry," Fran soothed. "She's a big girl. Maybe she went to the infirmary."

Enrico arrived with a steaming tray of entrees and served them with great flourish - grilled lobster tail for Birdie and filet mignon for Janet and Fran. Jamal grinned at his colorful pasta dish from the children's menu. Sue Ellen clapped as her veal parmigiana was set before her, although she did not remember ordering it and asked what it was. By this time she had switched to red wine and was dangerously close to being plastered.

Jamal reached for the bread basket and noticed the butter dish with two rounded mounds of whipped butter. "Hey, Birdie! Look! Those look like tescibles!"

The ladies hooted with laughter at the little boy's revelation. Janet choked on her water. Fran was so amused that she took a picture of the butter mounds. "I want to remember this moment."

"Girls don't have tescibles. Just boys," Jamal clarified, in case there was any confusion.

"I warned you," Birdie said with a smile. "The boy has no filter. Who wants a bite of my lobster?" she asked, looking around the table.

Fran said, "I'll try a bite."

"Dip it in this butter," Birdie instructed her.

Fran closed her eyes as she swallowed. "Mmm, that is absolutely divine."

Halfway through her meal Sue Ellen looked up and said, "Oops! I forgot to call Dillard!"

Fran was quick to lean in. "Sue Ellen, you just talked to him. Don't you remember?"

Sue Ellen's mouth formed an "o" as she thought about it.

"Close your mouth," Fran said crossly. "You look like a cartoon character. You're intoxicated."

"No, *you* are."

Fran glared. "You sound like a child."

"No, *you* sound like a child."

Birdie intervened. "Sue Ellen, why don't you finish your dinner and then have some coffee?"

Sue Ellen picked up her fork, dropped it, tried to catch it, missed it, and ate with her spoon instead. For several glorious minutes she was quiet, and then her head dropped and she was asleep, which was good timing because Enrico arrived to take dessert orders. No one woke her.

Enrico returned shortly with a tray on one hand and a pot of coffee in the other. "Here comes your dessert, Jamal!" his grandmother exclaimed.

At the sound of the word "dessert" Sue Ellen's head jerked up and her eyes flew open, taking in the scrumptious-looking desserts being distributed. But her look turned to dismay when only a cup of coffee was put before her. She slumped in her chair.

"Tha's jus' mean."

"Have dessert, then. I don't care." Fran quipped. "But you'll be breaking your promise."

"Oh." Sue Ellen tried to think. "But I really wanted some pineapple up-down side cake," she whined.

Birdie winked at Janet who grinned at Fran and, despite her drunken condition, Sue Ellen picked up on the nuances. "What? What did I say?"

"You said pineapple up-down side cake," Jamal grinned. "It's supposed to be pineapple upside down cake."

Sue Ellen blinked and took a sip of coffee. She gazed forlornly around the table at Fran's tall slice of cheesecake drizzled with raspberry sauce, Janet's tiramisu, Birdie's chocolate melting cake and Jamal's vanilla ice cream with a plump strawberry and a pineapple wedge. Fran quietly cut a generous wedge from her cheesecake and placed it on Sue Ellen's saucer, patting her drunken friend's hand.

Janet continued to check her phone, baffled as to why she hadn't heard from Aimee. *Where could she be? Would she have gone to the infirmary?*

Suddenly a large man with a ruddy complexion, straw colored hair and a bushy mustache appeared at their table. "Good evening!" he greeted them in a booming voice. "I'm Captain Mike Anderson. How is everyone this evening? Enjoying yourselves?"

Sue Ellen miraculously sobered up. There he stood, the ship's captain, in his white uniform with shiny gold buttons and an impressive array of bars on his shoulders, just as she had envisioned.

"Oh, Captain Anderson!" she gushed. "We've been hoping you'd stop by! I'm Sue Ellen. Sue Ellen Pack, from Arkansas."

Fran, smitten with the presence of this exciting man, bent her head and quickly and discreetly applied some lipstick, noticing that her lips felt strangely tingly.

Sue Ellen found her phone on the floor. "Please, captain, will you take a picture with me? I'd love to have one to show to the grandkids. You probably can't tell by looking at me but I have two grown sons and four grandkids," she rattled on.

"Sue Ellen..." Janet began, then closed her eyes and shook her head in surrender. The captain seated himself in a gracious manner and Sue Ellen leaned into him. "Hurry, Janet, take it!"

Janet took two photos and laid the phone back down on the table.

"And how about you, young man?" Captain Anderson addressed Jamal. "Would you like to take a photo with me?"

The little boy jumped eagerly from his chair. "Yes, sir! My name's Jamal!" The two stood side by side as four cameras flashed. Jamal looked up at the Captain with admiration, which made Birdie both happy and sad. What a difference a man would make in her grandson's life.

"Thank you, sir," Birdie said. "My grandson and I will cherish these pictures. And we are having a wonderful time on our cruise."

Sue Ellen was determined to keep the captain's attention. "I'd like to propose a toast to Captain Sanderson." She tapped her fork against her wine glass, knocking the bowl off the stem. Red wine pooled and then seeped into the white tablecloth. Miraculously, the stem and foot remained standing.

"Uh-oh," she muttered. "Did I do that?" She looked around the table.

Jamal's eyes darted back and forth. Fran shook her head sadly. Janet, completely mortified, frantically waved for Enrico. Birdie apologized profusely to the captain, using her napkin to dab at the purple splashes on his white uniform. At the far end of the table, Robert and Beverly got up and left, but not before Beverly got in one last jab at Sue Ellen. "If you ever sober up, come to room 715 and we'll have a lesson in Etiquette 101."

Fran fought hard to keep her anger in check but managed to commit the room number to memory. Sue Ellen attempted to stand and apologize. "I'm so sorry, Colonel Sanders. Here, let me help." She reached across the table, top heavy, and knocked another glass over. Janet had to look away.

"Sit down, Sue Ellen!" Fran barked. "Just sit down."

Sue Ellen frowned across the table. "Well, you don't have to be so shnarky. Shnarky." She tried again. "Snarky." Her lip quivered and she started to cry. "I've ruined our evening, haven't I? Usually I have impeckable…impeccable manners, don't I, girls?" She looked around the table for affirmation.

"On Opposite Day," Janet muttered, and Fran snorted.

But Captain Anderson handled the situation with grace and dignity. "It's quite all right, ladies, I assure you. My staff will have this laundered and pressed and hanging pristine in my closet by morning. They see to it that I'm always presentable to my guests," he smiled. "No harm done."

And then he nodded at Sue Ellen. "And might I say, you look very lovely tonight."

She wiped her nose and sat up a little straighter.

Captain Anderson then turned to face Fran, who smiled coyly up at him. "Are you allergic to seafood, ma'am?" the captain asked. "I would be happy to show you the way to the infirmary."

Fran batted her eyelashes. "Do what now?"

"You seem to be having a reaction..."

"Oh, good gosh! Fran!" Janet cried out, horrified.

"What?" Fran demanded in an aggrieved voice.

"Your lips! They're all swollen!"

Fran reached up to find her lips to be rubbery and twice their normal size. She flapped her hands in panic. "Somebody give me a mirror!" She gasped at her own reflection in Birdie's compact and tried to wipe at her messy red lipstick, and then she started to giggle.

Janet said gently, "Fran, maybe you should take this more seriously. The captain thinks you should be seen at the infirmary."

Fran looked up at the captain and tried to smile but only one side of her mouth lifted.

"I've seen worse," he went on, "but I think it's best that you get treated."

Fran gently prodded her mouth while shaking her head "no."

"Very well, then," Captain Anderson conceded, frowning curiously at Fran. He bid them all good night and went on his way.

"Well, that was awkward," Janet sighed, looking at the stained tablecloth and shattered glass.

"Which part?" Jamal asked, matter-of-factly. "So many things happened."

Sue Ellen swayed in her seat, having fallen asleep again.

"Miss Fran, now your eyes are puffy," Jamal noted with alarm. He turned to his grandmother. "Am I getting puffy, Birdie?"

"No, honey. You're fine. Miss Fran is having an allergic reaction to the lobster, I believe."

"But I ate some lobster, too!" he cried. "Remember? You gave me a bite!"

"You are not swelling, Jamal, I promise," Birdie assured him. "Here. Look in this mirror and see for yourself."

Jamal seemed satisfied with his own reflection, but had a question for Fran. "How you gonna' drink a juice box with those big lips?"

"I dan nah. I sudda tadda dat."

"Jamal, leave Miss Fran alone," Birdie said firmly.

"But she can't talk right."

"I can see you are concerned, Jamal, but her swelling will eventually go down. Fran, did you not know that you're allergic to shellfish?"

"One time Joel bot tum crab dib home and duh tame tang happened. But dat was yees ago."

Sue Ellen woke up and screamed, startled by her friend's appearance. "Frannie, what's wrong?"

"I'm taking you to the infirmary, Fran," Janet insisted. "C'mon, let's go."

"Better yet, I'll escort you." Captain Anderson had returned to check on his passenger. He offered an arm to Fran and she rose from her chair.

"Das vewy kind of you, tir."

Sue Ellen tried valiantly to get out of her chair. "Wait! I'll come, too!"

"You stay right where you are. Drink another cup of coffee," Janet instructed her, and then she appealed to Birdie. "I've got to find Aimee. She's not answering her phone and I'm worried about her."

"You go ahead. Go. I'll see that Sue Ellen gets back to her room," Birdie promised.

"Thank you. I've got a whole ship to search."

"Let us hear from you, okay?" Birdie asked.

"I will."

Janet headed straight for the Lido Deck, thinking Aimee might be lying in a deck chair getting some fresh air. She meandered around the pool area, feeling out of place in her dressy outfit. A children's movie was playing on the giant movie screen and there were about a dozen children in bathing suits, sprawled in chairs and munching on free popcorn. Some had ice cream cones. She walked briskly through the buffet area and then she took the stairs to the casino, where she wound her way among the slot machines, knowing that this was an unlikely place for her roommate to be. As a last resort she searched the shopping area on the Mezzanine, where most of the stores were now closed. Her stomach churned with anxiety.

It was after ten o'clock when Janet finally located Aimee. A partially open door to a small, dark library caught her attention and, on a whim, she peeked inside. Aimee was curled into a ball, sleeping in an upholstered chair under an air conditioning vent. Janet touched her cold, thin arm and gently jostled her. Aimee's eyes flew open.

"Hey. It's me. Janet."

Disoriented, Aimee blinked and tried to focus. She winced with the effort of sitting up.

"Are you okay? What are you doing in here?"

"Ugghh. I have such a headache," Aimee groaned.

"I've looked everywhere for you. I was worried sick."

"I'm sorry," Aimee mumbled. "Do you have any Tylenol?"

"No, but let's get you back to the room, okay? You can take something there."

They made their way back with Aimee leaning precariously on Janet. Janet gently helped her to lie down and put a pillow under her head. "Here, honey. Here's some Ibuprofen. And here's some water."

Aimee swallowed the pills and lay back down.

"I need to know what happened, Aimee. Why did you leave? Were you really sick?"

Aimee closed her eyes and nodded, and soon she was snoring lightly.

Janet lifted Aimee's head. "Aimee. Are you okay? Did you take something at dinner?" But the questioning was useless; her roommate was fast asleep.

Janet texted the others. *I found her. She's in her bed now. Something spooked her but I don't know what it was. She's not talking.*

10
The Hitchhiker

Sometime during the night the ship left the Gulf of Mexico and entered the Caribbean Sea, and the girls were about to get their first glimpse of Mahogany Bay, Honduras. It was early morning as the foursome gathered at the railing, speaking in reverent tones as the sun rose and the fog began to lift. Aimee was exceptionally quiet, grateful that no one questioned her about the night before. Janet must have asked them to leave her alone, she presumed.

In the distance the morning sun revealed banks of lush green vegetation rising right out of the azure sea. Excitement mounted, spirits lifted, and cameras began to click as the women attempted to capture the beauty before them. Despite her overwhelming craving for nicotine and her still-swollen lips, Fran was taken aback. "This is where I want to retire," she murmured. "This is it."

"What would you do for a living?" Janet asked, playing along. "You don't speak Spanish."

"I'd paint hermit crab shells and grow sugar cane. Smoke a little pot. I'd live the simple life."

"That sounds good to me!" Janet smiled. "I'll bet we could learn to make those macramé plant hangers, too, don't you?"

"Yes, and we could all roam around barefoot and get tattoos and wear coconut bras!" Sue Ellen got tickled with herself. "Just imagine me in a coconut bra!"

Aimee stood silent at the railing. She wore a ball cap low on her forehead and large sunglasses, baggy lounging pants and a long-sleeved tee shirt. She had twisted her hair into a knot on the back of her head.

Sue Ellen couldn't help herself. "Why are you dressed like a hobo, honey?"

"I don't know what you mean. I'm comfortable," Aimee replied, silencing the older woman. "Let's go get ready."

Their shore excursion was to include the entire day on a private beach, including lunch, away from the crowds and the pushy street vendors. At the allotted time they stood onshore in the hot sun with their group, waiting for their guide. He arrived and shouted, "Follow me!" and took off in long strides. They soon reached the long strip of sparkling white beach which was theirs for the day and the guide turned to face the group.

"Please keep track of time. At 5:00 sharp, everyone is to meet on that dock over there," he pointed. "You'll be picked up and returned to the ship by tender. *Do not be late.* The captain will not wait for you. Enjoy your day!" And with that, he was gone.

The girls removed their sandals and strolled along in the warm sand. Lofty palm trees in clusters of twos and threes afforded the only shade on the beach. They snagged four lounge chairs side by side and settled in for a heavenly day of relaxation.

"Take a picture of me, Fran," Sue Ellen called out. She stood between two swaying palm trees. Fran obliged as Sue Ellen changed poses a half dozen times.

"Oooh, I look good in that one!" Sue exclaimed, viewing the photos. "Thank you!"

"You're welcome. I hope a coconut falls on your head."

Aimee lay quietly in her chair, troubled by last night's events. Although she wasn't being hounded with questions, she felt the awkwardness between her and her travel companions. She owed them an apology and yet the words wouldn't come. It was all too embarrassing. So instead, she drifted off into a restless nap with her sun hat over her face.

Janet took a walk by herself to the far end of a long wooden pier where a group was snorkeling. She moved some sunglasses out of the way and sat down on a bench to watch. The tourists floated face-down in the turquoise water, kicking with large fins to propel themselves over the coral reefs. It looked like fun and she made a mental note to try it someday.

Sue Ellen and Fran went exploring and were surprised to discover an animal refuge housing tropical birds and monkeys in tall, roomy cages. Sue Ellen was drawn to a certain spider monkey with the face of a little old man. "Look at this little guy, Fran!" She attempted to take a photo but got too close and the monkey swiped at her hair, grabbing a handful in his tight little fist. Sue Ellen shrieked until some local boys came running, scolding the monkey and sending it scampering.

"Sorry, ma'am. That's Joe. Don't get too close to Joe. He likes the ladies."

"I can see that," she managed, cringing when the animal returned and pressed its front side against the cage, reaching for Sue Ellen with long, leathery fingers.

"Look at you!" Fran teased. "Your first day on foreign soil and already you're driving the men crazy."

"Not funny, Fran. He's creepy. Let's get out of here." Sue Ellen rearranged and patted her hair as they headed back to their spot.

At noon the foursome sat at a picnic table munching on seasoned rice with pork, beans, tortillas, and grilled corn, and cold lemonade to drink.

"Say, Sue Ellen, what do you remember about last night? Do you remember meeting Captain Anderson?" Fran loved to pick at her friend.

Sue Ellen swatted at a pesky fly. "Of course I do," she sniffed.

"Do you remember splashing him with wine and calling him 'Colonel Sanders?'"

"No, but I remember you swelling up like a giant balloon in a Macy's Day Parade! And you'd better not tell Dillard about me or else I'll post your blubber lips on Facebook."

"Too late. I already posted my blubber lips," Fran replied with satisfaction. "Eighty-six likes, so far. Mostly my students." With that, she stood and announced, "I'm going to go take a nap on the beach."

While Fran slept, Sue Ellen meandered along the beach and Aimee stared at the ocean. Janet waded in the warm water, looking for shells and digging in the wet sand, rousting little crabs and sea creatures.

Finally, Aimee couldn't stand it any longer. She sat up in her lounge chair and waved Janet and Sue Ellen back to the group. "I'm sorry, y'all. I owe you an apology and an explanation for my disappearance last night."

Fran woke up and they all stared at Aimee, waiting.

"Remember my house-sitting story? Worst weekend of my life? Well, I saw them in the dining room last night. The Bennetts. They came walking right toward our table."

"What?"

"They are on the ship! I know it was them. I recognized them right away and I was so shocked that I just bolted from the table."

Janet's mouth gaped. "Are you kidding me?"

"I am seriously freaking out! I know that we laughed about my house-sitting story, but it's not funny now. If that woman were to see me, there's no telling what she might say or do in front of everyone."

"So they didn't see you?" Janet asked.

"No, I'm sure they didn't. I left before they got close enough, and I never looked back."

Fran was putting it all together. "Aimee, I hate to tell you this, but they actually sat down at our table. I remember his name being Robert, and hers was Barbara, I think, or Betty. Something like that."

"Beverly," Janet corrected her. "They took those two empty chairs."

Aimee closed her eyes, dumbfounded. "Oh, my God. This just gets worse."

"They were assholes," Fran said. "Arrogant, rude people. We didn't like them, did we, Sue?"

"No, we did not."

Hesitantly, Aimee asked, "Was my name mentioned over dinner?"

"Your name never came up," Janet assured her. "It was a while before any of us even realized you had left," she added sheepishly. "We had all been drinking and, if I had noticed your absence, I would have thought you had gone to the ladies' room. Jamal eventually told us that you had gotten sick."

"Well, what were they like? What did they talk about?" Aimee seemed traumatized.

"They barely spoke to us," Fran assured her. "They kept their distance, like they were too good to be at our table. They mocked Sue Ellen."

Sue Ellen glanced quickly at Fran. "They did?"

Aimee sucked in a ragged breath. "Of all the cruises out there, *why* do they have to be on this one? What are the chances?"

The women sat shaking their heads, wondering the same.

"I don't even remember where I went or what I did," Aimee continued. "I have a tendency to get panic attacks and I could feel one coming on. My heart was racing and I felt sick. I needed to lie down somewhere in the dark, alone. I have these pills that I take."

"Why didn't you just go back to our cabin?"

"I don't know! I don't think straight when I get that way. I have to walk and keep walking. It's like I'm in a different world and just have to be alone."

"So you ended up in the library."

"Yeah."

"It's a miracle I found you there."

"I know. It was. And Janet, I'm feeling like this is going to ruin everything. Now that I know they are on the ship, I can't go anywhere! I can't roam around freely for fear of running into them. That's why I was dressed like a hobo this morning. It was a disguise."

"Nothing is ruined," Janet soothed her in a soft voice. "How were you to know this would happen? It's just a cruel, random coincidence and no one can blame you for trying to avoid those nasty people. But we can't have you hiding out and wearing disguises. We're here to have fun."

"But what if I run into them?"

Janet shrugged her shoulders. "Say hello. What are they gonna do?"

"Beverly is the type to make a scene. She'll yell at me about the birds, or say something to embarrass me. What if Robert comes on to me again?"

"Listen here, sweetie. That man has a lot more to be worried about than you do," Fran pointed out, "considering that vile proposition that he made. If his wife were to find out about that…"

Aimee's eyes grew large. "Well, I sure don't want to cause any trouble like that."

"You should just enjoy yourself and don't worry about them, honey," Sue Ellen said. "The chance of you crossing paths with the Bennetts again is slim to none."

Fran raised her chin defiantly. "Sue Ellen is right," she said. "Don't you worry about a thing. We've got this."

~

At the end of the day, at the allotted time, they gathered their towels and tote bags and trudged through the hot sand. To get to the meeting place they had to climb up a rise, walking single file along a path made of large flat rocks. Aimee brought up the rear, behind Janet. She kept her eyes on Janet's feet, careful to step wherever Janet stepped. A bit of movement caught her eye and she shrieked at the sight of a fuzzy brown tarantula clinging uncertainly to the hem of Janet's shorts. Her knees buckled, her eyes rolled back in her head, and she collapsed awkwardly into a heap on the ground, her knees spread-eagled.

Janet turned at the sound of Aimee's shriek and came charging back down the hill, followed by Fran and Sue Ellen.

"What happened?"

"What's wrong with her?"

"I don't know! Everything was fine! She looks like she's fainted."

"You ladies okay? What's going on?" A strikingly good-looking man stood panting before them, having been drawn in by the commotion. He stood well over six feet tall with muscled arms and legs, dressed only in black swim trunks, his shoulders glistening with sweat.

Janet swallowed hard, instantly recognizing him as the guy who had "given her the eye" on the ship. She crouched down and discreetly pushed Aimee's knees back together and gave her friend a little shake. "I think she's fainted. Aimee! Wake up!"

Aimee blinked her eyes and tried to focus on Janet's face, and then she began to scoot backwards, her heels digging into the sand.

"Janet, there's a spider on you! A big one!"

"Where?" Janet flinched.

"*There!*"

The tarantula had made its way to Janet's front side and was climbing up her tee shirt. "Holy shit!" she yelped, swatting it away.

"Jesus! That's a tarantula!" the man shouted. Then, embarrassed, he confessed, "I'm not a fan of spiders, either. Especially that size." He smiled, revealing nice teeth. His dark eyes had little creases at the corners. His nose was a bit crooked as if it had been broken, and a faint scar extended from his left eyebrow. *Ruggedly handsome*, Janet decided.

"Where did it go?" the man asked.

"Where did what go?" Janet replied dumbly.

"The tarantula. The one that was just hitchhiking on you."

"Oh. It's over there somewhere. I knocked it into those trees. It kind of freaked me out, too." *Understatement of the year*, she shuddered.

From the ground, Aimee cleared her throat and they turned their attention back to her. The man knelt down. "What's your name?"

"Aimee."

"I'm Jake. How do you feel, Aimee? Dizzy? Keep your head down for a few minutes. Here, drink some of this," he said, handing her a cold bottle of water. Janet could only stand there, feeling useless, while Sue Ellen and Fran moved in closer.

He turned to Janet. "Didn't I see you last night? Waiting for an elevator?"

Delighted that he remembered her, Janet couldn't help but smile. "Yes. We were on our way to dinner. I'm Janet." She grasped Jake's hand and held on a little too long as she studied him. "And my other friends over there are Sue Ellen and Fran." He turned and they waved at him.

"We all work together. We're teachers," Janet went on.

"Oh, yeah? Where from?"

"Arkansas. Conway. How about you?"

"Wisconsin. Madison."

"That would explain your accent."

Aimee tried to stand up and Jake lent her a hand. "Are you gonna be okay? You're not hurt?"

"I'm not hurt," Aimee replied, dusting herself off. "Thank you."

"Well, then, I'd better get going," Jake said. "My friends are probably wondering what happened to me. I had to run back for my sunglasses," he explained. "We were snorkeling."

Janet flushed at the realization that she had actually been watching him snorkeling, only yards away from where'd she'd sat on the bench. She felt like she was in a Hallmark movie.

"Thank you for stopping, Jake. That was really nice of you."

"Sure. No problem. Maybe I'll see you around, on the ship!" He waved and took off in long strides and no one said anything for a good thirty seconds, gawking as he effortlessly trekked up the hill.

11
A Sixth Sense

The ladies met for evening cocktails on the Lido Deck, this time at the ship's stern. They had never before been able to find empty chairs at the stern, a popular place where passengers liked to watch the frothy white water churning behind the ship's propellers. This evening, though, they found five unoccupied chairs which they pulled together facing each other. A small table in the middle held their drinks and key cards. Fran and Sue Ellen stood at the rail, taking photos.

Birdie arrived with a bright smile. "Ah, you saved me a seat! Thank you!"

"And here's a drink for you," Fran said, handing her a frozen Pina Colada.

"Thank you. I owe you one." She and Fran tapped their plastic cups together. "Last night was fun!"

"Where's Jamal?" Fran wanted to know.

"He is at Seuss at Sea where he will be happily occupied with story-telling for a while. How was your shore excursion today?"

"Fantastic."

"Wonderful."

"Wish you had been with us."

Birdie sighed. "I would have loved it, but Jamal would have been bored to lie on a beach all day. That boy likes to keep moving."

"So what did you find to do?" Janet asked.

"I dropped him off at Camp Ocean while I visited the spa, where I was treated to a facial and a hot stone massage." She closed her eyes and breathed in deeply. "It was heavenly."

"Lucky you!" Sue Ellen remarked.

"And then I took Jamal to the Build-a-Bear Workshop, and then we went back to the water park. That boy wears me out!"

Janet's phone buzzed and she stepped away from the table to take the call, clearly happy to hear from the caller. "I miss you, baby! Mwah, mwah, mwah!" She emulated a series of kisses which, of course, caught everyone's attention, never having heard such things coming from Janet's mouth. Despite their curious stares she continued cooing into the phone. Eyes widened as her voice grew higher and more animated.

"I hope you've been good while I've been away. I love you! Oh, yes, I do! Oh, yes, I do! Mwah! Bye-bye! Mwah!"

Janet ended the call and returned to the group with a happy sigh, surprised at the looks of contempt on her friends' faces. "What?" she asked.

"Was that Lee?" Fran demanded.

"Lee? No!" Janet's face turned red, not accustomed to being under scrutiny. "I was face-timing with Lucy. Geez! Mind your own business."

Aimee sat quietly, hunkered down with a beach towel around her shoulders and wearing a large floppy sun hat and sunglasses, her hair tucked under the hat.

"Why are you all bundled up, Aimee?" Birdie wanted to know.

"She's still not feeling well," Fran said, to save Aimee the job of retelling her story. "Tell us more about yourself, Birdie. I've never met anyone from Jamaica. Do you still have family there?"

"My mada still lives there, and my two brothers. My twin sister lives in Savannah, Georgia with her husband."

"You have a twin sister? What fun! Are you identical twins?"

"Yes, we are." She smiled. "Those were happy days, growing up on that island. The young people of Jamaica are like that, happy and carefree."

One by one they peppered Birdie with questions.

"What about your father?"

"My fada, he died many years ago. I barely remember him."

"So does your mother live alone?"

"Yes, but my brothers and their wives and children are close by. They all look after her. Mada is a seamstress and makes beautiful clothing. But she is quite old and her eyes are getting very bad."

"Do you worry about your family? You mentioned the violence and unrest…"

"Yes, I do worry about them. But Mada would never leave Jamaica. Her friends are there, her sons and grandchildren."

"Were you and your sister close?"

"We were born just minutes apart. I came first. They named me Ronica and my sister Raeni. Raeni and I were very close. Our older brothers gave us the nicknames, 'Birdie' and 'Chickie' because we had skinny legs. Jamal knows me by no other name."

"I love listening to you talk," Aimee said. "Your dialect is so expressive and lively." Janet noticed a trembling in Aimee's hand as she adjusted her sunglasses.

"Ya, mon," Birdie replied, and everyone laughed.

"The dialect is called Patois, am I right?" ee asked, pronouncing the word like pah-twa.

"Yes, that is correct. Some call it Jamaican Creole. The majority of Jamaicans speak it. But since we moved to Florida my Patois has given way to more understandable English. If I spoke now as I did in Jamaica you would not be able to follow."

"What was it like, growing up in Jamaica?" Fran asked.

Birdie paused to take a sip of her drink. "Most Jamaican parents are stern, even strict, and mine were no exception. We were expected to do chores, same as American kids, and go to church. When school was in session we were not permitted to watch television or hang out with friends. But don't get me wrong! We were a fun-loving and happy family."

"What was it like as you got older?" Aimee asked.

"After getting our education, we were expected to marry a suitable life partner and create our own families. Oh, and all family members have a say in any proposal of marriage."

"Are you serious?" Janet asked.

"Yes. I am serious. We are a tight bunch," Birdie chuckled.

"How interesting!" Sue Ellen remarked. "I love meeting people from other countries. You know, Fran here is Jewish."

Fran sighed. "Sue Ellen, that doesn't mean…"

"Tell us more," Sue Ellen went on. "Tell us about your husband. I mean, were you married?"

"Yes. My husband was a wonderful man. Very kind. He was an orthopedic surgeon. After three years of marriage I gave birth to our daughter, Mikayla. But sadly, my husband passed away when she was only a toddler. A traffic accident." Birdie looked sad. "And life became very hard after that."

After a stretch of silence, Janet spoke. "You told us that your daughter is deceased. Do you want to talk about that?"

"Mikayla was our only child and she was a wild one as a teen. Even with my family's support in her upbringing, she couldn't be disciplined. She got pregnant at a young age and gave birth to Jamal, all while still living at home. But she didn't shoulder the responsibility of motherhood very well." Birdie paused to stir her Pina Colada and took a thoughtful swallow while the others waited for more.

"She became a political activist which, in Jamaica, is a very dangerous thing to do. There are vigilante groups, right-wing and left-wing, and they engage in turf wars with assault rifles and grenades. I warned her against speaking out but Mikayla was never afraid to speak her mind. She was strong-willed to a fault, and it cost her her life. We buried her at age nineteen, with Jamal not yet two years old." Birdie's eyes glistened with tears. "I just do the best I can to give him all my love and a roof over his head. He's such a good boy."

"He's a very special little boy, Birdie, and you are raising him well. You should be very proud," Aimee remarked, and the others concurred.

"What is your mother like? She sounds like a strong woman," Fran asked.

"She is. Strong and bossy. And very gifted."

"In what way?" Sue Ellen wanted to know.

Birdie chuckled. "Ladies, I come from a long line of clairvoyant women. My mada is the most renowned psychic on the island of Jamaica. Not Black Magic or Voodoo or anything like that," she was quick to say, "although both are still practiced around the world. She has unique abilities inherited from her own mada and from generations of women who came before her."

"What kind of stuff can she do?" Sue Ellen asked. "Can she read palms and predict the future?"

"No, it's not like that. She's not a fortune-teller with a crystal ball. She just has this uncanny ability to perceive things that others might not. Her abilities go beyond the five ordinary senses. She has a sixth sense."

"I've heard of that," Sue Ellen said.

"Yes. And many people have a sixth sense, but it doesn't always manifest in the same way."

"What do you mean?"

"Well, some have the ability to know about things before other people know. They can predict important things with accuracy, like an earthquake, or the outcome of a horse race. Some have a powerful intuition about other people, like knowing that the ticket-taker at the fair just killed his wife. Still others are able to see dead people, like the little boy in that movie."

Aimee was intrigued. "So what is your mother's gift?"

"Mada is remarkably intuitive about other people. She senses things; she 'sees' things. And she has healing abilities, so people who are suffering come to her for help. She has even been known to cast away evil."

"This is fascinating!" Janet exclaimed.

"But Mada doesn't talk much about her psychic powers. She will help people when they come to her, mostly friends and family, and sometimes total strangers. But she doesn't advertise her gift."

"So if being psychic runs in your family, you must be psychic, too," Fran presumed.

Birdie shook her head. "No. I am not. Raeni and I always expected to inherit Mada's powers but surprisingly, neither of us did. And neither did Mikayla. It seems that Mada is the end of the line."

"How do you feel about that?" Janet asked.

"I'm fine with it. Relieved, actually. The gift brings with it a sense of obligation and enormous responsibility. Mada always says that it's both a gift and a curse."

The sky had turned a heavy gray as they talked, with a rumble of thunder in the distance. When fat drops of rain began to fall they jumped up in unison, grabbing their things.

"Let's go to my cabin!" Janet called out, and they all made a run for it.

~

Aimee removed her towel, hat and sunglasses and raked her long hair back with her hand.

"It must be nice to have such straight, silky hair," Birdie said to her.

"Not really," Aimee replied. "It looks the same every single day. It won't hold a curl. So boring."

"Would you like for me to do some cornrows in your hair? Just for fun?"

"You mean those tight little braids?"

"Yes! I used to braid Mikayla's hair all the time. I'm a pro at it," Birdie said.

"Do it, Aimee! That would look so cool on you!" Janet said, and the others agreed.

"But it will take forever, won't it?"

"I won't braid it to the ends. That *would* take forever. But I could do halfway braids, from your hairline to your crown. It will look good on you. Fun, and carefree."

Aimee so wanted to feel fun and carefree. With a spark in her eyes, she said, "Okay. Let's do it!"

Surprised that she agreed, the others settled in to watch. Janet sat cross-legged on her own bed while Sue Ellen and Fran perched on

Aimee's bed. Aimee took the room's only chair while Birdie stood over her, brushing her long hair until it was free of tangles.

Fran decided to tell a story. "This reminds me of when I was a little girl and I had frizzy, kinky hair which I hated. I had been hearing at school about girls ironing their hair. Remember when that was popular?"

There were nods all around.

"I begged my sister to iron my hair for me. It was a Saturday morning and my mother had left us at home to go to the grocery store, so we knew that we had about an hour to get it done."

"How old were you?"

"I was eleven, I think, and Martha was thirteen. Neither of us knew how to use the iron and it was one of those really heavy ones like they used to make. My sister apparently put it on the highest setting and ordered me to lay my head on the ironing board."

"Oh gosh, this doesn't sound like it has a good ending," Janet said.

"So I did what I was told. I stood on a book so that I could reach the ironing board and laid my head down and she brushed my hair out as best she could. *Don't move,* she said."

Birdie had stopped braiding, engulfed in Fran's story. Janet slowly shook her head.

"So I tried to hold still but she got too close to my forehead with the pointy end of the iron and I could feel the heat. It scared me and I yelped and jerked my head away which made her drop the iron. It landed on my foot and I wasn't wearing shoes."

"Oh, no!" Aimee cried. "How badly were you burned?"

"Pretty bad, but we didn't dare tell our mother. I had to tough it out with a burn that looked like a Christmas tree. Back then we were told to put butter on a burn so Martha buttered me up every morning and every night and mother never found out. It hurt like hell wearing shoes."

"Oh, you poor thing! What about your hair?" Birdie asked.

"My hair, the part that got ironed, was ruined. It turned crispy and broke off. You talk about a mess."

"What did your mother say about it? Surely she noticed what you'd done," Sue Ellen asked.

"When she got home from the grocery store she asked, *What's that smell? What's burning?* We had already put the iron away and didn't dare admit to having used it, so I blurted out that my sister had taken a cigarette butt from an ash tray and smoked it – a total lie. My sister got grounded for it."

"But your hair…"

"I cut the damaged hair off and ended up with the most hideous mullet you've ever seen. And this was before mullets were cool."

The room erupted with laughter. "You should see my bat mitzvah pictures. I looked like a Jewish Billy Ray Cyrus."

Sue Ellen laughed so hard that she fell off the bed and couldn't get back up. No one offered to help her so she stayed there, unwrapping a peppermint that she found under the bed.

Things got quiet as they watched Birdie's fingers work with surprising speed in Aimee's hair.

"Birdie, are you seeing anyone?" Aimee wanted to know.

"Who, me? No, there's no man in my life. Only Jamal."

"But I'm sure you have a lot of admirers. Do you think you will ever get remarried?"

She chuckled and shook her head. "Mada warned me long ago to never marry again."

Astounded, the girls wanted to know why. But before she could answer there was a knock on the door. Fran opened the door to Wayan, their steward.

"Hello," he nodded politely. "For you. Fresh-squeezed orange juice, if you like." He handed Fran an ice cold pitcher and four glasses from his push cart. Then, noticing Birdie, he added a fifth glass.

"Thank you, Wayan! Come in, please!" Janet called out from her place on the bed.

The slight man stood awkwardly in the doorway in his white jacket. "Ah," he smiled, pointing at Aimee's hair. "Like my sister."

"I wanted to ask you some questions, if you don't mind," Janet continued.

Wayan ventured further inside the room. "Is everything all right? Can I get you anything?"

"Oh, no, everything is fine. I was just wondering about your lifestyle. Why do you choose to live and work on a ship instead of working in Bali?"

"Oh…very little money in Bali. This job pays much better. Free room and board, I save my money, send some home to my family. One day I will return to Bali, maybe start a small business of my own. Maybe buy a small house."

"You seem to work so hard and your days are long. Do you get a day off?"

"A day off? No day off. Work seven days a week for ten months. Two months off to go home."

The women gasped. "How long have you been doing this?" Aimee asked.

"Four years I'm working on ship."

"Wow," was all Janet could manage.

Wayan continued to stand there, seemingly happy to chat. "I meet people from all over. Some nice. Some not nice. I learn many things."

"It does seem like an interesting job," Fran commented. "Where do you eat and sleep?"

"With the crew. I sleep on a bunk. The food is not so good but I have friends."

Wayan began to back toward the doorway. "I must go now. Enjoy your juice."

The ladies called out their thanks as he retreated and pushed his cart on down the hallway.

Janet was the first to comment. "Geez, what a life."

"I know!" Aimee declared. "Can you imagine living and working like that?"

"Well, according to Wayan, it's better than what he would be doing in his home country," Fran pointed out.

"Who wants orange juice?" Birdie asked as she poured five glasses.

"Finish your story, Birdie," Sue Ellen said. "You were about to tell us why your mother didn't want you to remarry."

Birdie sighed. "It was about four years after my husband died. I had grieved all I could grieve and my friends were pushing me to get out and meet people, go on a few dates. And I thought I might be ready. So I went to my Mada and asked her if she could feel the presence of another man in my life – perhaps another husband someday.

We were sitting on her porch, facing each other, and she was holding my hands. She closed her eyes and after several long moments she spoke. "You will meet a man. A good man. A kind man."

Birdie stopped braiding and sat down to take a rest beside Janet. "And then suddenly Mada became troubled and her hands felt hot. So hot. She looked up at me with eyes full of fear. I can still see that look."

"She saw something bad, didn't she?" Janet whispered. The girls were on pins and needles, waiting to hear the rest.

"At first she wouldn't say anything. And then she let go of my hands and covered her eyes. She said, 'Ronica, I see fire – so much fire! Flames are dancing all around this man. Smoke pours from his nose and his mouth. He is running, running.'"

Birdie shook her head, remembering. The girls waited for her to continue.

"So I ask my mada, 'What does this mean?' and she said to me, 'Ronica, fire means tragedy. Death. Heartbreak. Or worse, evil. You have suffered enough already. You must avoid this man of fire. You must avoid all men.'"

"All men?" Sue Ellen asked.

"All men. 'You must protect yourself, Ronica,' she said. 'Think of Mikayla. She needs you.'"

Aimee was the first to speak. "It must have been a very troubling vision."

Birdie nodded pensively. "I remember crying myself to sleep that night. I was still young – young enough to remarry and be happy again - and I did not want to believe what my mother was telling me. But to doubt her would have been disrespectful."

"So you've abided by her word, all this time?" Janet asked. "You don't date?"

"I don't date. But it's not so bad," Birdie said cheerfully. "I have my friends!" She stood up and picked at Aimee's hair and resumed braiding.

"But this makes me sad," Sue Ellen objected. "What if the love of your life is out there? What if your mada's vision meant something else?"

"How can I doubt her? Mada's prophecy is powerful and not to be taken lightly. Once she saved the life of my niece by insisting that she not board a plane, which ended up crashing in the Florida Keys. I trust her." Birdie gave Aimee's shoulder a pat. "There! All done! Go look in the mirror."

Aimee was thrilled with the result – an intricate pattern of delicate, scalp-hugging braids - truly a work of art. "Oh, Birdie! Thank you! I love it!"

"Will you do me?" Sue Ellen begged.

Fran scoffed. "Sue, Birdie is tired from standing and anyway, your curly perm is a hot look. Don't mess with perfection."

"And I've got to go get Jamal," Birdie added. "He's probably wondering where I am. His group finished ten minutes ago!"

"Hey, Birdie, we are signed up for shore excursions tomorrow in Belize. What are you and Jamal doing?" Janet asked.

"We are going to stay on the ship again. Jamal has made a list of activities. But maybe we can all meet up for dinner after."

"Thank you, Birdie. I do love my braids," Aimee said sweetly.

"You're welcome. Mi deh goweh now," Birdie said as she left the room, turning to smile over her shoulder.

12
Zip-lining

*G*ood morning, ladies and gentlemen! We are preparing for our arrival in Belize, which is a country situated just south of Mexico, bordering on the Caribbean Sea. Here's an interesting fact: the Belize harbor is too shallow to dock a vessel so the Captain will drop anchor a few miles out in the gulf. Those passengers doing shore excursions will be tendered to the shoreline by boat. Those who plan to stay on the ship can look forward to a full day of on-board activities for adults and children alike. Enjoy your day, folks, and stay tuned for further updates. Bye!*

After a quick breakfast the ladies rode the glass elevator down to the atrium, clutching their excursion passes and happily anticipating the day's adventures.

"Uh-oh, girls, my coffee just kicked in," Sue Ellen announced when they reached the lobby. "Does anyone have to use the bathroom besides me?"

"I'd love to go with you!" Fran said cheerfully, then turned to whisper to the others. "Not."

Sue Ellen didn't hear the "not" and struck out for the ladies' room while the others waited beside an enormous flower arrangement. She chattered all the way there, thinking Fran was behind her, and shut herself in the first stall. She heard the click of the lock on the stall beside her and began to hum as she busied herself with the flimsy toilet seat cover, tearing at the perforations and placing it on the toilet seat, only to watch it slide into the bowl. Irritated, she sat down on the commode, releasing a loud trumpeting noise.

"Mother of God! Excuse me!" she apologized. "I'm still gassy from those boiled eggs."

Much to her relief, Fran overlooked the transgression and made no comment from the other stall. So Sue Ellen quickly finished her business and washed her hands at the sink, calling out to her friend, "I've got a gift card for a pedicure at a new place that opened up back home, and I want you to have it. I was just looking at your feet and I hate to say it, honey, but you've got the toenails of a possum. I'm leaving it here on the sink, okay? Now hurry up – the girls are waiting."

With that, Sue Ellen exited the restroom to join her friends by the flowers.

"What took you so long?" Fran wanted to know.

Sue Ellen slowed to a stop, wide-eyed. "Wait. What? How did you beat me?"

"What are you talking about?"

"I just…you were…" She pointed to the restroom.

"I changed my mind. I didn't have to go."

Sue Ellen blinked, clearly confused. "Well, then, who was I talking to in there, in the other stall?"

Heads turned as a small, elderly Asian woman emerged from the restroom. She glanced suspiciously in all directions before she hurried to the elevator clutching the gift card, her sandals clip-clapping on the marble floor.

Fran shook her head. "Try to keep up, Sue."

~

The boat which would tender them to the shoreline of Belize was a large vessel with two levels of open seating and handrails. The driver, who was bare-chested and wore tattered shorts and a do-rag, revved the motor and steered the vessel with reckless abandon through the choppy waters. With every rise and fall, sea spray blew over the passengers and everyone squealed in unison, holding on for dear life.

Sue Ellen pointed to the front of the boat. "Look!" she hollered over the roar of the boat. "Somebody's throwing up."

Twenty minutes later, onshore, Fran and Aimee boarded a bus which would take them to explore ancient Mayan ruins for half a day. Janet and Sue Ellen stood in line to board a different bus, to go zip-lining and cave-tubing. But Janet's face was ashen.

"I don't feel so good, Sue," she said through gritted teeth. "I think I'm going to be sick."

"Are you seasick, Janet?"

Before Janet could answer she charged into the bushes and could be heard retching and groaning. The bus driver waited with the door open while Sue Ellen hovered hesitantly between Janet and the bus. "Are you okay now, Janet?" she called out.

"No!"

"Can I bring you a Kleenex? Some breath mints?"

"Just go, Sue Ellen. Go on without me." Janet vomited again.

"But, honey..."

"Tell the driver not to wait on me. Please, go! I'll get a ride back."

"Are you sure?"

There was no more talk - only the pitiful sounds of retching - so Sue Ellen climbed the stairs into the bus, looked over her shoulder one last time, and found herself a seat.

∼

A half hour later, Janet texted that she was feeling better and was about to take a different boat back to the ship. Sue Ellen sighed, already regretting her decision to go alone. The bus driver had grown tired of her constant jabbering and had donned head phones, and the man across the aisle feigned sleep for the same reason. She turned to smile at the young couple behind her, who politely said hello but were busy tapping away on their phones.

She leaned forward and asked the driver, "How much further?"

"We've only been driving for forty minutes, ma'am. It's a ninety minute drive."

Sue Ellen found a crossword puzzle book in her tote bag, settled back in her seat, and went to work. At some point she dozed off, her head bobbing, and was awakened by the sound of squeaky brakes and the driver's voice announcing their arrival. Quickly, she gathered up her things and exited the bus with the others. Two young men, locals, were holding signs and shouting directions.

"This way for cave tubing!"

"Follow me for zip-lining!"

Sue Ellen studied her excursion pass and saw that she would be zip-lining, first, so she joined that group. Two dozen participants formed a line and passed single file through a revolving gate, after which they were given a key and a bottle of water.

"What's the key for?" Sue Ellen asked the young lady.

"It's for your locker, to store your personal items. Don't lose it. See the number on the back? That's your locker number."

Sue Ellen did as she was told, stuffing her tote bag into locker 49, and then slid the coiled key keeper over her wrist. Their guide, Russell, shouted, "Follow me!" and the group struck out on a trail leading into the jungle, staying close together. Russell pointed at the dense greenery, calling certain plants by name, and warned the group not to step on the red ants or touch any vile looking mushrooms. They slapped at mosquitos as they trekked along, the air humid and heavy.

Then the trail started uphill, and there was much panting and sweating as they managed the unexpected incline, finally stopping at a check point to rest and have some water.

"It's important to stay hydrated," Russell instructed. "And be careful where you sit or you'll be sorry. The ants are aggressive."

Sue Ellen had started to sit but decided against it. "Are we almost there?" she asked.

"No, ma'am."

"Where are the monkeys? I expected to see monkeys."

"No monkeys here. Just gorillas and lions. They sleep during the day, so keep your voice down." Russell winked at one of the men, who grinned at Sue Ellen, who frowned at both of them.

There were sighs of relief when they finally reached the take-off point. Sue Ellen took her place in line and watched as, one by one, the participants went sailing over the tree tops, some doing Tarzan yells and others just screaming. She waited excitedly for her turn and when she was waved onto the platform, a female worker looked her over suspiciously.

"Um, ma'am, I don't mean to offend, but are you aware of our weight regulations?"

"Of course I am!"

"And do you meet the qualifications?"

"Well," she retorted, "I'm not in the habit of weighing myself every day. But I can tell you that I crossed an ocean, survived a harrowing boat ride, and climbed a mountain to get up here, and I dare you or anyone else to deprive me of my adventure."

"Step forward, please," the worked said. She strapped Sue Ellen into a harness and handed her a helmet and a pair of heavy gloves.

Before she knew it Sue Ellen was barreling down the zip-line. She screamed involuntarily and kicked her legs as she sailed toward the landing platform, abandoning all grace and dignity. She failed to raise her knees as instructed, but they applied the brake to slow her impact and nothing was hurt but her feelings.

She clumsily executed two more zip lines before reaching the final platform, never getting the hang of a proper landing but finishing without injury. She beamed as she removed her helmet and gloves and stepped out of the harness, wishing Dillard could have seen her in action.

A savory aroma wafted through the air and Sue Ellen followed her nose to a large pavilion where a complimentary lunch was being served. She craned her neck and saw the staff dishing up stewed chicken with rice and beans and a scoop of potato salad. Her mouth watered as she carried her plate to a table and sat down, helping herself to a bottle of cold beer from a tub.

Famished, Sue Ellen ate every bite of her lunch and drained her beer, then looked around contentedly while she shimmied to the loud Caribbean music. She wished Janet was with her; she always felt better when Janet was around to take charge of things.

"Excuse me, sir. Do you know when the cave tubing will start?" she asked a silver-haired gentleman who sat with his wife.

"In approximately twenty-five minutes, we're told."

"Thank you," she smiled sweetly. "I think I'll just walk a little of my lunch off."

Sue Ellen strolled lazily around the pavilion area, thinking of her friends and wondering what they were doing, until she spotted a bench in some shade and sat down. Yawning widely, she stretched out on her back and was soon fast asleep.

Hours later, an ant scurried across Sue Ellen's cheek and woke her. She was lying in full afternoon sun. Disoriented, she sat up and looked around. The place was devoid of people except for some young girls sweeping the pavilion and emptying trash.

"Excuse me! When does the cave tubing start?"

The shy girls shook their heads to indicate they didn't speak English.

"Oh, dear, I wonder if I've missed it," she fretted out loud.

She headed to the lockers but realized that her locker key was no longer attached to her wrist. She returned to the bench and looked all around. *What has happened to my key? Did I lose it on the zip line?*

Feeling a bit panicky, she returned to the lockers and found number 49, an easy number to remember since it was her street number back home. It stood wide open and empty, the key still in the lock. She sucked in her breath.

"I've been robbed! I've been robbed!" she hollered.

The startled clean-up girls ran to get someone in charge, and soon a man who appeared to have some authority arrived. "What is the problem?"

"Someone took my locker key and emptied my locker! All my stuff was in there!"

"Try to calm down, ma'am. I will file a police report for you. Sit down, please."

He left momentarily and returned with a note pad. After jotting down her name and other pertinent information, he said, "Okay. Can you tell me what was taken?"

Sue Ellen quickly ticked off the items. "Let's see. There was a beach towel, my eyebrow pencil, some Junior Mints, my room key card..."

The man frowned as he tried to keep up.

"My Bingo marker, some grape jelly packets, a crossword puzzle book..."

"Just your valuables, ma'am."

"Oh! Okay. My wallet, my coin purse..."

"What was in the wallet?"

"Well, my driver's license, my library card, my Silver Sneakers card, my Sally's card..."

"Any cash or credit cards?"

"No."

"What about your passport?"

Sue Ellen's eyes grew wide, and then she relaxed. "No, thank goodness my passport is on the ship."

"Do you need a doctor?"

"Do I need a doctor? What for?"

"Your sunburn. That's a bad one."

Sue Ellen looked down at herself. Her chest was beet red, as were her arms and legs. She reached up to feel her face and winced. "Ouch."

He waited for her response about the doctor.

"Did I miss the cave tubing?" she asked.

"Yes, ma'am. That group has already returned."

"Where are they? When do we leave here?"

"The bus left about twenty minutes ago."

"You mean the bus that was to take me back to the ship?"

"Yes, that bus."

"But no one woke me up! They left me!" Sue Ellen began to cry, a loud, ugly wail which scared a flock of birds out of a tree. "What am I to do? Will I ever see my family again?"

"Please calm down, ma'am. I'm sure we can get you home eventually. But for now, I'll have to ask you to come with me."

~

"I'm exhausted," Janet groaned, lying on her bed. "I haven't been that sick in a long time."

"I'm so sorry about that," Aimee sympathized from her own bed. "I know you were looking forward to the activities."

"Hopefully, Sue Ellen took a lot of pictures."

Aimee giggled. "You know she did! She should be back soon, right?"

"It's already past time for them to be back."

Fran was leaning against the door frame. "She'll be along. You know how she likes to talk and lollygag."

"Lollygag?" Aimee asked.

"It's a real word. Look it up."

Janet rolled over to face Fran. "What did you think of the ruins?"

"Very interesting," Fran said. "Glad we chose that excursion. But I'm dying for a cigarette." She popped a piece of gum into her mouth to fight off the urge for nicotine. "You two rest up. I'm going to the pool."

Fran closed their door behind her and headed outside with a novel tucked under her arm. When she reached the pool area Jamal spotted her and called out, "Hey, Miss Fran!"

"Hi, there!" she waved back.

"Watch this!" he hollered, and he held his nose and disappeared underwater, popping back up several yards away.

"Great job!" Fran called out with a big smile. She was growing fonder of the little boy with every day. *I would have been a decent grandmother,* she decided.

Birdie lounged in a poolside chair with a book and a frozen drink, wearing shorts and a tee shirt that read, "Get Nauti."

"Hey, I like your shirt. I want one."

"Come sit down," Birdie invited, removing her leg from the adjoining chair. "What did you think of Belize?"

"It was an excellent excursion. Aimee and I loved seeing the ancient ruins. You don't see something like that every day. Janet never made it to her excursions. She got sick on the tender and had to come back to the ship. She's resting in her room right now."

"Oh! I'm sorry to hear that. What about Sue Ellen?"

"She went on without Janet, for zip-lining and cave tubing. She's not back yet."

Before Birdie could ask anything else she was interrupted by shouts from Jamal.

"Hey, Birdie, watch this!" He did a handstand in the shallow end.

"Good job, Jamal!" she called out when he reappeared.

"You sure are great with that little boy."

"Ah, he is my pride and joy. The love of my life."

"He obviously adores you, too."

"He could use a father figure, but we do okay." Birdie drained her frosty drink and said, "I'm going to get another. Can I get you anything? You know I owe you one."

"Sure, I was planning on getting a beer. Corona."

Birdie nodded. "Jamal," she called, pointing to the tiki bar, "I'm going there. I'll be right back." He gave her a thumbs-up and disappeared under the water, tossing his head like a seal when he emerged.

Birdie returned with the two drinks and placed Fran's beside her.

"Thank you! What do you think of my tan?" Fran asked, holding out her arms.

"Looking good. What do you think of mine?" Birdie joked.

Jamal appeared, dripping with pool water, and reached into Birdie's tote for a beach towel. "May I go get an ice cream cone? I know where it is." He pointed in the general direction. "All you do is pull a handle and the ice cream comes out. I saw some other kids doing it."

"Yes, you may, Jamal. I'm sure you are ready for a snack."

As he sprinted away Birdie called out after him. "Don't run!"

Fran rested her head back and closed her eyes, the Caribbean sun warm on her body and the beer giving her a drowsy, feel-good effect. "I'm craving a cigarette so badly but it's been five days now so…it would be dumb to give in."

"You're going to make it, my friend. Congratulations."

"You know about my deal with Sue Ellen, right? She gave up sweets in return for my giving up cigarettes."

"Yes, I heard about that. How's it going?"

"We're both suffering." Fran laid back in a chair, calculating in her head the amount of money she was saving as a non-smoker, when Jamal returned with his vanilla cone, a good bit of it covering his mouth.

"Look, I made it all by myself."

"Hey, that looks good," Birdie said. "I'm hungry. I'm going to see what's on the buffet. You want anything, Fran?"

"I'm not hungry," Fran mumbled, lying back again.

"Okay. Jamal, you stay here with Miss Fran and finish your ice cream. I'll be right back."

Jamal stared at Fran as he licked the cone. "How come you don't have a husband?" he asked.

"I used to have a husband. He died."

"Can't you get another one?"

"I'm waiting for them to go on sale."

"You mean, so you can get one cheaper?"

"That's right."

Jamal considered that. "How much do they cost? Full price?"

"$12.99."

"How much on sale?"

"9.99."

"You should wait, then."

"I agree."

Having settled that, the two sat in silence until Birdie returned with a plate of food.

"I got coconut shrimp and some chicken fingers and French fries. Want a bite?"

Jamal shook his head and sat down on a beach towel, staring solemnly at his grandmother's plate.

"What's wrong? You sure you don't want some?" Birdie offered again.

The boy shook his head vigorously. He watched as she picked up a crusty coconut shrimp and tossed it into her mouth. "Mm," she murmured as she chewed. "That's yummy."

"Don't eat the shrimp, Birdie," Jamal said, barely above a whisper.

She picked up another shrimp by the tail and Jamal's eyes grew wide. His voice rose an octave as he said, "Don't eat any more shrimp, Birdie!" He reached for her plate but she held fast to it.

"Jamal, I offered you some! Don't be rude!" She bit into the shrimp and chewed, placing the tail on her plate.

"Birdie! Stop!"

Fran lifted her head to see what was going on just as Birdie began to gag. Her hands flew to her throat and her eyes grew large as she tried to cough.

Fran jumped to her feet. "Is she choking? She's choking! Help! Help us, please!"

Several people rushed over, including an employee who was cleaning railings along the deck. "Stand back, please," he ordered. Birdie's face was distorted and her eyes were wild. He took a stance behind her, one of his legs between hers, and reached around her torso and thrust his fists against her belly, just below her rib cage. The shrimp came flying out and she took a deep, rasping breath of air, and then another, and then her legs went weak.

The man gently guided her into a chair and waited until he was sure that she was breathing with ease. "Maybe you should go to infirmary," he suggested. "Just to get checked out."

"Oh, no, no, I'm just fine now," she assured him. "Thank you so much for coming to my rescue."

The young man hesitated. "Are you sure?"

"I'm sure. Thank you."

He nodded and returned to his work. Fran found a paper napkin and discreetly picked up the chunk of shrimp and tossed it into a trash receptacle.

"Are you okay now, Birdie?" Jamal asked, patting her on the leg.

"I'm fine, honey. I should have listened to you."

"You sure you're okay?" Fran asked.

"Yes. Just a little embarrassed."

"It seems the shellfish are kicking our butts on this cruise," Fran joked.

Birdie chuckled, and then she sat back and grew quiet, studying her grandson with great curiosity.

"Hey! There goes that guy!" Jamal pointed.

"What guy?" Birdie raised her head to see.

"That mean guy! The one who wore blue jeans on Captain's Night!"

"Oh, him," she muttered. "The jerk."

"His wife was mean, too, wasn't she, Birdie?"

"Yes, she was. Very rude, both of them."

Fran watched but said nothing as Robert sauntered past the lounging sunbathers with an arrogant smirk on his face. He was alone, wearing swim trunks and clutching a beach towel, seemingly headed to the ship's stern to sunbathe. He continued in that direction and did not return.

Now's my chance, thought Fran. *It's now or never.*

She excused herself with a white lie. "I think I'll go back to the room and rest for a while. I have a little headache. You two enjoy yourselves!"

13
Glitter

Dressed in capris and a white tee shirt and sunglasses, Fran reappeared on the Lido deck carrying a small suitcase filled with lotions, oils, wash cloths, gloves, and the glitter from Sue Ellen's tote bag. She proceeded to the ship's stern, rehearsing her lines along the way. She found Robert easily, lying face down with his blonde tousled hair lifting gently with the ocean breeze. He looked to be sleeping.

Fran spoke as cordially as she could manage. "Excuse me, sir. Can I interest you in a massage?"

When he didn't reply she cleared her throat and spoke louder. "Excuse me, sir. Can I interest you in a complimentary massage?"

Robert looked up and squinted against the sun.

"A free massage? Seriously?"

"Yes, sir," Fran smiled. "The Captain likes to take care of his guests."

"Sure. Go for it. I could use a little TLC."

Fran looked around. "Is there a wife or a girlfriend who might be interested in a massage, as well?"

"I don't know where the hell she is," he grumbled. "Haven't seen her all day."

Satisfied that they were alone Fran said, "Okay, then make yourself comfortable. I'm Cindy," Do you mind if I use a bit of oil?"

"The more, the better," he replied. He put his head down and closed his eyes in anticipation.

"I'll start with your legs and feet, and then I'll do your back and arms. Sound okay?"

"Sounds good. But don't be surprised if I fall sleep. I've got a serious hangover."

"No problem. Most of the guests do fall asleep. That's how good I am."

Fran reached for the rubber gloves which she had sweet-talked from a housekeeper and pulled them over her hands. She dribbled some oil on the backs of Robert's legs and gently rubbed it into his calves, her hands making circular motions until he was covered in oil up to his swim trunks.

In a business-like tone she ad-libbed, "I'm using peppermint papaya oil from the island of Wiki Tiki Wahoo. It's hard to come by, but today is your lucky day."

"Mm, hm," Robert muttered. "Rub harder."

Having been to spas before, Fran knew the basics of a good massage. She ran her hands up and down the length of Robert's hairy legs applying firm pressure, focusing on his calves. Robert moaned a little. Fran repositioned herself so that she could get to his feet, her oily thumbs kneading his instep.

Changing position again to reach his back, Fran used the flat of her hand to rub in circles on either side of his spine. He moaned again.

Grinning, Fran leaned into the massage with her body weight on his upper back, producing a slight pop of his spine. Then she began to knead his upper arms, working her way down to his hands and fingers. After a few minutes Robert's groans turned into open-mouthed snoring in the warm Caribbean sun.

Fran looked around to see if anyone was watching. Most of the other passengers had their eyes closed or were absorbed in a book. She reached inside the suitcase for the glitter and ever so carefully sprinkled it along the length of Robert's greasy body until he shined like a pink diamond.

Saving a little of the glitter for last, she rubbed Robert's neck until it was good and oily and then deftly ran her fingers through his hair, back and forth, back and forth, working the last of the glitter into his scalp.

Then she sat back and waited, holding her breath. He was out, snoring loudly with a little string of drool hanging from his lower lip. For the finishing touch, Fran quietly pulled some scissors from the little suitcase and, holding her breath, snipped a lock of his hair at the roots. He never even flinched. She snipped another lock, and then another, concentrating on the top of his head and leaving a ragged bald patch.

Satisfied with her work, she removed her gloves and tossed them into a trash can, repacked the suitcase and made a hasty retreat.

~

Ninety minutes later, the sun disappeared behind heavy gray clouds and a wind came up, rustling Robert's hair until he began to stir. He wiped at the drool on his lips and lifted his head, realizing that he was the only passenger still on the deck. Empty plastic cups rolled around under the chairs as thunder rumbled. He gathered up his things and sprinted for cover just as the rain came pummeling down.

He found refuge in a booth in the dining area. A table full of children looked up and snickered at him, some pointing. Still half asleep, he smiled and waved at them from his seat. An elderly couple strolled by, pausing to frown at him before continuing on, whispering to each other.

He decided to wait out the rain with a hot cup of coffee. With his glittery hair sticking out and his back side an iridescent pink, he sauntered to the coffee bar where two young ladies were adding condiments to their coffees. "What's up," he said, in his best Mr. Cool voice. They turned and gaped at his hair and forehead, a dazzling sight under the lights. Even his ears glistened. Not knowing what to think, they put their heads together and giggled.

Unaccustomed to being rebuffed, Robert turned away and muttered, "Come back when you grow up." Their giggles became hoots of laughter behind his back. Hesitantly, Robert looked around the big room and realized that he was the center of attention. Even the buffet line workers were grinning at him. The children were on their feet.

"Mister, how'd you get so shiny?"

"Yeah, who are you supposed to be?"

Robert looked down at himself to see that his hairy arms were coated in…glitter? A glance in a wall mirror revealed that his hair, too, was sparkling and standing on end. He turned to examine his back side and was confounded to see that he was a walking glitter bomb. "What the…?"

Suddenly he remembered the "free massage" by that strange woman. He'd been pranked. She had made a laughing stock of him.

Fuming, Robert stomped down three flights of stairs to the stateroom that he shared with his wife. He assumed that she was behind this; after all, their earlier argument had been a nasty one. Beverly wasn't in the room, though. No surprise there. He would get to the bottom of this.

Robert peeled off his swim trunks and kicked them across the bathroom floor and turned on the shower water. He lifted his face to the shower head while a rainbow of glitter went down the drain. Twice he soaped up and rinsed, then squirted a large dollop of shampoo into his palm. He shampooed and rinsed, then shampooed and rinsed again, but something felt wrong. His thick, bouncy hair, his best asset, felt ragged and thin.

Robert shut the water off and dried himself, starting with his hair. The tiny bathroom had filled with steam and he couldn't see in the mirror so he stepped from the bathroom to the large mirror which hung over the dresser.

"What the…?" Robert peered into the mirror in disbelief. His worst nightmare had come true. His hair was falling out.

And his arms and legs still sparkled.

~

Thanks to Travis Rand and his negotiation skills with the Belize authorities, transportation was arranged to return Sue Ellen to the ship before it sailed away without her. She arrived sunburned, hungry, and without her tote bag. She knocked on Janet and Aimee's door and Janet answered in her pajamas, blinking.

"Thank goodness you're back, Sue Ellen! They told us that you missed the bus. We've been so worried!"

Aimee sat up in bed and switched on a small lamp. "Oh, gosh, you are so sunburned!" Sue Ellen's sunglasses had left a raccoon pattern of pale skin in contrast to her crimson cheeks, nose and forehead. Blisters were beginning to form on her nose.

"Girl, what happened? Didn't you wear sunscreen?" Janet asked.

"I didn't think I needed it," Sue Ellen replied, not about to mention her long nap on the bench.

"You poor thing. I think maybe you should go to the infirmary," Aimee suggested.

"I already went, before I came upstairs. They gave me this medicated cream."

Aimee read the directions and scooped her fingers into the white salve and gently applied it to Sue Ellen's face, shoulders and arms.

"My tote bag was stolen. Thank goodness I had tucked my cell phone inside my bosom. Imagine if I had lost all my pictures!"

Janet patted Sue Ellen's knee.

"Ouch!"

"Sorry."

"Could I sleep in here?" Sue Ellen asked meekly. "Fran is already asleep and she hates being woken up."

"Of course you can," Janet replied. "You can have my bed. Are you okay with doubling up with me, Aimee?"

Aimee was already scooting over to the wall. "Fine with me."

After much moaning and flapping of sheets, Sue Ellen finally got settled and Janet turned out the bedside lamp. The three lay quietly in the darkness until Sue Ellen said wistfully, "I wish you girls could have seen me on the zip-line today. I was amazing."

∼

At breakfast the following morning, Sue Ellen set her coffee cup down and exclaimed, "Look what time it is! Who's going ashore with me?"

Fran shrugged. "I don't know. I'm not much on shopping. You know that."

"But didn't you hear what Travis said? Cozumel is supposed to have the best merchandise! I'm going to load up on gifts for the grandkids. Don't you even want a tee shirt or something?"

"Come on Fran," Janet said. "Let's go for a little while. I need to buy some gifts, too."

"Count me in!" Aimee chimed in. "I've been looking forward to this all week."

Fran's cell phone rang and she grappled for it. "Maybe it's Kabir! Oh, hello, Birdie. Yes, we're going. Let's meet in the downstairs lobby in thirty minutes." She ended the call and said, "I guess we're all going shopping."

Janet stretched her long torso and said, "I'm going for a run first, but I'll catch up with y'all at the marketplace."

It wasn't long before Janet was in her running gear, doing leg stretches on the running track. She inserted her ear buds and started to jog. A gentle morning breeze blew sea mist against her face, clearing her mind as she settled into the rhythm of her own heartbeat. It felt good to run, and by the time she finished her fourth lap she felt empowered and strong, like she could run forever.

"Hello!" a booming voice called out from behind, startling her even over the music in her ears. Jake caught up and ran along beside her.

She slowed to a jog and smiled, her chest heaving. "Hey!"

"Janet, right?" He fell into step beside her.

She nodded, gasping for breath.

"I had you pegged as a runner. You're in great shape." He said the words with sincerity, not like a come-on.

Between puffs of breaths she said, "My job…requires it."

Their feet pounded the track in unison and Janet stole a quick glance at his bronze shoulders and the dark stubble on his face.

"What do you do?" he asked.

"I'm a gym teacher. I teach middle schoolers."

"A teacher, huh? Cool." After a moment he asked, "How's your friend? The one with arachnophobia?"

"She's fine. Are you looking for her?"

"What? No! I was just asking if she was okay."

Pleased that Jake's company had nothing to do with her pretty roommate, Janet slowed down and the two fell into a comfortable walk.

"What about you? You don't really seem like the cruise ship type," she teased.

He chuckled. "Yeah, I'm really not. It was a drunken decision. I'm here with a couple of buddies. We just finished a tour in Afghanistan."

"I thought you might be military, what with your haircut. Which branch?"

"Army National Guard. I'm a helicopter pilot."

"No shit! Black Hawks?"

"Yeah. Crazy, huh?"

"Impressive! I'm glad to finally meet a real American soldier. I'll bet you're glad to be back in the States."

"Absolutely."

"Thank you for your service, by the way," she added, sneaking another glance at him.

"You're welcome."

Janet could feel the sweat trickling between her breasts and down her back. They walked in silence for a moment until a thundering of feet came up behind them. Two men ran past, grinning over their shoulders. One whistled loudly with his fingers in his mouth and the other shouted something inaudible.

Janet looked questioningly at Jake.

"My travel buddies," he muttered. "Assholes."

"Oh," she nodded. "How'd you break your nose?"

"That noticeable, huh? I wish I had a good story behind that, but I don't. I broke it playing flag football when I was seventeen."

"It gives you character. I broke my nose once, too, but my mom and a plastic surgeon made sure it wasn't noticeable. Me being a delicate lady and all," she joked.

"I'm glad I ran into you," Jake remarked. "I was hoping I'd see you again. Any chance you'd like to have a drink later?"

Janet's heart thudded in her chest. *Oh my God, he's asking me out.*

"Okay. Sure!" She tried to sound casual. "I'm going ashore to do some shopping but I can meet you later. What do you have in mind?"

"There's a pretty cool lounge on the Mezzanine, just past the casino. Do you know where that is?"

"I think so. I'll find it. What time?" she asked, trying not to appear too anxious.

"How's 5:00? That should give you plenty of time to shop."

"Sounds good. I promise to shower between now and then," she kidded, looking down at her sweat-stained jogging clothes.

"Great! See you later, then." With that, he turned to go.

"Hey!" Janet called out. "Have you tried the ropes yet?"

"Not yet."

"Neither have I, but it looks like fun!"

Janet hurried back to her cabin feeling giddy, her heart fluttering in her chest. *I have a date!* She would not tell anyone, she decided - not even Aimee. She didn't want to jinx it.

14
Rum Cakes and Tequila

Birdie and Aimee took turns holding Jamal's hand as they strolled through the mile-long waterfront shopping district of Cozumel, the morning Mexican sun already hot on their shoulders and necks. They ducked in and out of vendor tents and shops, admiring hand-painted pottery and hand-crafted jewelry and paintings by local artists. They sorted through tee shirts and rum cakes, coffees and chocolates, spices and organic vanilla.

Sue Ellen struck out on her own wearing a wide-brimmed hat to protect her sun-ravaged face. She was last spotted bent over a large bin of children's tee shirts, plowing through them like her life depended on it.

Janet met up with Fran in the marketplace and they shopped quickly and with purpose, returning to the ship by noon. Janet's purchases were displayed all over her bed. Rum cakes for her dad, chocolates for her mom, an assortment of Mexican coffees for both. She had even splurged on a halter top sundress and a pendant to go with it, recognizing her need to spruce up her wardrobe. Fran had purchased two bottles of Tequila and a sea shell necklace for herself, and a wind chime for her sister.

"I have to admit, the merchandise was cheaper than I thought it would be," Fran declared.

"I know, right? I think we got some good deals."

"I love a good bargain," Fran went on as she kicked off her sandals and laid back on Aimee's bed. "The best deal I ever got was when I went to Debra Patinka's yard sale. Remember her?"

"Sure, I remember Debra." Debra had been their school counselor until she changed schools for a position which suited her better.

"I bought an old chest of drawers which I planned to paint and put in my laundry room to hold supplies. I gave her ten bucks for it. A real steal. When I got it home, I took all the drawers out and found a Ziploc bag full of marijuana."

"You did?" Janet's eyes grew round. "What did you do?"

"I smoked it, of course! What do you think I did?"

"I don't know…I…"

"The stuff was old, I could tell, but I still got high. And then I ordered a large pepperoni pizza and ate the whole thing."

Janet shook her head at her friend. "You are just full of surprises, Fran."

"And one time I went to a going-out-of-business sale and found some capris for a dollar."

"A dollar?"

"Yeah! They were on the bottom shelf in housewares, behind some iced tea pitchers, and they were my size! I snatched them up, thinking I had really found a treasure, but when I got home I realized that both legs were stitched closed at the hems."

"Oof," Janet said. "That's bad. One time I bought a John Grisham book at the Goodwill for two dollars, and halfway through it a ten dollar bill fell out. I bragged about that for months. And now, I'm a lottery ticket winner. Who would have thought?"

"You must be living right," Fran replied.

"Oh, by the way, I bought a card for Wayan, for when we leave on Sunday," Janet said. "I thought we could all sign it and say something," she explained, tossing it on the dresser.

"That was thoughtful," Fran acknowledged. "Ugh. I would die for a cigarette right now," she grumbled.

"I know it's hard, Fran," Janet said gently. "But I'm so proud of you. Your willpower has been amazing. You can't give in now."

"Damn Sue Ellen," Fran said resentfully.

"She's doing you a huge favor, you know. You'll thank her someday," Janet reminded her, "when you live to be 104."

Fran tossed a piece of gum into her mouth. "Can't wait."

~

Jamal began to complain about being tired, bored with following the meandering cobblestone streets of Cozumel. To appease him, Birdie bought him a bright orange tropical tee shirt and a long rubber snake which looked remarkably real. Aimee surprised him with a safari hat which he promptly placed on his head, and she treated herself to a tie-dyed sundress, two tee shirts, and some spices.

They decided to rest their feet and have some lunch at a rickety looking wooden restaurant overlooking the ocean. The place was packed and the food smelled wonderful. They found seats on the outdoor patio. Much to Jamal's delight, a bird flew down and perched on the back of his chair before taking off again.

"He's probably looking for something to eat," Birdie guessed. "If he comes back, give him a chip."

While Jamal watched for the bird to return, the ladies looked over the menu. "This is fun," Birdie remarked.

"I'm having fun, too. I love to shop, and what a beautiful day for it! But some of those street vendors won't take no for an answer. Did you get harassed?"

"I did. The trick is, just keep walking and don't make eye contact."

"Believe me, I tried that, but it didn't work," Aimee said. "But it's still a great place to shop for gifts. There is so much unusual merchandise that we don't have back home. Did you see all the coral and silver jewelry?"

"Oh, yes," Birdie nodded. "I have a weakness for jewelry."

"I think you have a weakness for pottery, too. You were in that one store for a long time. Did you see something you like?" Aimee wanted to know.

"Oh, yes. Yes, I did. I'm just not sure my bank account can take the hit."

Aimee sighed contentedly. "I'm happy with what I bought. I wonder where Sue Ellen is. She's probably having the time of her life, buying presents for those grandkids."

The brazen bird returned as their food arrived. Jamal tossed a tortilla chip in its direction and the bird snatched it up and flew to the roof of an adjacent building. Jamal followed it with his eyes, fascinated. The bird returned twice before losing interest in the chips.

"Are we done shopping, Birdie? Because I want to go back to the ship."

"Can you hold out for just a little bit longer, my boy?"

"Hey, Jamal, I have an idea!" Aimee exclaimed, winking at Birdie. "I'm done shopping. Would you like to go get some ice cream with me?"

"Oh, he loves ice cream, don't you, honey?" Birdie said, playing along.

Jamal perked up. "Okay, sure!"

Birdie mouthed "thank you" to Aimee, paid the lunch tab, and took off to the pottery store.

~

As Aimee and Jamal sat licking their ice cream cones in a shady spot, the little boy turned to Aimee and said, "Do you have any kids?"

"No, I do not."

"Do you have a husband?"

"No, I've never been married."

"Why not?"

"Well, I guess because I haven't met the right man yet."

"I would marry you if I was older."

"Why, thank you, Jamal! That is a very sweet thing to say."

"You remind me of Harriet."

"And who is Harriet?"

"She's a dog. Our neighbor back home, Mr. Bunch, has three dogs, named Becky, Tillie, and Harriet. Harriet is my favorite because she's the prettiest and the smartest. Mr. Bunch teaches them tricks."

"What kind of tricks?"

"Like, jumping through a hula hoop. Do you know what a hula hoop is?"

"Yes, I do. I used to have one. What else can they do?"

"They can shake hands and roll over and fetch and all kinds of stuff. But my favorite trick to watch is the hula hoop. Harriet can jump really high."

"That's cool."

"But Mr. Bunch held it too high one day and she broke her front foot."

"Oh, the poor thing. Did her foot heal?"

"Not really. Mr. Bunch says it won't ever be the same. Now Harriet won't jump. She just sits and whines. I guess she's scared."

Aimee thought about that as she wiped ice cream from Jamal's chin.

"Mr. Bunch says she lost trust in herself."

"It sound like she did."

"I told him that he should teach her a new trick, something she's never done before."

"And did he?"

"Yep. He taught her how to dance. He plays music and she stands up on her back feet and turns in circles. The other dogs can't do it but Harriet can. And she seems happy again."

"So you had a good idea, didn't you, Jamal?"

"Yes, ma'am."

"You know, you're a pretty smart guy. And you look great in that safari hat."

"Sometimes my mama talks to me."

His remark caught Aimee off guard. "Your mama talks to you?"

"Uh-huh. But Birdie doesn't know it. I don't want to tell her, and you can't tell her, either!" He looked up at Aimee with pleading eyes.

"I won't tell. I promise." Aimee cleared her throat. "When does she talk to you? At night, in your dreams?"

"No, it's not like that. She's not a dream. She's really there. I can't see her, but I can hear her voice."

"What does she have to say to you?" Aimee gently prodded the boy.

"She talks funny. Sometimes I can't understand her. But mostly she says she misses me and she loves me. One time I had to get a shot in my arm, for school, and she told me it was okay to cry."

"Are you a Christian, Jamal?"

"Birdie and I go to church, if that's what you mean."

"You believe in Heaven?"

"Yes, ma'am. We talk about Heaven in Sunday school."

"Then you know that you and your mama will someday be together again. And Birdie. All three of you together in Heaven."

Jamal nodded emphatically. "I know. I'll get to dance with my mama."

Aimee smiled and put her arm around Jamal. "Yes, you will."

"Can we go find Birdie now?"

"Of course," Aimee replied, gathering up their trash. "It's almost time to meet up with her and Sue Ellen by that big fountain. Do you remember it?"

Jamal nodded. He led her straight to the fountain where Birdie waited on a bench with two well-wrapped pieces of pottery beside her. A pair of beautiful silver earrings hung from her ears.

She handed Aimee a small plastic sack. "For you."

"For me?"

Aimee opened the sack to find a set of delicate coral earrings. "Oh, Birdie! You shouldn't have! But I love these! Thank you so much!"

"No, thank *you*."

Sue Ellen showed up late, breathless and puffing, with three full sacks of gifts. She emptied the sacks right there on the bench to show what she had bought: four giant conch shells, maracas and flutes, a hand-carved wooden cat for her kitchen window, cigars for Dillard, coffee cups, and tee shirts for all. When Jamal showed her his snake Sue Ellen laughed, having bought one, too.

"Let's go. I'm beat," Birdie said.

"Me, too," Aimee agreed. "When we get back to the ship I'm going to get a Pina Colada and lay by the pool."

∼

It was mid-afternoon by the time Aimee made it to the pool to sunbathe. A live country music band was performing and the deck was crowded. She had just found an empty recliner when Travis breezed past her and then suddenly backed up. "Hey! How are you?" he greeted her. "Everything going well for you and your friends?"

"Couldn't be better!" Aimee smiled. "I'm not sure where they are right now, but we are having a fantastic time. Where are you off to?"

"I'm trying to round up some participants for tonight's Karaoke Night. The sign-up sheet is practically empty and I don't want to disappoint the audience."

"Oh," she replied, for lack of a better response.

"I don't suppose I could talk you into signing up, could I? Do you sing?"

"Yes, I sing," she admitted, cautiously.

"What about your friends?"

"I don't think they're the type. I'm not even sure I'm the type. But we were planning on going, just to watch," she replied, hoping that would satisfy him.

"I would be so grateful if you would perform. Any song you want, except for offensive rap songs, but you don't look like a rapper," Travis added.

Aimee scratched her head, considering the idea. "Okay," she nodded. "I'll do it."

"Awesome!" Travis grinned. "Can I sign you up, then?"

"Sure, go ahead."

"I'm sorry, I guess I never got your name."

"It's Aimee. Aimee Burke." She spelled first and last name for him.

"Okay, Aimee Burke. The show starts at 8:00. Thank you!"

"No problem," Aimee smiled sweetly. "Oh, wait! Do I have to sing karaoke, or can I do my own thing?"

"Not sure what you mean."

"If I can find an acoustic guitar, I'd rather do my own background music."

"Really? Well, I don't know why not. It's all about entertaining the guests, right?"

"So can you round up an acoustic guitar?" she asked. "One that's tuned?"

"Yes, I'm sure I can."

"Okay, then! I'm in!" Aimee grinned.

Travis gazed at her, his green eyes full of amusement. "Thank you. See you tonight," he said with a nod. As he hastened away he called out over his shoulder, "I like your braids!"

Aimee watched him go and then stretched back out in the afternoon sun.

Above her, on the upper deck, Robert stood at the railing, sporting a fedora to cover his butchered hair. He stared down at Aimee, admiring the pretty blonde and trying to recall where he had seen her before.

15
What's Your Facebook Status?

Janet had their stateroom all to herself as she prepared to meet up with Jake. She showered for the second time that day and donned a pair of navy blue shorts and a new tee shirt. She blow-dried her hair and arranged it as best she could, then she applied some mascara and blush and sprayed herself with Aimee's perfume. Satisfied with her appearance, she left the room and took the elevator to the casino level.

The time was precisely 5:00 when she stepped into the lounge and spotted Jake at the bar. He was seated on a bar stool, sipping a beer.

"Hey, you," she smiled.

"Hey, yourself! Have a seat."

"Thank you!"

"Is this okay? The bar? Or would you rather sit at a table?" He started to get up.

"No, no! This is fine. Really." Janet settled herself on a bar stool, catching a whiff of his cologne.

"I like to watch the bartenders make drinks," Jake explained. "I used to think I wanted to be a bartender, maybe have my own place."

"Really? Yeah, I can see you doing that. You look like you could take care of any unruly customers."

He grinned. "So what can I order for you?"

"I'll have a Bud Light, same as you."

"Cool," Jake replied, and signaled the bartender.

So far, so good, Janet thought. She glanced at herself in the mirrored glass and wished she'd thought to wear earrings.

"I don't know why, but you look familiar to me," Jake said, studying Janet curiously. "Like I've met you before, somewhere else."

"Really? Well, that can't be, because I've never been to Wisconsin."

The bartender placed a frosty bottle in front of Janet and she took a long sip.

Jake continued. "The thing is, my family actually lived in Arkansas, years ago, when I was a kid. We lived in Fort Smith. Do you know where that is?"

"Of course I know where that is! I was born in Fort Smith and grew up there!"

The two stared intently at each other, trying to ascertain if they knew each other from the past. Janet asked, "How old were you when you lived there?"

"I started first grade there but we moved away when I was in fourth grade. My dad got transferred to Madison and we moved over Christmas break. I cried in the car. Worst Christmas ever." Jake chugged his beer, remembering, and ordered another.

"This is such a coincidence!" Janet smiled. "Where did you go to school?"

"I think it was Bradley Elementary. Something like that."

"Bradford Elementary?"

Jake snapped his fingers. "That was it!"

"No!" Janet exclaimed. "This is too weird. That's where I went! How old are you?"

"I'm 31."

"So you were a grade ahead of me." She squinted her eyes and thought. "But I don't think I've ever known anyone named Jake."

"Back then I went by my middle name. My parents had named me Jacob Ryan but I didn't care for Jacob so I went by Ryan. After I got older I started calling myself Jake."

"Last name?"

"DeLuca."

Janet slapped her hand on the bar and shouted "Shut up!" which startled the bartender. "I'm sorry," she apologized, and lowered her voice. "Ryan DeLuca? You're Ryan DeLuca? Oh. My. God."

Jake was smiling and frowning at the same time. "So did we know each other? You remember me?"

"Of course I remember you! Your family lived one street over from my family and you used to come and play in my neighborhood because our street was a cul-de-sac and we had a basketball hoop at the end of our driveway. I had the biggest crush on you!"

The realization finally struck Jake. "You're Janet Kayler, aren't you. Holy crap, you're Janet Kayler! Your parents are Martin and Teresa Kayler, right?"

Janet was nodding enthusiastically.

"I *knew* you looked familiar! This is incredible!"

The bartender raised his eyebrows at Janet, asking if she wanted another Bud Light, and she did. So did Jake. They had a lot of catching up to do.

"You've changed a lot," Janet commented. "Look at you! Back then you were kind of skinny and you wore braces, didn't you?"

"I wore braces for three long years. Hated them," he chuckled, picking at the label on his bottle. "Yeah, I was skinny. But I started a growth spurt at fifteen and my mom was afraid I'd never stop."

"I can relate. As you can see, I had a growth spurt, too. Thank God it stopped at six feet. My mom was freaking out."

"You're beautiful," Jake replied, catching Janet off guard.

"I don't know about that, but thank you." Janet looked away, peeking at herself in the mirrored backdrop of the bar. Turning the conversation back on Jake, she said, "You were so cute back then. I remember your hair was always a little too long and hanging down in your eyes, and you were kind of shy. I was too young to have a boyfriend but I had a major crush on you. All the girls did. Remember Barbie Pennington?"

Jake rolled his eyes. "Sure do. She followed me around all the time, and she told everyone that I was her boyfriend and it used to make me so mad. Fourth grade boys aren't into that sort of thing."

"So how are your parents, and your sister? I'm sorry, I've forgotten their names."

"John and Marilyn, and my sister is Chelsey. Everyone is fine. Chelsey's married and lives in St. Louis. Mom and Dad are great. They both still play golf. They tee off every Saturday morning."

"Remember how we all went to the same church and your family always sat behind us, on the left side of the sanctuary? I always wanted to sit behind y'all, so that I could look at you during the service."

Jake swallowed some more beer and smiled, nodding, thrilled to be having this conversation with a long-ago friend. "Do you still have that little birthmark on the back of your neck?"

Janet gasped, astonished. "How did you know about that?"

"Because one time, at church, you wore your hair in a ponytail and I saw it, just behind your right ear. It looked like a little apple without the stem."

"Still there," Janet confirmed.

"Show me, so I can be sure you're not an imposter."

Janet turned sideways and lifted her hair for Jake to see.

"Yep, it's you, all right. What a freaking coincidence this is! You played basketball better than any of my friends. I'd walk over to your cul-de-sac, hoping to find you outside, and there you'd be, shooting hoops like a pro."

"I was a tomboy. Still am. I love sports."

The two grew quiet, comfortable in each other's company.

"Man, wait until I tell my mom about this. She always liked you, Janet."

"Yeah, I'll be texting my parents about this, too."

"So, how was Cozumel?" Jake asked, changing the subject.

"Crowded, hot, lots of things to spend money on. I'm not much of a shopper so I got in and got out."

"What did you buy?"

"I bought some things for my parents. Coffee, chocolates, rum cakes. And a little something for my dog."

"What kind of dog do you have?"

"She's a little dachshund, only ten weeks old. She's staying with my parents right now. Her name is Lucy," Janet gushed.

"Yeah? I have a five year old boxer named Boss."

"I think everyone should own a dog, don't you?" Janet asked.

"They're great companions," Jake concurred. "Boss is my best friend."

"So, what did *you* do today?" she asked.

"I went to the rock-climbing place but I couldn't get in. Crowded. Another time, I guess."

"What else?"

"Sat by the pool. Ate some pizza. Waited for you to get back."

Flattered, Janet felt her face flush.

Jake finished off his beer. "So, in Honduras, you said I have an accent. I might say the same about you."

"I don't have an accent!" Janet exclaimed.

"Really? Y'all don't have an ACK-ceeaant?" he mocked her southern drawl and they both laughed.

"Tell me more about yourself," Jake said. "I know you're a teacher now and you're here with your friends, but that's about all I know."

"Hm. Well, my family stayed in Fort Smith until I graduated high school. I went to college at UCA in Conway, and after I got my teaching degree I was hired at one of the Conway schools – a middle school. Once it became evident to my folks that I wouldn't be moving back to Fort Smith, they sold their house and moved to Conway. Remember, I'm an only child," she chuckled.

"You like teaching?"

"I love teaching. I just finished my fifth year. Kids today need more physical activity and that's my thing. I try to make it fun for them, you know? We have a good time. And they like me."

"Why wouldn't they? So, what's your Facebook status?"

"My Facebook status?"

"Yeah."

"Single. Never married. No kids. What's yours?"

"The same."

They both paused and focused on their beers, secretly pleased with the exchange of information.

Jake spoke next. "I stopped in St. Louis on the way down to visit with Chelsey and Chad, her husband. They just found out that they are expecting a baby."

"Oh, how fun!"

"Yeah. I'm going to be an uncle. How about that?"

"You'll be an awesome uncle," Janet predicted. "Uncle Jake. It has a nice ring to it."

"I was thinking, 'Uncle Awesome.'"

Janet laughed. "Even better. But wait, what about your friends? Didn't you drive down together?"

"Nope. They flew down. They wanted to experience Bourbon Street and do some partying before the cruise. Not really my thing."

Janet nodded thoughtfully, glad to know that Jake had skipped that part. "I just bought a house," she blurted out, as if to validate that she, too, was mature and responsible.

"First time homeowner?"

"Yep. It took everything I had. I'm mortgaged to the hilt. But it feels good. How about you? Do you own, or rent, or what?"

"Neither. I haven't been back in the states long enough to know what I want to do. I'm staying with my folks in Madison for now, until I figure out if I'm going to re-up or not."

"When did you get back to the states?" Janet asked.

"About three weeks ago."

Janet studied Jake, her mouth a bit slack.

"What?" he asked. "What did I say?"

"I was just thinking…I may have seen you on TV. I was watching the news and saw a big homecoming of Army National Guard soldiers, like three hundred of them. It was a big deal. Was that you?"

"It was. We landed in Milwaukee on May 23rd."

"Yes! Yes! I saw that! I remember because May 23rd was our last day of school and I drank a half a bottle of wine that night, watching TV with Lucy! Oh my gosh! That was you coming home!"

Jake smiled modestly.

"So was someone there to meet you? Your family? Or…someone else?" Janet caught herself, realizing that she knew nothing about Jake's personal life.

"Yeah, my parents and my sister were there, and some friends. It was so great to be home."

Janet smiled, remembering the broadcast so well. "I wish I had been there to welcome you back."

"You were there, sort of. In a way."

"So, how is it that you made the decision to join the military? I'm curious about that."

"Hm. Well, I attended the University of Wisconsin in Madison and played football for the Badgers for the first two years, until I blew my knee out. I earned a degree in Finance but wasn't motivated about how to apply it. I talked with my dad about the military and he actually encouraged me to sign up. And I'm so glad he did. I feel like I learned a lot of life skills there. I really grew up."

"And you were in for how long?"

"Five years."

"Are you going back?"

"I'm not sure."

"How is it that you ended up on this cruise?"

"Well, one night I was drinking beer with my buddies, Andrew and Grant. They were in my battalion. We'd been back in the states for about a week and Grant decides that we should go on a vacation. That's all he wanted to talk about – beaches, ocean water, palm trees, dolphins. Girls. Four rounds later, we had booked ourselves on a Caribbean cruise."

"Just like that?"

"Just like that. I regretted it the next day, of course, but then I thought, what the heck. Why not just go? Live a little."

"Do you still regret it?"

"Absolutely not. What about you? Do you cruise a lot?"

"Gosh, no. This is my first time. I won ten grand on a scratch-off lottery ticket."

"No shit?"

"No shit. I never win anything, but I got lucky. And I decided that I would use some of my winnings to treat myself and my friends to a nice vacation. We chose this." She swept her arm around to take in the surroundings.

"You paid their way?"

"I did!"

"That was a really generous thing to do."

Janet shrugged. "They are my friends."

Jake took Janet's hand in his and thoughtfully rubbed it with his thumb. He studied her face closely and asked, "Will you have dinner with me tonight?"

"Oh!" Janet was taken by surprise. "Sure! I mean, I'd love to, but I'm supposed to meet my friends at a karaoke thing that starts at 8:00."

Jake glanced at his watch. "Can you eat now?"

"I can always eat."

"Great. How about we try that steak restaurant?"

"Do I need to change clothes?" Janet asked.

"No. You're perfect."

16
Karaoke Night

While Jake and Janet were having dinner, Aimee lay stretched out on her bed with her hands behind her head, having showered and moisturized her face.

She wished she hadn't agreed to participate in the karaoke show tonight. Much as she liked to sing, she had never performed in front of a large audience. She didn't know what to expect and the idea made her uneasy. But then she thought of Travis and the gratitude in his eyes when she had agreed to sign up.

And then her thoughts drifted to Jamal and his story about Harriet, the dog, who restored faith in herself by learning a new trick. Maybe Jamal was right —maybe she was just like Harriet, the dog. And maybe it was time she tried something new. *I have a gift, and I'm going to share it,* she decided.

With a refreshing surge of energy Aimee rose from the bed and started getting ready for the evening. She rifled through her makeup bag and carefully applied her favorite products, taking great care to play up her eyes. As she wriggled into her new sundress and stepped into some sandals she wondered where Janet might be. She scribbled a note to her roommate. "Where are you? See you at karaoke!"

Feeling empowered, she flushed her anti-anxiety pills down the toilet and smiled as she left the cabin, the door clicking softly behind her.

∼

Fran, Sue Ellen, Birdie and Jamal found seats in the center section of the auditorium. Janet soon joined them, breathless and smiling. Jamal saved a seat for Aimee, who slipped in just as the lights dimmed.

Sue Ellen could barely contain her excitement. At the last minute she had secretly put her name on the list, planning to do a rowdy rendition of "Nine to Five" once the show got underway.

Travis greeted the audience with a booming "Welcome to Karaoke Night!" The lights dimmed and he introduced the first participant, a middle-aged man from Texas who sang a George Strait song. He did a respectable job and the audience applauded and whistled.

"He's not half bad," Fran nodded her approval.

Next, a young Hispanic woman did a terrific job belting out a Beyoncé song with some sexy dance moves. She was followed by an inebriated older gentleman who stumbled to the stage and attempted to sing a Johnny Cash ballad.

"Ladies and gentlemen, our next participant is a young lady from Arkansas. Come on up here, Aimee Burke!"

As Aimee rose from her seat and took the stage, her friends gawked at each other.

"Are you kidding me?"

"She's going to sing!"

"Did you know about this?"

Travis handed Aimee the acoustic guitar which she accepted with a smile. She looked stunning under the lights. She leaned into the microphone and spoke in a soft voice. "Thank you. As you can see, I'm changing things up just a bit. I'm going to do a Beatles song with my own background music. I hope you like it."

"I didn't know she played the guitar, too," Fran whispered. Janet raised her eyebrows, indicating that she didn't know, either. Sue Ellen sat rigidly and Birdie took Jamal's hand in hers. No one breathed.

Aimee's nimble fingers began to pick the guitar strings with the familiar opening melody of "Here Comes the Sun." And then she began to sing with a voice smooth as butter and pitch perfect.

Here comes the sun
Here comes the sun and I say
It's alright…

The audience was delighted with her song choice and some sang along. Fran's head swayed back and forth. Janet's eyes glistened with pride, never having seen this side of her roommate before.

Little darlin,' it's been a long cold lonely winter
Little darlin,' it feels like years since it's been here
Here comes the sun
Here comes the sun, and I say,
It's alright…

Four rows behind, Robert leaned forward in his seat, his eyes intent on the singer. *Aimee Burke. Where have I heard that name?* And that face. He had seen that face before, at the pool. No, before that. And then it hit him. She was the house-sitter – the young woman who had killed Beverly's birds and spilled the wine, and ultimately rebuffed his advances. Here she was, all dolled up with funky braids and minus the glasses, but it was her, all right. And she was looking fine.

Robert stole a glance at Beverly who was texting on her phone, oblivious to the circumstances, and he breathed a sigh of relief.

Here comes the sun,
Here comes the sun, and I say
It's alright…

As the last note lingered, Aimee smiled and bowed her head. The audience clapped ardently and her teary-eyed girlfriends stood in unison to applaud. Janet whistled loudly through her teeth.

Behind them, Beverly applauded, as well. She elbowed Robert. "Wasn't she great? I love that song!"

Robert hunkered down in his seat.

"Sit up straight!" Beverly scolded him. "You're not twelve."

Aimee waved as she left the stage, exhilarated and happy with herself. Her girlfriends swarmed her.

"Aimee! You have a fabulous voice!"

"You never told us that you played the guitar!"

"You're so talented!"

"What a great song choice!"

Jamal said, "You should be on 'The Voice,' Miss Aimee. You're really good." Aimee kissed him on the cheek and squeezed his hand.

Sue Ellen slipped out to remove her name from the list, realizing she wasn't as prepared as she'd thought. Aimee would be a hard act to follow. The girls sat through four additional performances, all mediocre, and the show came to an end with Travis taking the microphone.

"That's it for tonight, folks. Hope you had a great time! Let's give a big round of applause to everyone who participated!" He smiled directly at Aimee which made her blush. Robert and Beverly left the auditorium with Robert stealing glances over his shoulder.

"That was fun! Let's go have a drink!" Aimee proposed.

"Yes! Let's go celebrate!"

"I can't stay long," Birdie said. "Jamal is worn out from a very long day."

They found seats at their favorite tiki bar by the pool, and once they each had a drink in front of them, Sue Ellen turned to Aimee and said, "I have a confession to make, Aimee. I saw Robert today on the Lido Deck, and I pulled a mean prank on him."

"Oh?" Aimee looked up, her eyes wide. "What did you do?"

"Well," Sue Ellen replied smugly, adjusting her blouse and making sure she had everyone's attention, "you know that fake rubber snake that I bought this morning in Cozumel?"

Heads nodded.

"I dropped it into Robert's lap from the upper Lido deck."

Aimee gasped. "You didn't!"

"Yep! And you should have seen him come out of that chair!" Sue Ellen hooted. "He ran away screaming like a little girl. It was priceless!" Sue Ellen laughed hysterically, gasping for breath.

Fran high-fived her friend. "You did that, Sue? Good for you. I wish I'd thought of that!" She wasn't quite ready to admit to her own prank, tricking Robert into a "free massage." In hindsight, it seemed a little excessive, even to herself.

Birdie pulled Jamal to his feet to dance to the loud reggae music, much to the delight of everyone around them. They swayed from side to side, bobbing their heads and swinging their arms back and forth, clearly having danced together before. Birdie began to roll her hips in a circular motion, her hands in the air and her eyes closed and Jamal did the same, in perfect rhythm. Then they bent their knees, dropped their hands to their sides, and continued the hip-swaying. Jamal added a few kicks here and there.

The crowd clapped and whistled, egging them on while Sue Ellen did her best to film the duo.

"I've never seen anything like this!" Fran shouted over the music. "Just look at that little boy dance!"

"They make it look so easy!" Aimee exclaimed, tapping the tabletop.

When the song ended Jamal took a bow and plopped into a chair, panting, followed by his grandmother. She fanned herself with her hands.

"Wow!" Janet exclaimed. "That was amazing! I could watch you two dance all night long!"

"Well, this old gal can't dance all night long," Birdie admitted. "I'm good for one dance and that's about it."

"Dancing is in our blood," Jamal declared. "My mama was a good dancer, too."

"That's right," Birdie said. "She was the *best* dancer, and *she* could dance all night long!"

"You'll have to give me a lesson, Jamal. Will you?" Fran asked.

"Sure!" he grinned. "It's easy!"

Two crew members rushed past toting a mop and bucket and a broom and dust pan. A third crew member trailed behind with a spray bottle and a bag of something. "Where's the PVI?" she called out to the other two.

"By the cantina!" they shouted back.

The ladies looked on with curiosity. "What's a PVI?" Sue Ellen asked.

Janet had already figured it out. "You don't want to know," she replied, which peaked Sue Ellen's interest.

"PVI...PVI...what could that stand for?"

"They've obviously gone to clean something up, you nitwit," was Fran's response.

"I know, but what?"

"Think of words that start with a 'v,'" Janet played along. "Public, what? Fill in the blanks."

Sue Ellen's mind worked at it. "Vagina?"

"There you go!" Fran exclaimed with fake enthusiasm. "Public Vagina Incident. I knew you'd get it sooner or later."

Sue Ellen looked befuddled. Jamal, without taking his eyes off the game he was playing on his grandmother's phone, said, "I know what a vagina is."

Birdie rolled her eyes and shook her head while the others sipped their drinks and smiled at the boy's innocent remark. Suddenly, Janet remembered the card she had bought for Wayan and tossed it onto the table top.

"I bought this thank you card for our steward. Sue Ellen, you and Fran need to sign it. Aimee and I already have." They passed a pen around and after each had scribbled a note of thanks and best wishes, Janet dropped it back into her purse and cast her eyes around the table. "Ladies, I have some news. I'm seeing someone."

The others sat up in surprise. Sue Ellen begged, "Do tell!"

"Well," Janet began, "remember the tarantula, back in Honduras?"

"Oh, Janet, honey," Fran patted Janet's arm, "surely you can do better than that!" A round of laughter erupted.

Janet frowned. "Good one, Fran. Nice."

"Just kidding. Go on."

"So, the guy who caught up with us when Aimee fainted, remember him? Jake? Well, he and I have met up a couple of times since then."

"That good-looking military guy?" Sue Ellen asked. "You've been seeing him?"

"Well, at first we just happened to meet on the running track, but then we met for drinks, and I had dinner with him tonight."

"Oh, so that's where you were!" Aimee declared.

"Turns out, we knew each other back when we were kids. He lived one street over from me and we used to play basketball together."

The women peppered Janet with questions.

"How old is he?"

"Is he single? Divorced?"

"What's his last name?"

"What branch of the military?"

"Where's he from again?"

Janet basked in the attention, clearly happy with the enthusiasm she had roused in her friends and she shared everything that she knew about Jake. Fran reached over and gave Janet a hug.

"I'm happy for you, sister, but I'm jealous as hell. I was hoping to meet a lovely, older gentleman who would sweep me off my feet."

"There's still time, Fran," Aimee reminded her. "The cruise isn't over yet."

A glassy-eyed Jamal yawned widely, bored with the girl-talk. Birdie said, "I hate to be a party-pooper but my grandson needs a shower and a good night's sleep. It's been a long day." She stood, pulling the little boy to his feet. "Come on, pickney. Say good night to everyone."

Jamal did a few more dance kicks as they walked away.

~

The exhausted little boy held his grandmother's hand as they waited for an elevator. An elderly, stoop-shouldered gentleman shuffled by and Jamal watched the man with interest, never having seen anyone quite so old. An empty elevator arrived and they stepped on, followed by a sudden flurry of people who filled the car, forcing them to the back.

At level eight, Birdie took Jamal by the hand and called out, "Excuse us, excuse us, please." The crowd parted to let them through. Birdie hopped to clear the closing door but lost her grip on Jamal who held back, afraid of being pinned in the door. Birdie could be heard calling for him as the door closed and the elevator continued its ascent.

"Were you supposed to get off there, little fella?" a man with a big belly asked.

"No, sir."

"Wasn't that your mama?"

"No, sir."

"You're riding the elevator all by yourself, then?" the man asked. Everyone stared at Jamal, waiting for his answer, but fear kept him from telling the truth.

"Yes, sir. I know how to get to my room."

"You sure? What's your room number?"

"I'm not supposed to talk to strangers," Jamal said, flatly. He crossed his arms over his chest.

The man raised his eyebrows, as did the others. "You sure that wasn't your mama? She was calling for you."

"She wasn't calling for me. She was calling someone else's name."

The man looked around the elevator full of adults. "What's your name, son?"

"I'm not supposed to talk to strangers," Jamal repeated, and the man was silenced.

Everyone got off at the next stop, glancing worriedly at Jamal as they exited. He reached up to press a button when two giggling teenage girls jumped in and selected level eleven, and he decided to go wherever they were going. Maybe Birdie would be waiting for him and maybe she wouldn't be too mad. When the girls stepped out, another large group got on, including a woman in a wheelchair, crowding him to the back once again. This time he felt the car descending, stopping on five.

The woman in the wheelchair asked Jamal, "Do you need to get off here?"

Seeing no sign of his grandmother, he shook his head.

He continued to ride down and up and down again, avoiding eye contact but watching for Birdie as the doors opened. Three men dressed in swim trunks and tee shirts stepped on, bantering loudly with each other. They all had hairy legs and short haircuts, Jamal noticed, like the military guys he'd seen on television. Jamal could feel their curious eyes on him and moved shyly to the front of the car. The minute the doors opened he jumped off with no idea where he was.

He found himself on the level with all the shops and galleries and photography studios. Strangers eyed him curiously so he kept his head down and stayed close to the walls, watching for a sign of Birdie, until he came upon a set of stairs. Relieved to be able to avoid the elevators, he began to climb the carpeted steps, counting as he went along. *One, two, three, four, five, six.* Turn at the landing. *Seven, eight, nine, ten, eleven, twelve.* Each set took him to a new floor but every floor looked the same - hallways in all directions lined with cabin after cabin.

Birdie was still down on the eighth level, frantically pacing back and forth, praying with each elevator ding that Jamal would step off, and then she couldn't wait any longer. She called security and alerted them of a lost child and gave the officer a description of her grandson. Then she sprinted up the stairs to the tenth floor to rouse her girlfriends, but they had not made it back from the bar yet.

Her heart in her throat, Birdie considered her options. Should she wait by their cabin door, in case Jamal found his way back, or should she search for him?

She had to search.

Jamal was still climbing and had reached the top deck, about to head back down. He held onto the stair rail and tried not to cry. Suddenly, he heard his grandmother call his name. He raced toward the sound of her voice but tripped on the carpet and sprawled out on the floor. Before he could get to his feet an elevator dinged and he looked up, catching a brief glimpse of Birdie as the door closed behind her.

His eyes swam with hot tears as he studied a diagram on the wall, a cross-section of the ship's layout, deck by deck. Maybe this would show him the way back. But it was too high on the wall for him to make out the numbers and letters and even if he could, he wasn't sure of their cabin number. Wiping his face with the tail of his shirt, Jamal sat down on a step and yawned, and then he remembered something that Birdie had told him, after they had gotten separated one time at a school Open House. *Next time you get separated from me, or from anyone who is watching over you, just stop and stay where you are. Let them find you. The first place they will look is where they last saw you.*

The last time Birdie saw him was in an elevator. But there were so many, going up and down and up again. Where would she expect him to be? His tummy hurt and the tears flowed as he thought of how much trouble he was going to be in.

Feeling miserable, he took a ragged breath and rubbed at his eyes with his fists. When he looked up, an elderly couple stood before him. Jamal recognized the very old man he'd seen earlier, but now the man was accompanied by an old woman who appeared to be his wife. She held on to his elbow with one hand and clutched a cane with the other.

"What's wrong, little one?" the old woman asked in a trembling voice. "Are you lost?"

She had kind, pale blue eyes and thin, wispy gray hair pulled back with a clip. She was tiny and frail as a bird. Jamal was speechless.

"We're Mr. and Mrs. Silverstone. We live on the ship and we know our way around quite well. Would you like for us to help you?" Her tiny voice quaked, almost as if she were singing her words.

Mr. Silverman watched Jamal through thick, round eyeglasses which magnified his eyes in a comical way. His eyebrows were white and unruly, matching the thin strip of hair which circled his otherwise bald head. He smiled gently at the boy.

Jamal remembered what he'd been taught about stranger danger. His first impulse was to lie and say that he wasn't lost, as he'd done in the elevator. But he needed help and somehow he trusted this sweet couple.

The woman, Mrs. Silverstone, came closer. "Who are you with, my dear? Are you on the ship with your family?"

"I'm with my grandmother. Her name is Birdie Clarke."

"And your name?"

"Jamal."

Mr. Silverstone spoke for the first time in a surprisingly deep voice. "Jamal, you don't have to be afraid. We're going to help you find your grandmother."

The boy took a deep, shuddering breath and wiped at his nose.

"Charles, give him your handkerchief," Mrs. Silverstone said. Turning back to Jamal, she asked, "How long has it been since you last saw your grandmother, dear?"

"I don't know. She got off the elevator and I didn't. And when I did get off I didn't know where to look for her. I think she will be mad at me for being gone so long."

Mrs. Silverstone's face softened. "Oh, honey. I seriously doubt that. She will be overjoyed to see you."

Jamal's eyes rested on a stub where Mr. Silverstone's right hand should have been. Startled, he looked up, wide-eyed.

"I lost my hand in the war, son. A long, long time ago. I know it looks funny, but it doesn't hurt."

"How come it didn't grow back? Your hand?" Jamal wanted to know.

"Because my other hand is enough. That's why God gave us two."

Mrs. Silverstone rested her hand on Jamal's shoulder. "Do you know your cabin number, dear?"

"No, ma'am."

"Do you know which deck you are staying on?"

"No, ma'am."

"Well, then, we've got work to do!" Mr. Silverstone's big eyes twinkled behind his glasses.

"Can't you just call Birdie on your cell phone? I know her number."

Mrs. Silverstone chuckled, glancing at her husband. "I'm afraid we don't own a cell phone. We never felt the need for one."

Mr. Silverstone seemed to have a plan. "Tell me, son, you've been to the big swimming pool, right?"

"Sure!"

"And when you and your grandmother go to the pool, do you take the stairs, or the elevator?"

"We take the stairs."

"Up, or down?"

"Up. There's twenty-four steps in all."

"So you count them?"

"Yes, sir! Every time. I like to count."

"This is good information," Mr. Silverstone said. "Twenty-four steps would connect two decks. The pool is on deck number ten, so you must be on deck number eight."

Jamal waited hopefully.

"We will have you there in no time. Let's go."

"Will Birdie be there?"

"I certainly hope so!" Mrs. Silverstone smiled. "If not, we will wait for her. You have narrowed down our search considerably."

They began to walk, much too slowly for Jamal's liking. Mrs. Silverstone's bony hand gripped her cane and shook a little as they waited for an elevator. With a ding an elevator arrived and Mr. Silverstone pressed the button for level eight. Jamal trembled in anticipation of seeing his grandmother and, when the doors opened, there she was, pacing.

"*Birdie!*" he called out, racing to her and throwing himself against her legs.

"Oh, Jamal, Jamal, I was so worried! Oh my goodness, thank God you're okay!" She hugged him fiercely and then held him at arm's length. "You are okay, aren't you? Were you scared?"

"Yeah, a little."

She grabbed him again and squeezed until he pulled back. "Are you mad, Birdie?"

"Am I mad? No! Of course not!"

Relieved, Jamal said, "I'm sorry I didn't follow you. I was scared of that door closing on me."

"I know, honey. It wasn't your fault. How did you manage to get back here?"

Jamal turned around to point at the Silverstones but there was no one there. He blinked and looked around, turning in a circle. "Th- there was an old man and woman. Mr. and Mrs. Silverstone. They were just here, right behind me. They helped me find you." He stared at the spot where they should have been. "I guess they left," he said, "and I didn't get to say thank you." Jamal hung his head.

Birdie patted his shoulder. "I'll track them down and we can say thank you together. Mr. and Mrs. Silverstone, you say?"

"Yes. The man's name was Charles. I don't know the lady's name."

Birdie committed that information to memory and took her grandson by the hand. When they reached their cabin she helped him into his pajamas and tucked him into bed. "You must be exhausted," she said, kissing his forehead.

Jamal rolled over onto his side and closed his eyes, and soon his breathing became steady. Birdie picked up the phone and called security to let them know that Jamal had been found safe and sound. Then, she quietly slipped into her nightgown and into her own bed. She lay on her back in the dark, listening to Jamal's breathing and thinking about the Silverstones, whom she never got to meet.

17
I've Always Wanted a Shiner

Good morning, ladies and gentlemen! This will be our last full day at sea as we navigate across the Gulf of Mexico, headed back to the Port of New Orleans. Later today I will provide important updates regarding procedures for the removal of your luggage, but for now, just get out there and enjoy another beautiful day in the sun!

"What an incredible view!" Jake exclaimed. "You can see for miles! Look, there's another ship, way out there in the distance. Can you see it?"

"Yeah, I see it. I told you you'd like this!"

They were on the ropes course, poised one hundred fifty feet above the ocean in safety harnesses, resting after an hour of navigating rope bridges and swinging steps.

"You're a thrill-seeker, aren't you? I've never met a woman who enjoyed this sort of thing," Jake said.

"I'm always up to a good challenge, especially outdoors," Janet replied. "I can be borderline reckless."

He grinned. "Where have you been all my life?"

"Apparently I've been waiting for you to show back up."

Jake gazed at her intently. "You're amazing, you know that? Inside and out, you're a beautiful woman."

His compliment caught her so off guard that she was tongue-tied.

"You are, Janet. You're kind, and intelligent, and genuine. Not to mention adventurous. You make me happy."

Janet's heart soared. She swallowed hard before responding. "I feel the same way. I'm so happy that we've reconnected." Her eyes stung with tears. "It's going to be really hard to say goodbye tomorrow."

"I know. I keep thinking about that. I don't want this to end."

He reached up and pulled his military dog tags from his neck. "I want you to have these." He placed the tags and the chain into Janet's palm. "Something to remember me by."

"But Jake, these are...don't you need these?"

"I can get another set. I want you to have them."

"I don't know what to say," she whispered, curling her fingers around the warm metal. "This is so personal."

"It's supposed to be."

She turned the tags over, running her fingers over the plates stamped with vital information for Jacob Ryan DeLuca.

"This is the most thoughtful, special gift I've ever received. Thank you."

Jake pulled Janet against himself in an awkward, high-rise hug. She gripped a pole with one hand and attempted to embrace him with the other but lost her footing. She shrieked, grappling for support. The safety harness kept her from falling but she banged her head against a wooden beam. She winced in pain, gripping the beam with both hands.

"Damn. That hurt. That really, really hurt," she groaned.

"Shit. Are you okay? Let me see!" Jake cried out in panic.

"I'm dizzy," she mumbled, grabbing him around the neck. They held each other for a long minute, hearts thumping, and then Janet pulled away cautiously, the dizziness having subsided.

"Um, you know I dropped the tags, right?"

"I know. My fault for throwing you off balance."

"We have to find them!"

"Don't worry about the tags. They're down there somewhere."

She looked down at the vast expanse of people and beach chairs and potted plants.

"Don't worry," he repeated, kissing her softly on her injured eye, and then on her lips. "Let's get you down from here."

~

Janet sat in the shade with ice on her left eye while Jake looked around for his tags. When she couldn't sit still any longer she joined him. They wound their way throughout the area just below where they had been. Janet even approached a few people.

"Excuse me, did you happen to see anything fall from up there?" she pointed above. "Some tags on a chain?"

No one had seen anything. After an exhaustive search they sat down on the side of the pool, dangling their legs in the water. Jake raised Janet's chin with one finger. "You know you're going to have a shiner," he said.

"Finally! I've always wanted one."

He put his arm around her in a comfortable way and she rested her head on his shoulder. "Could they have dropped into the swimming pool?" she asked.

"I was just wondering the same thing. It doesn't seem possible, but with the ship being in motion…"

They stared at the pool, a sea of churning arms and legs. The notion of trying to search it seemed impossible. Janet dropped her chin.

"Babe, it's not your fault," Jake assured her, pulling her to him.

"But they are important. To you, and now to me."

Jake didn't reply, and when Janet looked up he was staring intently across to the other side of the pool. Someone or something had caught his attention.

"What are you looking at?" she inquired, following his gaze.

"There's someone over there I want to talk to. I'll be back in a minute."

Janet watched as Jake circled the pool and stopped in front of a teenage boy, apparently someone that he knew. Janet splashed her feet in the cool water.

"Hey, you," Jake said when he reached the boy.

"Yeah?"

The kid was gangly and looked to be about fourteen, with red hair and a mouth full of braces. He wore swim goggles on his face.

"What's in your pocket?"

"Huh?"

"I saw what you just did. Show me what's in your pocket."

"Screw you, man." He turned to walk away.

Jake grabbed the boy by the back of the neck and stopped him short. "You see that security guard over there? Do we need to have a talk with him?"

"No, sir."

"Then let's have it, pal. C'mon, I'm waiting."

The kid slowly reached down into the pocket of his swim trunks and produced an expensive looking gold watch.

"Hold it up where I can see it."

The boy did so, and Jake took a picture.

"Why'd you take a picture?" the boy asked, scowling.

"Why'd you steal it?"

"I didn't!"

"I saw you take it from that open beach bag over there, beside that sleeping bald headed man in the red trunks."

"You don't know shit."

"Is that right? I've got all I need to nail your ass. Let's go."

"Wait. I'll put it back."

"Damn straight you'll put it back. But first you owe me."

"What do you want?"

"Can you swim?"

"Duh!"

"Underwater?"

"Sure."

"My dog tags fell down here somewhere, from the ropes course. I think they may have landed in the pool."

"So?"

"So you're going to find them for me. You have until 8:00 tonight."

"Why is this my problem?"

"Oh, it's not about the tags, pal. It's about that stolen watch. What's your name?"

"Austin."

"Austin what?"

The boy hesitated, looking all shifty-eyed. "Austin Shepherd."

"Where are your parents?"

"Sitting over there with those people, playing cards."

"Okay, Austin. I'm Jake. Meet me back here at 8:00 tonight, with the tags. They're on a chain. They're important to me. I want you to comb every inch of this pool, including the drain. Especially the drain."

"What if I can't find 'em?"

"You'll find them and you'll bring them to me. That's your part of the deal."

"What's your part of the deal?"

"I'll keep my mouth shut about the watch. Remember, Austin Shepherd, I have evidence," Jake said, showing him the photo he took on his phone. "Now go put the watch back while the guy is still asleep. And I'll see you tonight at 8:00 sharp."

~

Not far from where Jake confronted Austin, Beverly wound her way through the lounge chairs while Robert followed, hoping for another glimpse of that little blonde. He had not given up on the idea of nailing her. In fact, he was obsessed.

"How about we go up there?" Robert suggested, pointing to the balcony.

"No, Robert," Beverly replied. "I might want to get in the pool. Let's stay down here. Look, there're two chairs!"

Robert wore sunglasses and a ball cap pulled snugly down over his forehead, not wanting to be noticed or recognized. He didn't need any more drama. He settled into his chair and waited for Beverly's incessant chatter to begin. His wife talked too much.

"I just called the store," she said. "The Gucci handbag sold. The one in the window."

Beverly owned a small boutique which her parents had bought for her, fittingly called *Daddy's Money*, a name which the family thought was cute but one which Robert abhorred. The shop was filled with overpriced merchandise for pretentious shoppers.

"Would you rub some tanning lotion on me, honey?" Beverly asked.

"I just got comfortable, Beverly!" Robert complained. "Can't you do it yourself?"

"But I want to lie on my stomach and I can't reach around to my back. Please?"

He made a big show of getting back up, tossing his ball cap on the chair for effect.

"Put your cap back on. Remember your hair."

Quickly he grabbed the cap and snugged it down.

"I still don't understand how you got your hair caught in a fan. What were you doing so close to a fan?"

"I told you. I was hot," Robert snarled as he began to rub lotion onto his wife's shoulders. "Drop it."

"Well, you need to be more careful. Why don't you get a short haircut? I've never seen you with short hair. You know, like that tall guy over there?" She pointed to a darkly handsome fellow with a military cut.

Without bothering to look, Robert mumbled, "Maybe I will," just to placate her. He quickly spread the lotion on her back and flopped back down on his chair.

"And you still have glitter on you, honey. Are you using enough soap in the shower?"

"Yes, Beverly."

"I even have it on me! How in the world did you end up in a children's art class, anyway? That doesn't sound like you. You don't even like kids."

"I already told you. I was bored and I volunteered to help out. There were a lot of kids in there and not enough helpers."

"But…"

"I have a headache, Beverly. Just let me lie here for one minute without talking, okay?"

"Oh, I'm sorry. I have some Advil back in the room. It's in my makeup bag on the dresser. The black bag with the white polka dots. Wait, no, it's probably in the bathroom. I think that's where I left it. But if it's not in the bathroom then it will be in my purse. Not the black purse. The burgundy one."

Robert feigned sleep.

"I know you're not asleep already, Robert. Why do you always do that? Pretend to be asleep when I'm talking? It's rude, you know."

Robert jumped out of his chair in exasperation. "I'm going to get something to eat."

As he stalked away, Beverly raised her head and called out sarcastically, "No, thank you, honey. I'm not hungry just yet." Then she stuck out her tongue and lay back down.

After a moment the scraping of a chair caught Beverly's attention and she opened one eye to see a young woman standing beside her.

"Excuse me, is this chair saved?"

"No! Go ahead. It's all yours," Beverly replied sweetly.

"Thanks."

Beverly watched with mild interest as the slender blonde woman made herself comfortable, removing her sunglasses to apply some sun block to her face. Beverly sat up on one elbow.

"Hey! I saw you sing last night! That was you, right? At karaoke?"

Aimee smiled modestly. "Yes, that was me."

Now Beverly sat up straight, happy to have someone interesting to talk with. "You were wonderful! You have the voice of an angel."

"Well, thank you! I'm really not used to performing in public."

"And you play the guitar! I'm jealous. I have no musical talent whatsoever."

"I've always been a music buff," Aimee explained. "I'm still learning the guitar." She laid her head back and closed her eyes. "Oh, this sun feels good. My roommate keeps our room so cold."

Beverly returned to her face down position and asked, "Do you cruise often?"

"No, this is my first time. I'm here with some friends of mine. What about you?"

"My husband and I are cruising in celebration of my birthday. He just went to get something to eat. I should warn you, he's not in a great mood. He's got a hangover."

"I didn't take his chair, did I?"

"No, he's sitting over here on this side. You're fine."

Beverly peeked again at the newcomer, envious of her smooth, flat belly, long legs, and golden tan. Ordinarily, she would be judgmental, looking for flaws, but she didn't have the urge to do so with this sweet and quiet woman who presented no threat.

"Who did your braids?" Beverly wanted to know.

"What? Oh, a friend who I met on the ship. She's from Jamaica. What do you think?" Aimee asked, reaching up to touch the tight rows.

Beverly replied, "I mean, I couldn't pull it off, but it looks good on you. Are you single, then?" Beverly asked.

"Yes, I'm single."

Beverly waited for more but Aimee said nothing else.

"Sometimes I wish I were single. Husbands can be a real pain in the ass. At least, mine is."

Aimee wasn't sure how to respond so she didn't. The woman went on about her marriage. "We went through a really rough patch not too long ago. He became distant so I, well, you know, I turned to someone else for companionship. A woman has needs, you know?"

Aimee remained quiet, suddenly uncomfortable with the direction the conversation was going. She wished this woman wasn't talking so loudly.

"And then about the time I started feeling guilty about it, I found out that he was bonking someone else, too. How dare him! I mean, look at me! I'm older than he is but you certainly can't tell it, and I come from money."

She stopped talking long enough to take a sip from her insulated drinking cup.

"So I threatened to call my lawyer and have him written out of my inheritance and wouldn't you know it, he came crawling back. I've got him on a tight leash now," she scoffed and took another sip.

"What's that you're drinking?" Aimee asked, anxious to change the subject.

"Oh, this? It's cranberry juice from the breakfast bar mixed with vodka. I know you're not supposed to bring liquor onto the ship but I smuggled in an eighty dollar bottle of Grey Goose. Shhhh!" she added, raising her finger to her lips. "Don't you tell on me, now!"

Aimee smiled conspiratorially but, having no interest in this woman's personal business or her illicit vodka, she pretended to get a text on her phone. "Oh, gee, I'm sorry but I'm gonna have to run. My roommate has locked herself out."

Aimee began to gather up her things when a shadow fell across her and she looked up. Slowly, she stood, shoulders back, and said, "Hello, Robert," and then she tossed her hair and walked away.

Robert's eyes cut to his wife before he dropped into his seat and waited for the onslaught.

"You know that girl? That singer?" Beverly asked, incredulously.

Robert closed his eyes and shook his head.

"But she knew your name! I heard her call you Robert. She said, 'Hello, Robert.'"

"I don't know her, Beverly, but she looks like the girl who came and watched our house when we went to your grandfather's funeral."

"The one who killed Brad and Angelina?" Beverly let that sink in.

Robert was slow to respond. "I think her name is Aimee or something like that."

"She's very pretty," Beverly added, testing the waters. She waited for Robert to comment but he remained silent, which, to Beverly, was a familiar red flag. "You slept with her, didn't you?"

"What? Why would you think that? I've been with you this whole week!"

"I mean, before. After she ruined my carpet and killed my birds. I'm not stupid, Robert. She slept with you and you let her off the hook."

"Jesus, Bev!"

"We talked about suing her for damages, and then suddenly you just dropped it. You acted like it had never happened."

"That's why we have insurance, Beverly. They took care of it."

"No, they took care of the carpet, but they didn't cover the dead birds, remember?"

Robert groaned, his eyes closed. He wanted so badly to say that he didn't give a rat's ass about those two noisy, messy birds, but he kept his mouth shut.

"You said you'd take her to court over it but you never did. It was easier to sleep with her, instead, and call it even. Am I right?"

Robert merely shook his head in aggravation, not willing to give his wife the satisfaction of an answer.

"You always do this, Robert!" Beverly's voice rose several octaves as she railed against him. "You always find a way to justify having sex with other women! You think I don't know, but I do. It's disgusting!"

Robert cast his eyes around and pulled his ball cap further down. Through gritted teeth he hissed, "Stop yelling. You're making a scene."

"Did you pay for her to come on this cruise?"

"That's ridiculous. It's a complete coincidence that she's on the ship."

"Really, Robert? I'm supposed to believe that it's a coincidence that...what's her name...*Aimee*... just happens to be on the same cruise? Do you think I'm stupid?"

"Shut up, Beverly. You don't know what you're talking about."

"I was actually lying here *sunbathing* with that slut, being all nice to her. Ew!"

Her chin quivered as she waited for a response but got none.

"*Fine.* If you're not going to take care of this, then I will. I will not have that skinny little bitch ruining our vacation."

"This is not a vacation, Beverly. This is a freaking disaster. Anyway, we'll be back in New Orleans in the morning. What's the point?"

"The point is, I'm your wife. Haven't you put me through enough?"

"Calm down, will you?"

"Just wait until my parents hear about this. They paid for this cruise, you jerk! For my birthday. Which is today, by the way."

Robert winced. He'd bought her a card but forgot to give it to her. "Happy birthday," he mumbled.

"That's all you have to say?" she demanded, fury in her eyes. The question hung in the air.

"Happy birthday to you?" Robert added, trying to be funny.

"Fine. I'm calling Daddy." And with that, Beverly grabbed her drink and flounced away.

18
A Woman Scorned

Beverly's call home wasn't helpful at all. Her father had flown to London on business, according to the maid, and her mother was hosting an important fundraiser. Beverly was on her own to deal with this latest humiliation in her life.

She marched straight to a lounge and ordered an apple martini, her mind scheming with all sorts of nasty plots for revenge. She had had enough of her cheating husband's shenanigans. *If he can be deceitful, so can I*, she told herself. First, she would stir up some trouble for Aimee, and then she would deal with Robert through her lawyer.

Beverly asked the bartender for a pen and began to scribble on a bar napkin. Several wadded up napkins later, she had crafted something which satisfied her. She folded the napkin in half and dropped it into her purse, finished her martini with a gulp, and clumsily made her way out of the lounge. She found their state room empty, which actually made things easier. She folded her note several more times and pushed it into the front pocket of Robert's jeans which had been lying in a heap since Captain's Night. Then she enjoyed a hot shower and shampooed her hair.

When Robert returned, reeking of whiskey, Beverly was curled up in bed reading a novel.

"Well, well, look what the cat drug in," she said. "Thanks for ruining my birthday cruise, by the way. I hope you're proud of yourself."

He ignored her, stepping out of his clothes and kicking them into a corner.

"You are such a pig. Look at this room!" she said with disgust, getting out of bed. "Your jeans have been lying here for days." Beverly snatched up the jeans and pretended to be surprised when the folded note fell out.

"What's this?" she asked. She picked it up and smoothed it out on the dresser top next to Robert, who was clipping his nose hairs.

"Oh. My. God. You two are planning to kill me?" she asked.

"Huh?" Robert grunted, his eyes not leaving the mirror.

"This note! It's from your girlfriend! Were you going to tell me about this, or were you two just going to throw me overboard and live happily ever after?"

"What are you talking about, Bev? Nobody's going to throw you overboard."

"According to this, you just might!"

Robert sighed and sat down and read the note, then read it again.

Robert,

Ever since that time we were together…I can't stop thinking about you. And I know that you care about me, too. I could see it in your eyes today, at the pool. Let's get rid of Beverly. We can throw her off the back of the ship and no one will ever know what happened to her. Let's do it tonight.

Love, Amy

Robert, smiling, turned to his wife. "You wrote this, didn't you?"

"What?"

"You wrote this, and you planted it in my jeans. Classy, Bev."

"What are you talking about?"

"This reads like something a ten year old would write."

"Well" she huffed, "I guess I should expect this reaction from you. I'm calling security. My life is obviously in danger."

She punched the button on the telephone before Robert could stop her. "Yes, hello, this is Beverly Bennett in Room 715. I have reason to believe that my life is in danger and I'd like to file a report, please." There was a pause. "Beverly Bennett. Room 715," she repeated. Another pause. "Yes, I'm here now. With my husband." Pause. "Okay. Thank you."

She hung up and narrowed her angry eyes at Robert. "Don't you dare leave," she hissed.

Within minutes there was a knock at the door and two men wearing security badges introduced themselves. The shorter one said, "I'm Officer Compton. This is Officer Larimore. Are you Mrs. Bennett?"

"Yes, please come in. This is my husband, Robert." Both cops glared at Robert, who glared right back, exhausted now from all the drama his wife had caused.

"We understand there's been a threat."

Beverly produced the napkin and stated, "This was in the pocket of my husband's jeans." She waited until both officers had read it.

"So, who is this Amy? A passenger on the ship, I presume?"

"She is the devil in disguise, that's who she is! And she's been after my husband for months. Tell them, Robert. Tell them how she has stalked you and harassed us, and now she has followed us on this cruise, for Pete's sake!"

"Mr. Bennett, is that true?"

Robert glared quizzically at Beverly. "Um, no?"

"Is that a question, sir?"

Robert sighed loudly. He didn't have the gumption to cross Beverly. He knew that if he didn't back his wife's story she'd divorce him, which meant he'd have no more access to her money, not to mention a sizeable inheritance when her parents passed away.

Beverly narrowed her eyes at her husband.

"The woman has caused us some problems, yes," Robert concurred.

Beverly scoffed. "Problems? She clearly wants me dead! What do you plan to do about this, officers? I want to press charges and I want a full-blown investigation."

Robert started to speak up but Beverly cut him off. "And I want your best people on it."

"You're looking at us." Officer Larimore gave her a thumbs-up.

"We will look into the matter immediately, Mrs. Bennett," Officer Compton assured her. "What is this woman's last name?"

Robert answered the question. "Burke. With an 'e' on the end."

"And Mrs. Bennett, how did you come into possession of this?" He held up the crinkled napkin.

'It fell out of my husband's jeans when I picked them up. Just a few minutes ago."

"Mr. Glitter? I mean, Mr. Bennett?"

Robert cursed under his breath.

"Mr. Bennett?"

Robert retorted angrily, biting off his words. "I don't know what to say, okay? This is the first time I've seen that thing."

"How very strange," Compton said, pursing his lips.

"Very strange, indeed," Larimore concurred.

After an embarrassingly long silence, Officer Compton tucked the wrinkled evidence into his shirt pocket.

"So what happens next?"

"We will look into the matter, Mrs. Bennett. We take the safety of our passengers very seriously. Thank you for contacting us."

"But wait! That's it?"

"We'll be questioning Miss Burke, of course, and then we will get back to you," Larimore assured her.

"You do plan to place a guard at our door." It was a statement, not a question.

"Not unless we deem it necessary," Compton said.

Beverly frowned, clearly frustrated. "When will I hear back?"

"Later today."

The officers nodded and let themselves out. Officer Compton hesitated in the hallway and turned back.

"Don't go anywhere, Mr. Bennett," he said, gravely.

"Right. Where would I go?"

∼

"Miss Burke?"

"Yes?" Aimee was just leaving her room when the two officers arrived.

"I'm Officer Larimore and this is Officer Compton, ship security. We'd like to have a word with you, if you don't mind."

"Sure," she said, surprised. "What is this about?"

"There's been a complaint filed against you."

"A complaint? Who filed a complaint?"

"Would you like to talk here, or would you prefer our office?"

"Your office, please." Aimee wasn't about to let two strange men into her room.

"Sorry to inconvenience you," Officer Larimore said. "Bring your purse, please."

Baffled, Aimee followed them to the security offices. Officer Compton pulled out a chair and she took a seat, nervously bouncing her leg.

"Does this have anything to do with the Bennetts?" she asked timidly.

In answer to her question Officer Compton handed her the napkin. "Does that look familiar?"

Aimee read the words quickly and then snorted with laughter. "Are you serious right now?"

The men exchanged looks. "Yes, Miss Burke. We are taking the matter very seriously."

"Is this supposed to be from me? Because I didn't write this," she declared flatly.

"I see," Compton said, raising his eyebrows.

Larimore stepped in. "Mrs. Bennett claims that you've been stalking her husband and causing them marital problems. Is that correct?"

"What?" Aimee was stunned. "No, it's not correct! I house-sat for them one time, and things didn't go well. Some birds died. I may have splashed wine on their carpet. But that's all in the past and I haven't seen either of them since. That is, until I came on this cruise."

"And how is it that you happen to be on the same cruise with them? Seems rather suspicious."

"I'm sure it does. But I promise you – it's totally by coincidence. I'm here as a guest of a friend who won some lottery money. I about fell over when I saw Robert in the dining room on Captain's Night. I immediately left the restaurant and I never went back. I've managed to avoid him ever since. Like I said, the house-sitting weekend didn't go well and I was embarrassed and humiliated about the damages. I offered to pay for everything but Mr. Bennett had other ideas." Aimee rolled her eyes.

"Go on."

"Well, he propositioned me while his wife was out in the car. He suggested that the two of us get together to 'smooth things over.' If you know what I mean."

"We do." Both men nodded, their eyes on the floor.

"I rejected him, on the spot. I told him that it was wrong and that I'd rather pay the damages, even if it took me the rest of my life. My rejection probably hurt his ego, but I don't think he's behind this. I think Beverly is. I've never stalked anyone in my life. And I sure as hell would not stalk a man like Robert Bennett."

"So what happened today to get things stirred up?"

Aimee sighed. "Today I had the unfortunate experience of choosing a pool chair right beside Beverly. Except I didn't know it was Beverly, and she didn't know me, either."

"Oh?"

"We'd never really met face to face so how was I to know? She was half-drunk and very obnoxious. She talked too much and made me uncomfortable so I got up to leave and suddenly, Robert appeared. That's when I realized who she was."

"And then what?"

"I said, 'Hello, Robert,' and then I left. I never looked back. I can only imagine what happened between them after that. And I certainly did not write that letter. It seems to be a lame attempt to set me up."

"So who do you think wrote it?"

"I think it's obvious, don't you? Beverly wrote it!"

"And what makes you think so?"

"Well, first of all, this is not my handwriting. I'm left-handed so my handwriting tilts to the left. This tilts to the right. Second, I've never been to this lounge," she said, referring to the logo on the back side of the bar napkin. "I like the tiki bar by the pool."

Then she crossed her arms. "But most importantly, this is *not* how I spell my name. My name is spelled A-i-m-e-e." She produced her driver's license again as proof.

A long silence followed, both men weighing the odds.

"This is ridiculous," Aimee finally declared.

Larimore cleared his throat. "Thank you, Miss Burke, for your time. I think we are beginning to see the bigger picture now."

"You're welcome."

"Anything you want to add?" Compton asked, glancing at his notes.

"Yes. I'd like to say that I have no wish to cause trouble for the Bennetts. Beverly's vindictiveness is understandable, although it should be directed toward her cheating husband, not toward me. He's a despicable, lying womanizer. And I think she knows it."

~

Aimee was dismissed, and the Bennetts were summoned to the security office for an update on the alleged murder conspiracy. When the officers informed them that Aimee Burke had been questioned and released, Beverly was incensed.

"But she clearly wants me dead! At the very least she should be thrown into the brig until we get home. She's a danger to society!"

"We don't think so, Mrs. Bennett. We listened to her side of the story, which is very different from yours, and well, to be honest, the letter does not appear to be legitimate."

Robert squirmed in his chair but offered nothing, knowing better than to cross his wife.

Beverly pushed on. "Are you saying it's a fake letter? But that's absurd! What makes you think so?"

Officer Compton handed her a note pad and a pen, which she took with her right hand. "I want you to write down the name of your husband's alleged stalker."

She scrunched up her nose. "Is this some kind of lie detector test?"

"No, ma'am."

"But I don't see what…"

"Just write it down. First and last name."

Beverly huffed, did as she was told, and shoved the note pad back over. The two officers studied it and came to a quick conclusion. Compton cleared his throat.

"Don't you find it peculiar, Mrs. Bennett, that the person who you claim to have written a note threatening your life would misspell her own name?"

Beverly hesitated. "That doesn't surprise me. She's not very bright."

Compton frowned at Beverly's persistence.

"Just how many ways can you spell Amy?" Beverly wanted to know.

"Apparently there's at least one other way. Miss Burke's identification shows that her name is spelled A-i-m-e-e."

Beverly turned all shades of red and struggled for a rebuttal. When she couldn't think of one she pulled her husband to his feet and said, "Let's go, Robert. It's obvious they are not taking us seriously."

Once out the door, she turned back angrily. "Don't say I didn't warn you. That woman is a pathetic, cold-hearted homewrecker and if I get thrown overboard tonight I'm going to hold you and this cruise line responsible! So you'd better hope nothing bad happens to me."

She slammed the door behind her, leaving Compton and Larimore shaking their heads.

"She's a nut job."

"Yeah, she is. A first class wacko."

"And what's with all the glitter?"

19
Golden Boy

Aimee was irritated after being interrogated about the fake letter. She took the stairs, hoping to find Janet in their room, and almost collided with Travis who came racing down the steps two at a time.

"Are you always in a hurry, Mr. Cruise Director?"

"Oh! Aimee!" Travis halted, panting. "Yes, I'm always in a hurry. Never a dull moment. What are you up to?"

"I've just been acquitted of a being an accomplice to a murder plot, so I'm going back to my room."

"What?" Travis asked, his forehead creased in confusion.

"Never mind," she chuckled. "I'll tell you about it some other time. Where are you headed in such a rush?"

"Actually, this is my normal pace. I've forgotten how to walk. I'm on my way to the bridge. Hey, would you like to see it?"

"The bridge?"

"The wheelhouse, where the navigation of the ship takes place. I'm not allowed to take you inside but you can get a peek at it."

Aimee hesitated, not expecting such an invitation. "If you think it's okay, yes, I'd love to see it."

"Follow me," Travis said. "But don't get your hopes up. Captain Anderson is not likely to be there. I mean, he may be, but there are others who navigate the ship for the most part. The Captain only takes physical control when we are docking and undocking, or if the weather gets crazy."

"I didn't realize that! What does he do the rest of the time?" Aimee asked as she trotted alongside Travis.

"Believe me, he's got plenty to do. Just consider that he's responsible for the safety of the ship itself and also for the safety of thousands of passengers and crew members. He's on-call 24/7, often for months at a time. It's a highly stressful job."

"Yikes. I never thought about it like that."

"Plus, he likes to get out and mingle with the passengers when he can."

They continued along in silence through an area unfamiliar to Aimee until Travis stopped short. "Here we are! Take a look." He moved aside so that Aimee could peer through a small, obscure window which gave her a direct view of the expansive, glass-enclosed area which was the wheelhouse. A mind-boggling display of instruments covered the walls, and there sat the big steering wheel, just like she had seen in pictures.

"Wow! So much equipment! Look at all of this!"

"It's quite an operation to navigate a ship of this size. All of those instruments you see keep it running safely and efficiently and on course. Radar, echo sounders, mirrors, a speed regulator, and those big guys are the wing controls," he said, pointing.

Before she could ask about wing controls, two uniformed crew members passed by the window in front of Aimee, causing her to jump back.

"Those men are navigation officers. They report to the captain. Just as I do."

"This is amazing," Aimee whispered, taking it all in. "I guess I shouldn't take a picture, right?"

"Better not."

"Okay, but thank you so much for showing this to me, Travis! It's very impressive."

"My pleasure. C'mon, I'll show you the way back."

When they turned around, Captain Anderson stood before them with raised eyebrows.

"Hello, sir!" Travis addressed him. "Captain Anderson, I'd like to introduce you to my friend, Aimee Burke. Aimee, this is Captain Mike Anderson."

The Captain extended his hand to Aimee to greet her with a spark of amusement in his eyes. His large hand felt warm and solid.

"I was just allowing Aimee a quick peek at the wheelhouse," Travis explained, "from the window, of course. Hope you don't mind."

"Of course not. Any friend of yours is a friend of mine. I guess Travis explained to you that passengers aren't allowed inside, but…"

"Oh, yes, sir, he explained that to me. I'm honored just to see it from here, and I'm equally honored to meet you in person."

"Well, aren't you a treasure! I'll bet you're from the south, judging from your accent."

"Yes, sir. Arkansas."

"And what do you do in Arkansas?"

"I'm a music teacher. I teach at a middle school."

"Ah," the captain said. "So you must be the passenger with the beautiful singing voice! Am I right, Travis?"

"Yes, sir. She is the one."

Turning his eyes back on Aimee, the captain said, "Do you know that he practically tore the place up looking for an acoustic guitar and then spent a half hour tuning it?"

Travis blushed. "Not helping, sir."

Aimee laughed. "Well, he found a good one. I was very pleased with it."

"I hope you are enjoying the cruise. Are you traveling alone, or…?"

"I'm here with some girlfriends. It's our first cruise, and we are having a blast."

"Wonderful! Then I hope to see you again next summer."

Aimee spoke up. "How do you do it, Captain? And you, Travis? How do you spend so much of your time living on a ship and yet manage to have families back home? I don't understand the logistics of how that works."

As she waited for a response she saw Captain Anderson make meaningful eye contact with Travis. They both started to speak at once and then Travis refrained. "Go ahead, sir."

"Your friend Travis is not a married man. That bogus wedding band on his finger is my doing."

Aimee frowned, not understanding.

"I make him wear it, my dear, as a means of keeping the women away."

"Still not helping, sir," Travis muttered, staring at the floor.

"We have a very strict policy that ship employees are not to socialize with passengers, and vice versa. But when your cruise director looks like Travis, you have to get creative. He draws attention wherever he goes."

Aimee laughed out loud and turned to Travis. "So, really? You wear a fake wedding ring?"

"Boss's orders."

Secretly pleased with this new information, Aimee suddenly had so many questions for Travis but they would have to wait.

"It was a pleasure meeting you, Aimee Burke. Please do come back and cruise with us again," Captain Anderson said. "Meanwhile, I promise to get you and your friends home safely. Good day, Aimee."

"Good day, Captain Anderson."

Travis and Aimee resumed their stroll down the hallway. Aimee spoke first. "He seems like a terrific guy."

"He's cool," Travis replied.

"You seem to be his golden boy."

"What? No! No way."

"So, where did you find a guitar?"

"What? Oh. It's my guitar. I just couldn't remember where I had stored it."

"Really? So do you play?"

"Used to. Not in a while, though. I work sixteen hour days so…"

"Why do you do it, Travis? You're young. How old are you, anyway?"

"I'm thirty-three."

"Do you not miss having a social life?"

"This is my social life. It's a fun job, for the most part, but it comes with a lot of responsibility. Good thing I have a knack for multi-tasking."

"But, I mean, don't you want to get married one day? Have a couple of kids?"

Travis remained thoughtfully quiet.

"I'm sorry, am I being too personal?"

"I was married once. For a short time, while I was still in college. But it didn't work out. At all."

"Children?"

"No. God, no. I would never take on a job like this if I had children."

"So, you must really love your job, then. I admire that."

Travis chuckled. "Ironically, this is my last season. I'll be resigning at the end of the summer."

Aimee's eyes cut to Travis. "What? Does the captain know?"

"He does. And he's been very supportive. The man is like a father to me."

"And what are your plans? What will you do going forward?"

Travis pushed an elevator button. "I'll try to find a job in the real world. This is not the real world, by any stretch of the imagination."

Aimee's heart thumped a bit. So much had changed in the last ten minutes. "I don't even know where you're from, Travis."

"I really don't know, either!"

"What do you mean?"

"I grew up in Gulfport, Mississippi. But when Katrina hit the coast my parents lost their home and they moved further inland. I was at Ole Miss at the time. And then my marriage floundered. So I was looking around for a job and…"

"You took the cruise director position," Aimee finished his sentence.

He nodded. "The opportunity presented itself."

The elevator door opened on the tenth floor and, surprisingly, there was no one waiting to get on, so neither of them moved. Travis pressed a button to hold the elevator and they stood in silence, gazing at each other. "You know we're probably on camera right now," he stated.

"What? No, I d-didn't know…"

"Yep. There are cameras all over the ship."

The elevator door dinged in protest, trying to close.

"So if I was to do anything inappropriate it would be caught on camera, and the captain would hand me my ass on a silver platter."

"Travis, are you having inappropriate thoughts?" Aimee teased, her eyes sparkling.

"Maybe," he smiled.

The elevator dinged again, annoying Travis immensely. Aimee stepped out and turned around. "Will I see you again?" she asked, surprising herself.

"There's no way I'll let you off of this ship without seeing you again," he replied. "Where will you be around 9:00 tonight?"

"My friends and I are getting together by the pool."

"Great. I'll find you there." Travis smiled as the door closed.

~

The sun had already set as the group gathered by the pool for the last time. Birdie arrived first and dragged two large tables together, making enough room for everyone. Aimee joined her, followed by Sue Ellen and Fran, then Janet and Jake holding hands.

Nearby, Jamal lay sprawled in a lounge chair watching *Toy Story 3* on the big outdoor screen. Beside him, in the adjacent chair, a little girl about his own age sat cross-legged, her eyes glued to the screen as she munched popcorn.

"I've already seen this like, six times," Jamal said importantly.

"Me, too," she replied. "I like Jessie the best."

"I like Buzz Lightyear. He's cool." After a stretch of silence Jamal asked, "What's your name?"

"Alison."

"I'm Jamal."

"That's a funny name."

"It is?" While Jamal considered that, Alison announced, "This is my second cruise to ever be on. And we're going on another one next summer. To Alaska."

"You are? Next summer?"

"Yeah. My mom already booked it."

Jamal frowned while he thought about that. "She should probably cancel it."

"How come?" Alison turned to Jamal.

"I'm not really sure. But I think next summer is going to be weird. People won't be allowed to go on cruises."

"That's silly. I don't believe you," Alison said uncertainly.

"Okay." Jamal turned back to the movie, not caring one way or the other. Alison returned to her popcorn, Jamal's remarks forgotten as cartoon toys sailed along on a conveyor belt, legs in the air and arms flailing, headed for certain doom in an incinerator.

"Don't worry, they get saved," Jamal assured his new friend.

"I know. I told you, I've seen it before," she replied crossly.

Meanwhile, the adults had settled in around their table, the mood subdued and sentimental, a time for reflection and goodbyes. Janet leaned on Jake's shoulder, still feeling sad about the lost dog tags. "What are your buddies doing tonight?" she asked.

"Oh, I can only imagine. They hooked up with some giggly girls from Alabama a couple of days ago."

Sue Ellen was particularly quiet. Not only was their cruise about to end, but no one had remembered her birthday. All day long she had expected something. Perhaps a little gift from her traveling companions, or at least a greeting card from Fran, who surely knew that today was her best friend's birthday. She hadn't even gotten so much as a text from Dillard. She felt wounded, but pride kept her from crying.

Fran proposed a toast. "To good friends and good times. And to Janet, for making this fabulous vacation possible."

"Aw! It has been fun, hasn't it? Hey, Birdie, when do you and Jamal leave the ship in the morning?" Janet asked.

"We're in the 8:30 group. The first group. How about you?"

"9:30 group. So I guess this is really goodbye."

"I'm feeling very sad," Birdie said, "but how lucky we were to meet you fabulous ladies from Arkansas! Our dinner together on Captain's Night will be my favorite memory."

"My favorite memory will be zip-lining over the jungle," Sue Ellen said, hoping to draw attention to herself.

"I loved our private beach day."

"Shopping in Cozumel."

"Aimee singing on stage."

Jamal came trotting up to Birdie. "I'm done watching the movie," he announced.

"Good! And I imagine that you are full of popcorn and Coke and you won't sleep a wink tonight," she predicted.

The little boy's eyes darted around the table, landing on Sue Ellen's phone. "Can I look at your pictures, Miss Sue?"

"Of course you may," she replied. "Just let me show you how to…"

"I found them," he stated, holding up the phone to show her. He sat down to scroll. "Gosh, you took a lot of pictures. Who is this man?" Jamal asked, pointing to a waving pot-bellied man wearing sandals and white tube socks.

"That's my husband," Sue Ellen replied. "His name is Dillard. Isn't he handsome? That was the day we left Janet's house."

Without commenting, Jamal swiped through the photos one by one. A pile of suitcases. The back of Janet's head in the car. Blurry images taken through window glass. Jamal swiped faster, looking for something more interesting. Janet pumping gas. Fran with a bag of chips. Two waffles on a Styrofoam plate. Fran making a face. Then finally, a photo of the cruise ship.

"This is where it gets really good," Sue Ellen said, looking over Jamal's shoulder. He swept past multiple selfies taken at the railing with the ocean behind her.

"These all look the same. What's wrong with your mouth?" he asked.

"Oh! I was saying 'prune.' That's how you …"

"Save it, Sue. He doesn't care," Fran interjected.

"When does it get good?" the little boy wanted to know.

"Right here," Sue Ellen pointed.

Elevator buttons. Fran sticking out her tongue. Towel animals perched on the seat of a tiny commode. Jamal swiped faster. A slice of pizza on a plate. A camera-shy steward. A tray of desserts. A drink with a monkey and an umbrella on top. Somebody's feet. More selfies.

Jamal tried to return the phone but Sue Ellen pushed it back. "No! Keep going!"

Two mounds of butter on a white plate. Captain Anderson cheek to cheek with Sue Ellen. Jamal in the swimming pool. Birdie waving from a recliner. Aimee and Janet licking ice cream cones. Aimee singing on stage. Jamal dancing with Birdie and a poorly filmed video of the same. Janet's black eye. Selfies of Sue Ellen modeling a big floppy hat.

Travis' voice boomed across the P. A. system for the third time that day, reminding passengers about their luggage. *Don't forget, folks. Set your luggage outside your door in the hallway by 11:00 tonight for pickup.*

"Let's not forget to do that," Sue Ellen said to Fran.

A smiling staff member suddenly appeared carrying a large birthday cake with candles. The group began to clap and Sue Ellen's mouth dropped in surprise, and then she burst into tears.

"I thought you all forgot!" was all she could manage.

"Of course we didn't forget," Fran said as the girls piled cards and presents on the table. "But the cake is all Dillard's doing."

"Dillard?"

"Yep. Dillard and your sons. They wanted to surprise you."

Janet added, "I'm sorry that you had to wait all day for it, but we wanted everyone to be together."

Aimee began to sing the obligatory happy birthday song and the others joined in while Sue Ellen sat beaming.

"You're supposed to make a wish and blow out the candles," Jamal reminded her.

Sue Ellen closed her eyes, made her silent wish, and blew the flames out. "I'm just so happy right now!" she said, eyeing the cake with lust.

"Go ahead," Fran urged her. "Have a piece. Have a big piece."

"Oh, I couldn't," Sue Ellen replied. "I don't want to break our agreement."

"Screw the agreement. We both kept our word, and it's your birthday, for Pete's sake. Hand me that knife, Janet."

As Fran was slicing the cake Sue Ellen stated, "I do feel like I've lost a little weight." She looked around the table for affirmation.

Aimee took the hint. "You do look thinner, Sue Ellen."

"Yes, I noticed it, too," Janet said kindly.

Birdie nodded emphatically. "For sure."

Fran placed a large slice of cake in front of her friend. "Here you go. Enjoy that. You deserve it."

Sue Ellen happily took the first bite of cake, savoring the sugary sweetness.

"I just love you girls," she mumbled around it. "You make me so happy."

20
Conch Shells

Jake was having a nice time, happy to be with Janet on this last night of the cruise. He sat with his arm draped around her shoulder, the two of them talking softly together. He watched as a middle-aged couple strolled by with a teenage boy who hung back several yards, obviously not wanting to be seen with his parents. The boy clutched a small white sack rolled down from the top. They sat down together at a table and the boy glanced nervously around.

Jake whispered to Janet, "I'll be back in a minute." He strolled over and greeted the boy politely. "Hello, Austin."

"Hey."

"You must be the parents," he smiled, offering his hand to the older man. "I'm Jake DeLuca. Austin and I met earlier today."

"That's what I hear. I'm Ted Shepherd. This is my wife, Linda."

Austin silently handed the sack over to Jake who peeked inside and nodded.

"Good job, Austin. I appreciate your help, buddy."

"Okay," Austin mumbled, looking down.

Jake nodded to Ted and Linda. "Nice to have met you. Have a safe trip home."

When Jake turned to walk away, Ted spoke sharply. "Wait! Don't you have a little something for Austin for all his trouble? Surely you intend to pay him."

Jake stopped in his tracks. *Uh-oh.*

"No, sir. Austin and I had a deal. Didn't we, Austin?"

Austin rolled his eyes and sunk deeper into his chair.

"What kind of deal?" both parents asked at once, turning to their son.

"Nothing. Let's just go, okay?" Austin whined.

"Mr. Shepherd, Austin and I had a deal, all right, but there was no money involved," Jake explained.

Ted's eyes darted back and forth between Jake and Austin. He suddenly stood and pushed his chair back with his leg, in an aggressive stance. Austin and his mother were wide-eyed, not sure what was about to happen.

"Dad, let it go. Please," Austin begged. "This guy looks like he could beat the crap out of you."

"Are you suggesting that I can't take on this jerk? I'm a pretty tough guy, son."

"Sure, Dad, but he's right. He never offered to pay me anything. He asked me to help out so I did. That's it."

"So you're going to take sides with this cheap-ass, huh? Well, let me tell you something. I didn't raise you to let guys like this take advantage of you. You spent most of the day in that pool, looking for that piece of crap."

"I was just helping."

"You'd better learn right now, Austin, that everything comes with a price. You do something nice for someone, you should get something in return. What's fair is fair."

"I disagree, sir," Jake interjected. "Not everything comes with a price. Sometimes you just have to do what's right. What's honorable."

With that, he nodded at Austin and turned to go.

"Screw you!" Ted shouted.

Jake paused, then continued on his way. *Nice guy*, he mumbled. *No wonder the poor kid doesn't know right from wrong.*

Janet looked up when he returned. "What was that about?"

"I'll tell you later. Here are the dog tags."

"What? Really?" She peeked into the bag. "But how…"

"I'll tell you later tonight," he repeated, draping the chain over her head.

"There's going to be a 'later tonight?'" she asked hopefully, clutching the tags.

"Damn right there is." He pulled her close and kissed her hair softly.

Fran disappeared for a few minutes and then returned with a lit cigarette and plopped down in her chair. She took a long pull and tapped the ashes on the deck floor, shocking everyone.

"Fran Goldstein! What do you think you're doing?" Janet exclaimed.

Fran looked up at Janet with a blank face. Sue Ellen struggled to swallow a big bite of cake and stood up, looking like she might cry. "Fran! You told me it was okay to eat some cake! I didn't know you were going to have a cigarette! You promised to quit smoking!"

"The hell I did!" Fran quipped.

"But Fran, you…"

"Put that out, right now!" Janet demanded. "This is a non-smoking area. Where did you get a cigarette, anyway?"

"I bummed it off of Martha. What's the big deal?" Fran looked around the table, as if Janet were being ridiculous.

"It's not even your brand!" Sue Ellen admonished her, visibly upset.

Janet took Fran's cigarette and snubbed it out in a plastic cup.

Perturbed, Fran said, "What'd you do that for? Martha won't let me bum another one."

"Who's Martha?" Aimee wanted to know.

"My sister. She's right over there. We look alike, don't we?" Fran waved at a strange woman at the bar, who wiggled her fingers back.

"Geez, Frannie. That's not your sister. I *know* your sister. Come with me. Let's get you some coffee." With that, Sue Ellen marched Fran toward the coffee station, throwing a worried look over her shoulder at the others. A long and awkward silence followed.

"Do you think Fran is okay?" Aimee ventured to ask.

"I don't know. She's been saying and doing some weird things," Janet commented.

Jamal, bored with the adult company, turned to his grandmother. "Birdie, can I walk around by myself if I stay where you can see me?"

"Of course, honey."

Jamal wandered over to a man who was sitting by himself at the far end of the pool. He wore Bermuda shorts and an island shirt, with sandals on his feet. He was dark like Jamal and looked to be the right age to be his grandfather. Jamal stopped beside the man's chair.

"Hi. I'm Jamal."

"Hello, Jamal. My name is Howard."

"I'm six and a half."

"I'm fifty-eight and a half."

"Do you have tescibles?"

"I do."

"How many you got?"

"I've got two, last time I checked."

"That's how many I've got!" Jamal exclaimed. "But I'll probably get more, when I get older."

"No, I think two is the limit. Don't expect more."

"How come?"

"Because two is what God intended."

"Oh. What are you doing here all by yourself?" Jamal asked.

"Well, I'm enjoying the last evening of my vacation. How about you?"

"Me, too. We have to go home tomorrow."

"Where's home?"

"Tallahassee. That's in Florida. Where are you from?"

"Albany. That's in Georgia."

"Are you on vacation from your job, Howard?"

"No, I'm retired now. I used to be a fireman."

"A fireman? That's what I want to be when I grow up!" Jamal was clearly excited about his new friend.

"Well, how about that! Fire-fighting is an honorable profession, and an important one. If you can save even one person's life, it's well worth it."

"Did you save anyone?"

"Yes. Lots of people."

"Did their house burn down?"

"No," the man settled back in his chair, remembering. "Two tall office buildings burned down in New York City, where I lived at the time. It was a terrible, terrible thing. But it was years ago - before you were born."

Jamal studied the man intently. "So are you a hero?"

"I guess I might be in some people's eyes."

"Did you have to run through fire?"

"I did. Lots of fire. Lots of smoke."

"Did you get hurt?"

"Yes, I was burned. See this?" Howard turned sideways to show the little boy his scars. "But I was one of the lucky ones. Many of my comrades didn't make it."

Night was falling. Jamal stared at the reflection of lights on the swimming pool water. A small yellow ball, left behind, lobbed against the side of the pool.

"Do you have a wife, Howard?"

"No, son, I do not."

Jamal took his new friend by the hand, pulling him from his chair. "You need to come and meet Birdie."

"Who's Birdie?"

"She's my grandmother. She's right over there," Jamal said, pointing. "You'll like each other. I know you will."

"How do you know?"

Jamal shrugged. "I'm not really sure. I just know."

Howard followed the boy to the table of adults where Jamal announced, "This is my friend, Howard. He's a fireman."

"Retired fireman," Howard added, and then shook hands around the table.

Birdie said, "Please, sit down if you'd like."

"I don't want to impose…"

"No imposition," Jake said. "Join us, please."

Jamal made sure that Howard sat down beside his grandmother, and it wasn't long before the two were deep in conversation. Jamal looked very pleased with himself.

Aimee, meanwhile, was on the lookout for Travis. She wasn't sure when he would arrive, from which direction he would come, or how long he would stay. She wondered if he would sit down at their table, or if he would attempt to lure her away. She found herself looking around for hidden cameras. *How will we manage any private time?* She glanced around the table feeling left out and lonesome. It was getting late now.

He's not coming.

A tap on her shoulder made her jump and there stood Wayan. "From Mr. Travis," he said softly, handing her a small, sealed envelope.

"Thank you, Wayan! Thank you so much." She wanted to ask about Travis but didn't dare in front of everyone.

"I hope you have a good life, Miss Aimee. Maybe I will see you again one day." He smiled, and then he was gone.

Aimee was relieved to see that no one at the table seemed to have noticed the exchange. Their attention was on Howard who had produced a deck of cards and was performing card tricks for Jamal. She quietly retreated to a small table in a corner where she sat down and opened the envelope.

Aimee,

I'm so sorry. There was a medical emergency in the auditorium and I can't get away. Lots of paperwork. I'll find you in the morning. I promise.

Travis

Aimee was pleased to see that Travis had added his cell phone number, and her heart beat wildly with the implication. She read the note again and then folded it in half and slid it into her pocket, already anticipating the morning.

The night sky glimmered with stars. The Lido Deck emptied and became quiet as passengers drifted back to their cabins. Jamal fell asleep with his head on a folded beach towel on the table. Sue Ellen nodded off, as well, her head jerking every now and then.

Finally, Birdie announced, "It's time for us to say goodbye. I need to get this little guy to bed." She opened her arms to hug her friends one by one, promising to stay in touch.

"May I walk you to your cabin?" Howard asked, to which Birdie replied, "Yes, that would be nice. Would you mind carrying Jamal? He's gotten too big for me."

With the sleeping boy on his shoulder, Howard addressed the others. "This was my lucky night. If this young man had not dragged me to your table I would not have met you nice folks. I had a wonderful time." And with that, he and Birdie walked away, looking very much like a family. Birdie turned once and blew a kiss.

Fran wiped away a tear. "I'm going to miss them." Then she jostled her roommate. "C'mon, Sue Ellen. We've got to go pack our things."

Janet leaned over to Aimee and whispered, "I may not be back tonight. Would you please set my bag out in the hall with yours?"

Aimee smiled companionably. "Of course. Have fun," she whispered back.

∼

Tired as she was, Fran efficiently packed her one small suitcase and set it outside the door, keeping out a few toiletries and a change of clothes for the ride home tomorrow.

Sue Ellen, on the other hand, was flustered with the task. "I'm not going to have room for all of the gifts I bought!" she moaned. "What am I going to do, Fran?"

Fran considered Sue Ellen's dilemma. "What were you thinking when you bought those four giant shells? Why didn't you just buy the kids some tee shirts and leave it at that?"

"Because tee shirts aren't fun! They can hear the ocean in those conch shells! And I got the maracas and flutes because all kids like noise-makers."

"But aren't Eugene's boys like, fourteen?"

"Well yes, but…"

"And I hate to break it to you, but you can't really hear the ocean in a conch shell. That's just a myth."

"Is not."

"Is, too. And it's pronounced *conk*, not *conch*."

"Says who?"

"Says Merriam-Webster. And the way I see it, you're going to have to leave them behind."

Sue Ellen gasped. "What? But I can't! Are you nuts?"

"Well, will they fit in your smaller suitcase?"

"I've already put all of my shoes in there."

"Then you're just going to have to wear a lot of clothes home. Whatever won't fit in the big suitcase you'll have to put on."

"Are you serious?"

"Of course I'm serious. It's called layering. And it's very much in style."

"But won't I get awfully hot?"

"You don't have a choice, Sue Ellen."

"But don't you have some extra room in your suitcase?" Sue Ellen whined.

"As you can see, my bag is already in the hallway and it is packed full. Go ask Janet or Aimee."

Sue Ellen peeked across the hallway at 10284. She put her ear to the door and heard nothing.

"I think they are asleep already," she told Fran. "I'll just wear what I can't pack, like you said."

"Glad you see it my way. Because even though it's your birthday I was about to smack you."

Sue Ellen tugged her bulging suitcases into the hallway beside Fran's. Then she fell into bed and was snoring within minutes.

Fran quietly turned out the lights and left the room, descending three sets of stairs until she reached the seventh floor. Cabin number 715 was easy enough to find. Outside its door sat two expensive pieces of luggage with the monogrammed initials, BB, and a leather duffel bag.

Fran didn't have a solid plan, but as soon as she spied the room service tray littered with escargot shells and gutted crab claws, a smile crossed her face. Unaware that she was on camera, she bent over and removed a plate from the room service tray. She unzipped Beverly's suitcase, emptied the leftovers inside, and quickly zipped it back up. Then she picked up another plate, emptied it into Robert's bag, zipped it back up, and nonchalantly strolled away.

A security employee watched with fascination on his computer screen. "Hey, man," he said to his associate, "Did you see that?"

"See what?" the other man responded, sliding over in his rolling chair to look at the screen, showing a smiling woman with short, dark hair walking down a hallway.

"That lady there! She's on the seventh floor. Here, I'll show you what she just did."

He backed up the footage and they watched it together.

"Are you kidding me? What the hell just happened?"

"You saw what I saw."

"That was *awesome*! I thought I'd seen everything!"

"She must have a beef with those people."

"Should we send someone after her?"

"Nah. We've got bigger fish to fry."

21
Unfinished Business

Janet and Jake were lying on his bed on their backs, shoes off, while Jake regaled Janet with stories about his high school years when he played drums in a garage band and sneaked his dad's beer from the refrigerator.

"So, did you consider yourself a badass?" she teased.

Jake snorted. "Hardly. Although, to my credit, I did have one scrape with the law."

"Really? Tell me!"

"I was sixteen and had just gotten my drivers' license. It was a Saturday morning and my mother asked me if I'd run an errand for her. She handed me her car keys and a twenty dollar bill and instructed me to drive to a garden center and pick up an American Boxwood for her. Do you know what a boxwood is?" he asked.

"Sure. I plan to put some in my front yard."

"So anyway, she had already bought five that morning but she needed one more. They were on sale, she said, and told me that I would find them all the way at the back of the nursery. She told me to get a nice, round one that was full on all sides. I was happy to have an excuse to drive her car so I took off with the radio blaring, hoping some of my friends would see me driving."

Janet smiled, wondering where this story was headed.

"So I got the boxwood, the best one of the bunch as far as I could tell, and I set it on the passenger seat. Then I headed back home, although I took a different route so that I could go past the park where my friends played basketball. I honked, and they waved, and I was feeling pretty cocky until I pulled up to a four-way stop. Something moved in my peripheral vision and I glanced over at the boxwood to see a snake slithering out of it."

Janet gasped. "Oh, no!"

"It scared the shit out of me. My immediate reaction was to stomp the gas pedal, and I broadsided a patrol car in the intersection."

"You didn't!"

"I did. And as I sat there in shock, the snake crawled over my leg and I really freaked out then. I threw open the car door and took off running with two cops running after me. They were hollering at me to freeze and when I did, I got tased."

Janet didn't know whether or not to laugh. But then Jake turned to her and grinned and she lost it. When she finally caught her breath she asked, "What happened? What did you do?"

"Oh, it was a big mess, as you can imagine. They handcuffed me and called my parents and told them that I had tried to flee the scene of an accident. My parents got there within five minutes, looking mad as hell. I told them all about the snake and, sure enough, they found it on the floorboard, all curled up in a ball. The cops didn't take me to jail, and luckily no one was hurt, but our insurance rates skyrocketed. My friends, of course, had witnessed everything and I was totally humiliated. I was the brunt of their jokes for weeks at school."

Janet patted Jake's arm. "That must have been traumatic for a sixteen year old, but it's a great story."

"It was a grass snake, by the way. Totally harmless," he added, and Janet giggled some more. Then she became quiet, twisting and playing with the dog tags around her neck. "Can I ask you a personal question?"

"Sure."

"I'm sure you've had plenty of girlfriends. Have you ever been in love?" She turned to him and waited for his answer.

"I do like the ladies, and I've done my sharing of dating, but I've never been with anyone for very long. Once a girl starts putting the squeeze on me, I kind of drift away. Grant says I'm too picky. Maybe I am, but what's wrong with that?"

"Nothing! Nothing's wrong with that. But you haven't answered my question."

"Have I ever been in love? No. Not in the true sense of the word." He hesitated. "What about you?"

Janet closed her eyes and inhaled deeply, then exhaled.

"Is that a yes?"

"Let's just say I thought it was love. I *wanted* it to be love. I was in a relationship with this guy, Lee, for fourteen months. We broke up just a few weeks ago."

Jake had not been expecting this news. "No kidding," he managed. "Sounds serious."

"Not like you might think. The more I look back on it, the less authentic it seems. He was nice, but we had very little in common and, in my opinion, he was emotionally immature."

"Who broke up with whom?"

"I broke up with Lee."

"Any regrets?"

"Nope. No regrets. Except that I was too hard on him. It was a bad breakup."

"Are you in contact with him? None of my business, but…"

"He's texted twice. He doesn't know I'm on a cruise, unless my mother told him. Which she may have by now."

"So do I need to beat this guy up, or what?" Jake was smiling now.

"No, that won't be necessary, tough guy that you are."

Janet traced her fingers along his biceps. "How come you don't have any tattoos? I thought all guys in the military got tattoos."

"I never felt the need, I guess."

Janet kissed Jake lightly on the mouth. He responded by gathering her into his arms, kissing her back with intensity. His five o'clock shadow felt rough and sexy against her face, and he smelled of sea salt and fresh air. When he released her they rolled to their backs again, staring at the ceiling.

"Just my luck," Jake exclaimed. "I'm lying in bed with the woman of my dreams and she's leaving me tomorrow morning."

"What should we do, Jake? I mean, what's next? I don't want to say goodbye."

He thought for a moment. "How about this. How about you stay here with me tonight and we'll talk it through. We'll figure out how to make this work."

Janet scooted closer, laying her head on his shoulder. Within seconds, they were both sound asleep.

~

Janet woke up first. Jake was pressed against her back, his arm draped over her. She could feel the heat of his body behind hers and his breath in her ear. She lay very still, savoring the moment, afraid to wake him.

For the second time that morning the public address system bellowed the now familiar instructions, causing Jake to stir in his sleep.

"Jake," Janet whispered. "I've got to go."

"No," he murmured.

"Really. I need to go back to my room and get ready."

Jake rubbed at his face. "What time is it?"

"I don't know."

Janet looked for her sandals and stole a look at herself in the mirror. She raked her fingers through her messy hair. Then she sat down on the end of the bed. "We fell asleep. We didn't talk about what happens now. With us."

"Have breakfast with me. We'll figure it out over breakfast."

"Okay. I'm gonna run take a shower. Should I meet you at the buffet?"

"Yeah, meet me there in thirty minutes. Now get out of here before I pull you back into bed." He lunged at her playfully but she jumped away, giggling, and closed the door behind her.

Meanwhile, on the tenth floor, Sue Ellen was up and ready to go, layered to the max with extra clothing. She knocked on the door across the hall and Aimee answered.

"Where's Janet?" Sue Ellen asked, looking around.

"Janet is, well, preoccupied," Aimee replied. "Why do you have so many clothes on?"

"What do you mean, preoccupied?"

"Well, I mean, she's not here."

"So where is she? We're about to leave."

"She's with Jake, okay? Please don't tell her I told you."

"She spent the night with Jake? Oh, my! This is more serious than I thought!"

Fran appeared in the doorway. "What's going on? What did I miss?"

"Janet spent the night with Jake! Aimee just told me!"

"Sue Ellen," Aimee scolded her. "This is none of our business."

The room phone rang and Aimee answered it. "Hello? Oh, I'm sorry, she's not here right now. What? Yes, I think I can locate her. Yes, I'll have her call right away. Thank you."

To Fran and Sue Ellen she said, "Guest Services is trying to reach Janet. Should I call her on her cell?"

"Did they say what it's about?" Fran asked.

"No, but the woman said it was important."

"Then I think you should call her," Fran decided.

Aimee dialed Janet but the call went straight to her voice mail. *Hi. You've reached Janet Kayler. Please leave a message.*

"Her phone is turned off. Now what?"

At that very moment Janet burst through the door, surprising everyone. "Good morning! Are y'all having a meeting without me?" she joked. "Sue Ellen, why are you dressed like a street person?" She yanked back the shower curtain but Aimee took her by the elbow.

"Janet, I don't know what it's about but Guest Services is looking for you. They just called."

"Oh. It's probably about my bill or something. I'll call after my shower."

"They said it was important."

Janet paused, then went to the phone on the dresser and pushed the button. "Hi, this is Janet Kayler in Room 10284, returning your call. My mother? Okay. Okay. I'll call her right now. Thanks." She glanced at her own cell phone and cursed. Three missed calls from her mother.

"Excuse me, y'all," she mumbled, and went out into the hallway for privacy. The words she exchanged with her mother were indistinct, but the quiet sobbing that followed could only mean bad news.

"Daddy had a stroke this morning while he was walking Lucy," she announced stoically when she returned to the room. "He's in intensive care. I need to go home. Now."

"Oh, Janet, honey, I'm so sorry," Aimee said. "What can we do to get you home?"

"I don't know. We're not scheduled to leave the ship until 9:30, and then we have to get our luggage and go through customs. What time is it now?"

"It's only 7:45," Fran said.

"I can't wait that long! What if he dies? My mother needs me." She crumpled onto her bed, her head in her hands.

At that moment her cell phone rang and she snatched it up. "I can't do breakfast, Jake," she said, and told him the news while the others sat in silence. "Okay. Okay. Yeah, I'm sure. Thank you. Call me back."

Janet addressed her friends. "Jake offered to take me home right away. He's gone to check on how to manage that. I'm sorry, y'all. Will one of you drive my car home?" She searched in her purse for her car keys and held them out.

"I will," Aimee said. "What else can we do?"

"I don't know! I can't think! Where's my suitcase?" she asked, looking around.

"I put it in the hallway last night with mine, like we talked about."

"Oh, no..."

"Don't worry, I kept a few things out for you," Aimee said, handing Janet a small sack. "A change of clothes and your toothbrush and contacts, stuff like that. Go ahead and take your shower."

Janet's phone rang again. It was Jake. "Really? Okay. Okay. Bye."

"I'll have to skip the shower. I'm to meet him downstairs in ten minutes." She was changing clothes even as she said so, then she brushed her teeth and her hair. "Thank you, guys. I'm so sorry to take off like this. Did I give you the car keys?"

Aimee held them up. "Just get yourself home safely, Janet, and be sure to keep us posted about your dad, okay?"

There were quick hugs all around.

"Take care, honey," Fran said.

"We'll be praying for your daddy. What's his name again?" Sue Ellen asked.

"Martin. Martin Kayler." Janet turned to go and then turned back in a panic, holding up the sack. "What about my…"

"Your passport is in there, and your wallet. Go."

Janet left the room and then turned back again. "Don't forget to give Wayan his card."

"I'll make sure he gets it," Aimee assured her.

Jake was in the lobby, pacing, when Janet arrived. He embraced her and said, "I'm so sorry, babe." Then he nodded toward the Guest Services counter. "Just show them your credentials. We're both approved for expedited departure."

After doing so, Janet trotted behind Jake who seemed to know where he was going. They arrived at the luggage retrieval area where a staff member helped Jake find his duffel bag. When Janet inquired about hers Jake said, "There won't be room for your suitcase. Aimee will have to get it," a reply which puzzled Janet but this was no time for questions.

They sailed through customs and then jumped into a parking deck elevator. Janet leaned against the wall, feeling a little sick as the elevator ascended. When the door opened Jake held it for Janet, then grabbed her hand as they hiked to his parking spot where a shiny black Harley Davidson sat waiting. Janet stared at it, shifting from one foot to the other. "What are we doing?"

"That's my motorcycle," he replied, stating the obvious. "I guess I never told you. But don't worry, I'm a safe driver. I'll get you home to your family."

Janet stammered, "But, I just, I thought…"

"Have you never been on a motorcycle?"

"No. Never."

"Well, if I know you, you'll love it."

The bike looked both menacing and magnificent at the same time. Jake opened the rear storage compartment and reached for his helmet. He placed it carefully onto Janet's head, wary of her bruised eye, and fastened the chin strap. "Feel okay? Too loose?"

She gave her head a shake. "Feels good and snug. But what about you?"

"I'll go without one until we get out of town, and then I'll stop and buy one somewhere."

He shoved his duffel bag into the compartment and added Janet's small bag, then swung his leg over the seat and started the bike with a thunderous rumble. The smell of gasoline fumes erupted and the engine settled into a guttural rhythm. Jake motioned for Janet to get on. She mounted the low slung seat and Jake showed her where to place her feet, and then she put her arms around his waist.

"Ready?" he asked.

"Ready," she replied with a thumbs-up.

Jake revved the motor and they were off. He smoothly maneuvered the bike down the parking deck ramps and then through the port facility, pleased to see Janet smiling in the rear-view mirror. Once they reached the open highway, he patted her knee and turned the big Harley loose, leaving New Orleans behind.

~

The removal of three thousand passengers with their luggage was a daunting task, but one which had been perfected over the years by the cruise line. Nevertheless, there were always problems – passengers who refused to wait for their assigned time to disembark, passengers disgruntled over their final bills, passengers who couldn't locate their luggage.

Travis, as usual, was in the thick of things, but despite his attempt to focus he couldn't stop thinking of Aimee. The feeling of unfinished business gnawed at him and he cursed himself for not getting her phone number. He paced, edgy and distracted, barking orders at crew members.

Travis' uncharacteristic behavior was not lost on Captain Anderson, who ordered the young man to report to the bridge immediately. When Travis appeared in the doorway, the captain lifted a hoodie from a wall peg and handed it to his best employee. "Here, son," he said with a twinkle in his eye. "Put this on and keep your head down. I'll give you fifteen minutes to find her."

With a look of surprise and a nod of gratitude, Travis sprinted in the direction of the gangway, shrugging into the hoodie along the way. He knew that Aimee and her friends would be with the 9:30 group, which had just been called. Surely he could catch up with her as she stood in line or in the luggage area. Trying to be discreet, he hastily scanned the long line of passengers, wishing he had made better arrangements for a goodbye.

About the time his anxiety level had risen to the point of desperation, his cell phone buzzed, showing an unfamiliar number with a 501 prefix and his heart lurched.

"Hello?" he answered hopefully.

"Travis? It's me. Aimee."

"Where are you? I'm looking for you right now!"

"We're almost to the front of the line. I...I just wanted to say goodbye. I hope it's okay that I called."

"Jesus! Yes! I'm walking in your direction now."

"Okay. I'm wearing a pink ball cap."

"I see you now."

Aimee hung back a bit, allowing Fran and Sue Ellen to move on ahead while she waited for Travis, but she almost didn't recognize the man who slipped in line beside her. Under his hooded sweatshirt he muttered, "Captain gave me fifteen minutes to find you and say goodbye. Now ten minutes."

Aimee's eyes danced. "Are you serious? He did that?"

"I told you. He's like a father to me. And he likes you." Travis reached down and looped his fingers through Aimee's. There was no time for shyness. "You know I'm going to kiss you, right?"

"Here?" she asked, looking around.

"No. Not here."

Sue Ellen and Fran were ahead of Aimee by a half dozen people so neither noticed that she was now holding hands with a stranger. The line spilled into a large warehouse room full of hundreds of suitcases, backpacks, baby strollers and duffel bags, all tagged the night before by the crew.

"Let me see your luggage tag," Travis said, taking it from Aimee's hand.

"Mine should be easy to spot. It's a silver hard side with a bright pink scarf tied around the handle. Look! There is it over there!"

To get to her luggage they had to separate and step around a bickering couple. The woman was complaining loudly. "You mean we have to find our own luggage? This is ridiculous! Just look at all these filthy suitcases!" she protested, sweeping her arm around the room.

While his wife complained, Robert's eyes followed Aimee.

She took the handle of her suitcase and turned to smile brightly at Travis. "Now would be a good time," she said playfully.

Travis pulled her into a corner and into his arms and they kissed warmly and affectionately, and then eagerly, their hands in each other's hair. Twenty feet away Fran and Sue Ellen stood gawking.

Robert, too, was watching. He sighed sadly and turned to Beverly who was shouting at him from across the room, having found her expensive luggage. He followed her out, but not without one last pitiful glance over his shoulder.

Travis and Aimee finally pulled apart and Travis frantically glanced at his phone. "I've got to go. Right now."

"I understand," she replied, flushed and starry-eyed. "We have each other's numbers now. Thank you for finding me, Travis. I'll miss you. A lot."

He took her by the shoulders and looked into her eyes. "As far as I'm concerned, this is not over. I'll be in touch. Later today."

"Okay!" she nodded happily.

"I'm crazy about you," he whispered against her ear. "Have a safe trip home."

After another quick kiss, Travis hustled off to fulfill his duties.

Sue Ellen and Fran stood waiting with their suitcases as Aimee coyly approached them. Fran spoke first. "You're smiling like the cat that got the canary. You've got some explaining to do, Missy."

"Yes, I do, but first I need to find Janet's bag. Help me, will you?"

"No! You have to tell us now!" Sue Ellen insisted. "Who was that man you were kissing?"

"Shhh! We'll talk in the car. I promise I'll tell you everything."

The threesome found Janet's suitcase and made their way to the Bronco in the parking deck. Aimee dug for the keys, relieved to hear the chirp of doors unlocking.

"Remind me next time not to buy so many presents," Sue Ellen grumbled, peeling off layer after layer of clothing right there in the parking deck. "And to think they confiscated Dillard's cigars."

They climbed in, Fran claiming the passenger seat up front. Aimee adjusted the mirrors and the seat and turned on the GPS.

Fran turned around. "Take your Dramamine now, Sue Ellen, so you'll fall asleep and we won't have to listen to your driveling all the way home."

Aimee's phone rang. "It's Janet!" She shushed the others. "Hello?"

"Hey. It's me. Have y'all left yet?"

"We're in the parking deck now. About to leave. How are you? Any news on your dad?"

"My mom has been texting me. She says he is stabilized and holding his own but he's not responding to stimuli."

Aimee swallowed. "They can do wonders with stroke victims these days, Janet. I'm sure he will come around. Please don't think the worst."

"Yeah, I know. I'm just so worried about permanent damage, but it's too early to tell," Janet said. "He's such a good guy," she added, choking on her words.

Aimee teared up, too. "How is your mom?"

"She's upset, of course, but her sister is there now so she's got somebody with her."

"I've been praying, Janet, and we're all thinking of you. Where are you and Jake?"

"We're at a Walmart somewhere in north Louisiana, buying a cheap motorcycle helmet," she chuckled. "It's the only place we could find open on a Sunday."

"You're buying what?"

"A motorcycle helmet. Jake drives a Harley and he insisted I wear his helmet. So now we're buying another one for him."

Aimee laughed out loud, prompting frowns from Fran and Sue Ellen.

"There's one more thing," Janet noted. "When my dad collapsed, Lucy got spooked by the ambulance and she ran off, leash and all."

"Oh, noooo. Oh, Janet, I'm so sorry! Hey, I'll bet someone has already found her and will take care of her until you get home. She's wearing a dog tag, right?"

"Yeah, but no one has called." Janet's voice trailed off. "Anyway, Jake is waiting for me. I'll talk to you later today."

"Okay, Janet, y'all be careful. Thanks for calling and please keep us updated on Martin. And Lucy."

"I will. Bye."

"What did she say?" asked Fran.

"Martin is stabilized and holding his own but isn't responding to stimuli, yet. She says it's too early to know anything about permanent damage. And her aunt is there with her mom."

Fran looked out the window, her heart hurting for Janet.

"And she said that Lucy ran off when the paramedics showed up. The ambulance scared her."

"Oh, no! What else did she say?" Sue Ellen asked.

"They are traveling on a motorcycle. Jake's. Can you imagine Janet riding on a Harley all the way back to Arkansas? That's why I laughed."

"Yes. Actually, I can imagine that," Fran nodded.

"Me, too," Sue Ellen agreed.

Aimee backed the vehicle out of its parking space and started down the parking deck ramps. "Our vacation is over," she said sadly. "But didn't we have fun?"

"I want to go again next summer!" Sue Ellen exclaimed.

"It was the best time I've had in years," Fran said. "I just wish it hadn't ended this way for Janet."

The three exited the parking deck and found the freeway. They drove in silence for several minutes as they thought about their friend. Sue Ellen finally spoke up.

"Okay, Aimee. Tell us about your mystery man."

∼

Meanwhile, on the Lido Deck, Wayan stepped inside cabin 10284 to survey the work done by housekeeping and to add his own finishing touches for the next passengers. He would miss the nice ladies from Arkansas. As he placed wrapped chocolates on the pillows he spotted the bright blue envelope leaning against the bedside lamp, his name written on the front.

He sat on the bed and loosened the flap of the envelope with his finger tip and pulled out a cheerful card. Upon opening it, a flurry of one hundred dollar bills fell into his lap. Astonished, he counted them. There were ten in all.

22
Sloppy Joes and Tator Tots

Jake slowed the Harley as they pulled into the front parking lot of Conway Regional Medical Center. With no trouble finding a space, he parked the bike and they hurried inside, stopping at the information desk. Teresa Kayler, Janet's mother, was just crossing the lobby with a cup of coffee in hand.

"Mom!" Janet called out.

"Oh, honey!"

Teresa set her coffee down and embraced her daughter. She was an attractive woman, tall and dark-haired like Janet. They hugged and patted each other's backs.

"How's Daddy?"

"He's holding his own. He seems to be out of the woods but still isn't responding," Teresa replied. "Your being here will help," she added, glancing curiously at Jake.

"Oh, mom, this is Jake DeLuca. Jake, you remember my mother, Teresa Kayler. Mom, Jake used to live in our neighborhood in Fort Smith. Back then he went by the name Ryan. We used to play together."

As Janet spoke, her mother began to nod. "I remember you. My, you've sure grown up!"

"Jake was on our cruise," Janet continued breathlessly, "and we ran into each other and he offered to drive me home today because of Daddy."

Jake stepped forward and offered his hand with a kind smile. "Hello, Mrs. Kayler, it's a pleasure to see you again. I'm so sorry for what's happened with Mr. Kayler."

Teresa studied Jake closely while taking in Janet's black eye and the motorcycle helmets in their hands.

"Thank you. I appreciate that. Did you bring Janet here on a motorcycle?" Teresa asked cautiously.

"Yes, ma'am, I did," Jake replied.

"It's okay, Mom. He's a careful driver."

"But where's your vehicle?"

"My friends are driving it home. Let's go see Daddy." She took her mother by the elbow and turned her toward the elevators.

As they walked, Teresa whispered, "What happened to your eye?"

"Just a freak accident. We were on a ropes course and I lost my balance and hit a pole. I'm fine." Once in the elevator, Janet continued. "Jake's family lives in Wisconsin now. He's in the military."

"I see," Teresa commented. "Well, I do appreciate your driving Janet all the way home. You've come a good bit out of your way. How are your folks?"

"My folks are fine, thanks. And I'm happy I could bring Janet home. No trouble at all."

"Is Daddy going to be okay, Mom?"

"The neurologist says he will. Luckily, the ambulance was on the scene right away and he got medical treatment on the way to the hospital. He had what they call an ischemic stroke which they are treating with medication to break up blood clots. It's unlikely that Martin will need surgery, but it will be a few days before we'll know about disability."

The elevator dinged and the doors opened onto the brightly lit floor of the ICU.

"This way," Teresa waved them on.

Martin lay with eyes closed on the narrow hospital bed, covered with white sheets up to his neck. Janet teared up immediately upon seeing him; she had never known her daddy to be hospitalized for any reason. Jake lingered in the hallway until Janet insisted he come inside the room.

"Hi, Daddy, it's Janet. I'm here," she struggled. "Can I hold his hand?" she asked her mother.

Teresa nodded.

"Daddy, you're in the hospital, and you've had a stroke. But you're going to be just fine," Janet said, rubbing the back of his warm hand. "I have a friend with me. Jake. You'll like him. He brought me here to see you." Her voice caught in her throat. Jake gently rubbed the back of Janet's neck, and Teresa could see that there was more than friendship between the two.

Martin lay motionless and Janet was on the verge of tears. Suddenly, she felt his fingers squeeze hers ever so slightly. She gasped.

"What is it?" Teresa asked, alarmed.

"He squeezed my hand!"

Overjoyed, Teresa cried, "I knew it! I knew once you got here, he would come around!"

Jake quietly watched the women, feeling a little out of place. "Mrs. Kayler, is there anything we can do for you? Anything at all?"

"Teresa."

"I'm sorry?"

"Call me Teresa, please. And yes, you can go by the house and make sure I turned off the oven. I was about to bake some muffins for breakfast when this happened."

"Sure thing. Anything else?"

They were interrupted by the nurse on duty who stepped in to check Martin's monitors and to replace an empty bag on the IV pole. "You can have a few more minutes with Mr. Kayler, but then I'll have to ask you to leave," she said apologetically. "He needs to rest." She ducked out of the room with a courteous smile.

"Mom, what about Lucy? I've been checking my phone all day long and no one has called." Janet's eyes filled with tears.

"Honey, she'll turn up. I didn't want to tell you this but they found her leash with the collar attached. So she has no identification on her. But she can't have gone far with those little legs. Someone has her, I'm sure."

"So what should I do? Should I put signs up?"

"Go by my house first, check the oven, and see if she's there. Ask around. Our neighbors know that we were keeping her. Then go by your house. If no one has seen her, call animal control and call the local shelters. She'll turn up. I just know it."

"But today is Sunday. They'll be closed."

"Go. Pray. I'll stay here with Martin. I'm not leaving," Teresa assured her.

"Okay, but we'll be back later tonight. I'll bring your toiletries and a change of clothes."

"Oh, that would be wonderful! Come here, honey." She reached for Janet and hugged her fiercely. "I want to hear all about your cruise." Then she turned to Jake and embraced him, as well. "I'm glad you're here," she mumbled into his tee shirt.

∼

As the two pulled up in front of the Kaylers' home, Janet whooped at the sight of little Lucy in the front yard, all alone, lying next to the front porch steps. The little dog wriggled with excitement at the sight of her owner.

"Lucy! Where have you been, baby girl?" Janet snatched her up and held her tightly against her chest, kissing the puppy's head over and over.

"Oh, my gosh, I'm so glad you're okay, little girl!"

Jake grinned at the two of them, happy for the good outcome. He thought of his own dog and how it would crush him if his boxer were to disappear.

"Go on inside and do what you need to do," he said. "I'll stay out here and play with Lucy."

"You're the best!" Janet called out, and ran up the stairs two at a time.

Lucy stared up at Jake and trotted over to sniff his shoes.

"You're a cute little thing, you know that?" He scooped her up and held her in front of his face, touching her wet nose with his own. He could smell her puppy breath when she licked him with her pink tongue.

Soon Janet appeared in the doorway. "All set. Let's go to my house and I'll fix us some dinner. You must be exhausted from all that driving."

"Sounds good. How far is your house?"

"It's about a half mile, that way," she pointed. "Not far at all."

"Let's go," Jake said, digging for his motorcycle key.

Donning their helmets, Janet settled in behind him with Lucy between them, Janet's arms pinning her in. She directed Jake to her neighborhood and, just minutes later, he pulled onto her street and into her driveway, killing the motor.

"Nice place," he nodded, removing the helmet.

"Thanks. I'm still unpacking, but it's home."

Lucy left a little deposit in the grass before scampering toward the front porch, attempting to climb the bottom step but falling backwards. Jake chuckled, picking her up. "Your little legs aren't made for climbing, Lucy. Just wait 'til you meet Boss. He can jump anything."

Janet's shoulders slumped as she stood at the front door. "Uh-oh. We have a problem."

"What's that?'

"I don't have my keys. I gave them to Aimee to drive my car back."

Jake looked around, pondering the situation.

"Oh, wait! I have a spare house key! Daddy insisted that I hide one behind this shutter," she exclaimed, plucking it from its hiding place. At the thought of her thoughtful and protective father she felt a lump in her throat.

"I like the way your dad thinks."

"Welcome to my home," Janet said as she headed straight to the kitchen, turning on lights. She filled Lucy's food and water bowls and found her red play toy. Then she rummaged through the refrigerator and freezer. "How about sloppy joes?"

"That sounds great!" he replied, "If it's not too much trouble."

Janet wrapped her arms around Jake. "Are you kidding? You've been amazing. Thank you for bringing me home."

He rubbed her back in little circles. "You have hat-hair."

Janet giggled. "Yeah, I caught a glimpse of myself in the glass windows of the hospital." She leaned over and gave her dark locks a good shake. "But the helmet kept the bugs out. I hope."

"I would love you even with bugs in your hair," Jake said, and then flinched at his slip of the tongue.

Janet pretended not to notice. "Do you like Tator Tots?"

"What are Tator Tots?"

"You'll see," Janet smiled. "They're better than French fries." She found a package of frozen hamburger meat and placed it in the microwave to defrost, then turned on the oven for the tots. "How about a beer?"

"I'd love a beer. I was about to ask."

"Here you go," she said, handing him a Bud Light. "Go ahead, look around if you want. There's a pool out back."

"First I need to…"

"Bathroom's on the right down that hall."

While Janet prepared dinner Jake made himself at home, wandering around the back yard and checking out the pool while sipping his beer. He sat down in a patio chair and removed his tee shirt, enjoying an evening breeze. Janet watched from the kitchen window, overwhelmed by all that had happened in the past week. As she stared at Jake she felt such a rush of desire that it made her heady. She was falling in love, and fast. But it wasn't just Jake's good looks that made him so attractive. He was a man of integrity, a man who valued family and seemed to have deep respect for women. A man who measured up to her daddy, sitting right here on her patio. She marveled at her good fortune.

"Dinner's ready," she reported from the door. "How many can you eat?"

Jake wriggled back into his tee shirt and came inside to inspect the toasted hamburger buns. "Three," he decided. "Those must be Tator tots," he nodded at the pan of sizzling nuggets. He popped one into his mouth and chewed appreciatively.

"Careful! They're hot! And you're supposed to dip them in ketchup."

They filled their plates and sat down together at the table. Janet handed Jake another beer.

"This is nice," he murmured, wolfing down the first sandwich and reaching for another.

"You want cheese? I have some shredded cheese if you want."

"No, I'm good. This is perfect. I was famished."

"I was thinking, Jake. Why don't you plan to stay here with Lucy while I go back to the hospital? You need to rest. You can watch TV or whatever."

Jake considered the offer. "I'm happy to go with you."

"There's no need, not until daddy makes some progress. I don't plan to stay more than a couple of hours."

"Then I'll stay here. Okay if I take a shower?"

"Of course! Make yourself at home."

Fifteen minutes later Janet kissed Jake on the cheek and said, "Okay, I'm leaving now, and you'd better be here when I get back."

He chuckled and replied, "I'll probably be sacked out on the couch with Lucy."

"There's ice cream in the freezer. See you soon!" she waved and then, for the second time, realized she didn't have her keys. "Oh. I guess you'll have to drop me off," she said sheepishly.

Jake jumped up. "Let's go!"

∼

Jake sat on Janet's couch with a dish of cookie dough ice cream, Lucy tucked in close beside him. The TV was turned to "America's Funniest Home Videos" but he muted the sound when his phone buzzed.

"Hi," he answered.

"Hi, yourself. What are you doing?"

"Lucy and I are watching TV. How's your dad?"

"He's about the same. No better, no worse. I got another little squeeze from his hand, and so did mom."

"Ah, that's a good sign."

"Mom is going to run me home in a little while, so you don't have to come get me."

"Well, that's nice of her, but it's no trouble for me," Jake said.

"She says you need to rest after driving 'that big hog' all day."

"She said that?"

"Yeah. Oh, and Aimee called. The girls made it home just fine. I told her to keep my Bronco at her house and I'll get it tomorrow."

"Is it okay if I park my motorcycle in your garage, then?"

"Of course. Hey, I just saw a nurse go into Daddy's room, so…"

"Go. Get an update. I'll see you later."

Jake moved his bike into the garage and closed the garage door. He returned to the living room and no sooner had he gotten settled against the pillows when there was a knock on the front door.

"Who could that be, Lucy?" He strode to the door and pulled it open to find a lanky young man holding a large bouquet of red roses, and a broom. The broom looked to be brand new and was tied with a red bow to match the roses.

"Hello," Jake said.

The visitor stepped back in surprise, speechless. Jake easily assessed the situation; this had to be Lee, Janet's ex.

"Can I help you? Are you looking for Janet?"

"Well, yeah, I mean, I was driving by and I saw lights on and, I mean, I know she went on a cruise or something, but, is she back?"

Jake extended his hand. "I'm Jake DeLuca," he said.

"I'm Lee Harris. Janet and I were…" He faltered for words.

"She told me about you. Would you like to come in?" Jake stepped away from the door, and Lee timidly stepped inside, not knowing what to do with the flowers.

"Here, I'll put them on the kitchen table," Jake said. When he returned he said, "Have a seat," and then he asked, "What's with the broom, man?"

"Oh, this," Lee chuckled, embarrassed. "There's a story. You had to be there." He set the broom by the front door.

"Janet is home from the cruise but she's up at the hospital. Did you hear about her dad?"

"Martin? No, what about him?"

"He's had a stroke. It happened early this morning. He's at Conway Regional."

"Gosh, is he gonna be okay?"

"Too early to tell. Janet will be home soon if you want to ask her. You want a beer or something?"

"No, thanks." Lee took a chair and stared curiously at Jake. "So, who are you?" he managed. "You're not from around here."

"Funny story. Janet and I knew each other when we were kids. Lived in the same neighborhood, in Fort Smith. It was a real coincidence that we ran into each other on the cruise."

Lee absorbed this information, trying not to jump to conclusions.

"I drove her back to Arkansas when she heard the news about her dad. It was the quickest way to get her home."

The two watched the television in silence until Lee spoke again. "Okay, so..."

At that moment the front door opened and Janet stepped inside, having already seen Lee's vehicle in the driveway. "Yikes," she said.

"Lee and I were just getting acquainted," Jake said.

Janet faced Lee. "What are you doing here?"

"I saw lights on and thought you were home. I brought you a new broom and...some flowers." He looked away.

Embarrassed, Janet picked Lucy up and made her way to the kitchen on the pretext of feeding the little dog. Jake hopped up off the couch and followed her.

"I know this is awkward, but talk to him, Janet. He seems like a nice enough guy. He had good intentions."

"He's so *presumptuous!*" she hissed.

Jake half-smiled. "He's just hopeful, babe. I can't blame him. You told me that it ended badly, so maybe this is a chance to talk it out. If it's over between you two, you need to make him understand why."

"Oh, it's over, all right."

"Then let him have some closure."

Janet looked up into Jake's eyes. "Okay. You're right."

Jake rinsed dishes in the sink while Janet invited Lee to sit with her on the patio. Lee sat slump-shouldered with his knees wide apart, his hands clasped between them. Janet pulled her chair around to face him, her face earnest but kind. Jake returned to his television show.

~

Twenty minutes later, the lovebirds were on the couch and Lee had gone home. Jake draped his arm around Janet, pulling her close.
"You smell nice," she murmured.
"Soap."
She looked up into his eyes. "Thank you. I feel better now."
"You're welcome. And he'll be fine, don't worry."
After a moment Janet said, "My mother told me to tell you something."
"What's that?"
"She said to tell you that she likes you very much, and she hopes that you will stay for a few days."
"Score!" Jake smiled. "Now I just have to win your dad over."

23

The Silverstones

Birdie walked barefooted to the mailbox of her Tallahassee home and retrieved a handful of envelopes and some junk mail. As she nonchalantly rifled through the stack she noticed a return address bearing the cruise line logo. Anxiously, she tore open the letter.

Dear Ms. Clarke:
  Thank you for your letter inquiring about the passengers who assisted your grandson on the evening of June 21st. By your account, your grandson wandered alone throughout the ship for approximately ninety minutes.
  First, we are grateful for his safe return, and we sincerely regret what had to be a frightening experience for both of you. We pride ourselves on the safety and security of our passengers and are confident that, had he not been discovered by fellow passengers, our cameras would have located your grandson.

You have requested contact information for Mr. and Mrs. Silverstone to thank them for their kind assistance. However, after an extensive search in our database, we find neither Charles Silverstone nor any passengers with that surname who sailed that week. Furthermore, we have no permanent residents on our ship.

However, and quite by coincidence, we did find record of a Charles and Anna Silverstone who, years ago, sailed with us for an extended period of time. Mr. Silverstone was a distinguished army veteran and Mrs. Silverstone was a writer. Both are deceased.

I'm sorry that we are not able to help you in your search. Best wishes to you and your family and we invite you to sail with us again soon!

Yours truly,

Walter L. Brannon
Guest Services

24

Six Months Later – Wedding Bells

Janet squeezed her dad's arm. "This is it, Daddy! Are you going to be okay?"

"Of course I'll be okay. I wouldn't miss this for the world." Martin gave her a lop-sided smile. His stroke had left him with partial paralysis of his face and a limp in one leg.

"I promise to walk slowly, like in rehearsal, and you can lean on me if you need to," Janet offered.

"Don't you worry about me, honey. This is your big day and I won't screw it up."

"I know, but..."

The mother of the bride sat perched on the arm of a couch. "You look mighty handsome, Martin," she smiled at her husband. "And Janet. Oh, my, that dress is stunning on you."

Janet twirled in front of the floor length mirror in the bride's dressing room of their church, pleased with what she saw. She had chosen a pure white gown of sleek matte silk with an open boat neckline and three quarter length sleeves. With no embroidery, no lace, and no beading, the gown was all about simplicity, true to Janet's style. Her hair had been gathered up into a soft up-do.

"Thank you, Mom. I'm glad we settled on this one."

"It's the perfect gown for a winter wedding. Are you nervous?"

"Yes. And no. I'm just ready to do this! Daddy, have you seen Jake yet?"

"I spoke with him just a bit ago. He's pacing around like a nervous cat, but he looks spiffy."

"Spiffy?" Janet smiled at her dad's choice of words. "What time is it now?"

"It's time to get these two married!" Jake's mother exclaimed from the doorway.

"Hi, Marilyn! Come on in here!" Teresa patted the couch cushion.

Marilyn DeLuca reached for Janet and hugged her gently. "Janet, look at you! Aren't you just beautiful!" Marilyn and her husband, John, had grown quite fond of Janet in the short time they had gotten reacquainted with her as an adult woman. She seemed the perfect match for their son.

"Where's Chelsey?" Janet asked, referring to Jake's sister.

"She and Chad are already seated in the sanctuary. Chelsey is afraid she might go into labor during the ceremony."

Janet's eyes grew wide.

"I'm only kidding, honey," Marilyn assured her. "I think."

"Well, I'm going to get out of here," Martin said. "I'll see you in the lobby, sweetie," he said to his daughter, giving her a hug. "I'll be waiting for you." Slowly, he shuffled from the room on his cane. Janet watched him go with a lump in her throat.

Jake and Janet had decided against having a wedding party. They wanted a simple ceremony with minimal fanfare. Martin would walk Janet down the aisle and everyone else would be seated as guests.

The wedding planner, an older woman and a friend of Teresa, stuck her head in the door. "It's time, honey," she said to the bride.

Janet's heart lurched and she took a deep breath. "Mom," she faltered, reaching for her mother's hand.

"Baby, you're going to do just great. All you have to do is smile and walk. I've never been more proud of you, and I'm so happy for you. Now let's go. Daddy's waiting."

Soft classical music played as Jake stood at the altar, looking sharp in a dark suit with a pale blue tie. His hair had grown out and was styled with a bit of gel. He smiled warmly at Janet's mother as she was ushered in, and he winked at his own mother and father on the front row.

On the bride's side of the sanctuary, the third and fourth pews were filled with Janet's best friends. Sue Ellen and Dillard sat side by side wearing their Sunday best. Aimee and Travis sat shoulder to shoulder, holding hands. Howard had made the trip from Georgia and sat on one side of Birdie while Jamal sat on the other, with Fran next to him.

Birdie leaned across Howard to whisper to Sue Ellen. "You look fantastic! I almost didn't recognize you!"

"I've lost thirty pounds," Sue Ellen whispered back. "I joined Weight Watchers. And I got a new hairdo!" She patted her short, stylish bob, the permed ringlets now gone.

"You look beautiful," Birdie assured her, and Sue Ellen beamed at Dillard who nodded in agreement.

Excitement was in the air as the guests waited for the ceremony to begin. When the soft music turned into the traditional wedding march, everyone rose and turned to face the back of the church where Janet stood with her father.

The two began their procession down the aisle with Martin using his cane for support. Janet felt like she was in a dream, her eyes trained on Jake up ahead. Her hand shook as she gripped her bouquet, an elaborate combination of pale blue and white blossoms with long satin ribbons trailing to the floor. As they neared the front of the church her eyes glistened at the sight of her dear friends on the left side, all beaming and wiping their eyes. Upon reaching the altar, Janet turned and handed her bouquet to her mother, and the two women embraced briefly.

"Who gives this woman in marriage?" the minister asked.

"Her mother and I do," Martin replied. Janet kissed him on the cheek and held her breath as he released his grip on her arm and carefully made his way to the front pew, where he sat down beside Teresa.

Jake, meanwhile, was struggling with emotion, trying to suppress a big lump in his throat. His bride looked stunning, her face glowing, her makeup beautifully done. He offered his arm to her, as they had rehearsed, and she stepped up to take her place beside him. Sensing his nervousness, Janet mimicked a soft kiss with her lips to help him relax and they smiled at each other, completely and madly in love.

∼

The reception following was a rowdy affair. A local band had been hired and the church's large family life center resonated with dance music. Tables draped in white cloths were laden with appetizers and finger foods and two bartenders stood ready to keep the liquor flowing.

Sue Ellen and Dillard were the first ones on the dance floor, followed by the school principal and his wife and a drove of others.

Janet and Jake sat at a table with Aimee and Travis, who were very much in love, having made the best of a long-distance relationship. Travis, no longer with the cruise line, was sporting a short beard and Aimee had gained a little weight which looked good on her. Gone were her Caribbean braids; her long, straight hair had been shortened to a casual, shoulder-length style.

Aimee leaned over to Jake. "Did Janet tell you? Travis is thinking about moving to Arkansas! He likes it here."

"Cool!" Jake replied, turning to Travis. "What kind of work are you looking for?"

"If I can swing it, I'd like to open a small seafood restaurant, or maybe an upscale coffee house. Seems like something I'd enjoy."

"And he would be so good at it!" Aimee cut in. "Travis likes having a lot going on. He's so hyper," she giggled.

"She's right. I am. And I think Arkansas is great. It feels like home. You want some more champagne, babe?"

"Please," Aimee smiled. Once he was out of earshot, she leaned in to her friends. "Oh, my God. Isn't he just so sweet? I'm crazy about him!"

Sue Ellen appeared, red-faced and panting, with Dillard trailing behind her. "I haven't had this much fun since our cruise!" she gasped. "Dillard, honey, would you go get me a plate of food? You know what I like." Dillard dutifully headed for the buffet table as Sue

Ellen sat down. "Just no olives!" she called out after him. He waved without turning around.

Fran joined the table with her own plate of food and a bourbon and Coke. "Congratulations, you two," she smiled at the newlyweds, kissing Janet on the cheek. "I couldn't be happier for you."

"Thank you," they replied in unison.

"When do you leave for your honeymoon?"

"In the morning. We fly out of Little Rock at 9:40."

"Where are you headed?" Travis asked, catching the tail end of the conversation as he returned to the table.

"Colorado. Crested Butte," Jake replied. "It's a popular ski resort that we've heard a lot about it. We both want to learn to ski."

"And to snowboard," Janet added. "I can hardly wait!" She hugged Jake's arm, her solitaire diamond ring sparkling under the lights.

Before anyone could question them further, a band member announced that it was time for the newlyweds to have their dance. The lights dimmed and the dance floor cleared. Alone on the floor and feeling very special, Jake and Janet embraced and swayed back and forth to their chosen song as cameras flashed.

"You look gorgeous," Jake murmured. "I'm so lucky."

Janet was learning to accept Jake's compliments gracefully. "Thank you, babe. You look pretty amazing, yourself. By the way, I promise not to get fat on you."

"With the exception of pregnancies," Jake clarified.

"Pregnancies, plural?"

"That's what I said."

Janet rested her head on Jake's shoulder and sighed happily. "What do you think the dogs are doing?" she asked.

"Boss is trying to hump Lucy but, you know, she's so short."

Janet laughed out loud. "You think they'll be okay while we're in Colorado?"

"Janet, your mother feeds them pancakes. They'll be fine."

"I love you," Janet whispered. "I'm so happy."

He kissed her forehead. "I love you, too."

"Jake, have you ever thought that life is just a big game of chance? That so much of what happens to us is based on what-ifs?"

Jake pulled back to peer at his wife. "Getting philosophical on me?"

"Think about it! I won ten thousand dollars on a lottery ticket – a small fortune for me - but only because I was thirsty. If I hadn't been thirsty I wouldn't have gone inside the gas station for an Icee, and I wouldn't have bought the lottery ticket. And without the lottery ticket I wouldn't have been on the cruise and we wouldn't be married now. So the question is, did God make me thirsty?"

Jake replied thoughtfully, "The Bible says, yes. Jeremiah 29:11 – *For I know the plans I have for you.*"

"Okay, so, based on that same line of thinking, did God orchestrate that tarantula to jump on me in Honduras? Because if it weren't for the tarantula, Aimee wouldn't have fainted and you wouldn't have stopped to help and I'd never have met you. Have you ever thought about that?"

"Actually, I have," he nodded.

"So, are we to believe that a freakishly large insect changed the course of our lives? Is life really that hit or miss?"

"Apparently so," Jake was smiling now.

"All my life I've lived by the logic that there are practical explanations for why things happen, that there is an order of things, a pathway of making personal choices which lead us to our destiny. I thought that I would meet my soulmate at a teachers' conference, or at church, or volunteering at the soup kitchen, doing all the right things and lining up my destiny. But then a big hairy spider came along and shattered that logic."

"You were hard on the spider, as I recall."

Janet grinned. "I was, wasn't I? By the way, that wasn't my first encounter with a tarantula. Remind me to tell you that story some time. Totally different outcome."

"I'll look forward to it."

Their song ended and the music ramped up and a barrage of guests hit the dance floor. Aimee and Travis showed off their moves through two consecutive fast songs before collapsing into chairs. A tipsy Sue Ellen tried to bump hips with anyone who would let her, while Dillard danced with himself, munching on a chocolate covered strawberry. Grant and Andrew, both plastered, flirted shamelessly with the ladies. Grant pulled Fran to the dance floor and Andrew reached for Birdie, who obliged after a nod from Howard.

Jamal and Howard sat alone at the table. Howard pulled his chair closer to Jamal and cleared his throat. "We like each other, don't we, Jamal?" he asked.

"Sure, we like each other."

"You and Birdie and I get along just fine, don't we?"

"Yes, sir." Jamal glanced warily at Howard, wondering if he had done something wrong and was about to get a scolding.

Howard offered Jamal a piece of gum from a pack, and took one for himself. "I've been thinking," he said as he folded the paper wrapper, creasing its length. "I've been thinking," he repeated. "What if we were to come together as a family? You know, the three of us, sharing a home."

"You want to move in with my grandma?"

"No, no! What I mean is, what if she and I were to get married? What would you think about that?"

Jamal studied the table top while Howard continued to make sharp creases in the gum wrapper. "Would that make you my grandfather?"

"Well, I imagine I can be anything you want me to be. Your father, your grandfather, or just your good buddy. You can still call me Howard, if you'd like, but I'll settle for whatever you come up with."

Jamal pursed his lips and considered the idea. "What does Birdie think about it?"

"Oh, she doesn't know a thing about this! And you can't tell her, either. See, I wanted to make sure it was okay with you before I ask her to marry me."

"Oh," Jamal replied. He tugged on his lower lip. "Well, do you love her?"

"I do, son. I do. She's a fine woman and I would take very good care of the both of you, if she were to say yes."

"I think she will say yes."

Howard beamed. "I hope you're right. So, do I have your approval to ask Birdie to marry me?"

"Sure, you can ask her. Let's go ask her right now."

"No! Not right now, son. I need to buy a ring and do this properly, you know, at the right time."

"Why?"

"Because she deserves a ring and a proper proposal, in a quiet place. Not here."

"Okay. Is that all?" Jamal asked, itching to get on the dance floor.

"That's all. But remember, this is between you and me. Can you keep a secret?"

"Yes, sir, I promise I won't tell Birdie."

Jamal jumped down from his chair, hesitated, and then threw his arms around Howard before making a beeline to the dance floor. The crowd soon widened to form a circle around the little boy who stole the show.

Janet's eyes shined as she watched Jamal and surveyed her happy guests, pleased to see so many fellow teachers. Jake was posing for pictures with his Army buddies across the room. The band slowed its tempo and Janet watched as Howard left his chair and offered his hand to Birdie for a slow dance. Fran, too, was watching with a wistful look on her face. Janet quickly crossed the room to sit beside her friend.

"They make a handsome couple, don't they?" Fran said, nodding at Birdie and Howard.

"They do, indeed."

"Funny how that happened," Fran continued. "I mean, how Jamal introduced them. Wonder how he knew they'd be right for each other?"

"I'm sure I don't know. Kids tend to see things for what they are, without overthinking like we adults do," Janet chuckled.

"Janet, remember how Birdie told us that story about her mother? About how she saw a 'man of fire' in Birdie's life?"

"Yes, I remember," Janet said. "An omen of gloom and doom."

"Ironic, isn't it, that Birdie ended up with a 'man of fire,' anyway."

"I'm not sure what you mean."

"Howard was a firefighter, for Pete's sake! He pulled people from the flames of those smoke-filled, burning towers, all those years ago."

Janet slowly turned her head to Fran, her eyes wide. "So Howard is the man of fire? The man that Mada saw in Birdie's future?"

Fran only raised her eyebrows, giving Janet time to consider the idea.

"Of course! You're right, Fran! How did you ever make that connection?"

Fran took a sip of her bourbon. "It seems obvious now, doesn't it?"

"Mada was wrong, then."

Fran gazed at Birdie and Howard, dancing with their foreheads touching and their eyes closed.

"Let's just say that Mada was right *and* wrong."

A microphone squawked and all eyes turned to the stage, where Aimee stood grinning with the band. Janet and Fran grabbed each other's hands.

"She's going to sing!"

"Travis' doing, no doubt!"

The band launched into a sexy intro and, fueled by champagne, Aimee belted out a Taylor Swift number in a breathy, sultry voice which brought the crowd to their feet. Travis clapped the loudest and the longest, fist-pumping the air for the woman he loved.

"Wow. You think you know someone," Fran remarked. "That girl is just full of surprises."

Janet and Jake were summoned across the room to the cake table for photographs, leaving Fran, Sue Ellen, and Birdie at the table. Aimee plopped down, breathless from her song.

"Bravo, Aimee! I do believe you have found your calling," Birdie exclaimed.

"Yes, you are quite the diva once you've had some liquor," Fran remarked. "That was fun to watch!"

"Look at us!" Sue Ellen smiled. "All of us together again. Well, except for Janet over there."

"Ladies, I have some news," Fran blurted out, and all eyes turned to her.

"I won't be back after Christmas to finish the school year. I lost my job."

There were gasps all around. Sue Ellen's face went slack as she absorbed the information. "Wh-what?"

"They're putting me out to pasture, so to speak. I found out yesterday," Fran explained.

"But they can't do that!" Sue Ellen contended angrily. "Why would they do that?"

Fran lifted her jaw. "It's okay, Sue. It's time I quit teaching, and I think you know that." She reached for Sue's hand and patted it as her friend began to cry.

Aimee and Birdie exchanged glances, not sure what was happening.

Fran took a deep breath and continued. "I've been making a lot of mistakes lately. At home, at school…" Her voice trailed off and she struggled for composure. "One of the Rayburn twins argued with me over a math problem which I had marked wrong on her worksheet. I sent her to the principal's office. Turns out, she was right."

"But that's no reason to…"

"That's not all, honey. I left school one day when the lunch bell rang, thinking it was time to go home. I drove all the way to my house before I realized the school day wasn't over." Fran's voice cracked. "And then I couldn't find my way back. I'm sure you heard about that."

Sue Ellen had heard about it. Now she was full on bawling, her face beet red.

"Don't cry, you knucklehead. No more tears, okay?" Fran handed her a cocktail napkin and then realized that Birdie and Aimee were struggling with their emotions, as well.

"Hey, guys! I think it's for the best, really. A blessing in disguise. But promise me you won't tell Janet. I don't want her to know, at least not yet. This is her wedding day and I won't spoil it for her."

Chins trembled around the table. "Promise me!" Fran demanded. "Promise you won't say a word to Janet."

Heads nodded slowly.

"I'll be just fine. I'll start that vegetable garden, and I'll go visit Martha in Bella Vista. Heck, I might even get a dog. Or a cat. It is what it is, and I intend to make the best of it. Life goes on."

They all joined hands and sat quietly together, Sue Ellen taking ragged breaths. Truth be known, not a day had gone by that she had not puzzled over Fran's shoplifting incident, among other things.

Jamal appeared and tugged on his grandmother's sleeve. "Is it time yet, Birdie?"

"Not yet, honey. Janet will let you know. We're about to have some wedding cake. Come with me!"

The cake stood tall, like the bride - four deep layers of pink champagne cake frosted with vanilla buttercream. Jake's groom's cake was of rich chocolate with a cappuccino mousse filling and topped with an impressive model helicopter.

"Which cake would you like to try?" Birdie asked her grandson.

"I want to try the helicopter cake!"

The server smiled at him. "Okay, hold your plate out. Use both hands. Here it comes!" She placed a generous slice on his glass plate and then tucked a fork into the pocket of his jacket.

"Thank you," Jamal said. "That's a really cool helicopter."

Martin Kayler happened to be standing nearby and heard Jamal's comment. "It is a nice reproduction, if I do say so myself," he said to the boy. "I made it myself."

"You did? The cake, or the helicopter?"

"The helicopter. It started out as a million pieces in a box."

Teresa Kayler stepped up beside her husband. "It took him hours," she smiled. "But he was determined."

"I'm very proud of my son-in-law. Did you know that he's a helicopter pilot in the Army?"

"Wow! I didn't know that!" With that, Jamal took off in search of Jake, hoping to hear some stories.

"Be careful with that plate!" Birdie called out after him.

The newlyweds sat side by side at the family table, sampling their cakes. Janet took a bite and Jake planted a kiss on her mouth before she could swallow. Her eyes were starry from the champagne and Jake's hair had flopped onto his forehead.

"I can't wait to get you out of here," he said.

"When do you think we can leave?" she asked, swallowing.

Before he could answer, Jamal appeared at Jake's elbow with chocolate icing lining his mouth. "That man over there said you fly helicopters. Is it true?"

"It is!" Jake answered, turning to grin at the boy.

"Will you take me on a ride sometime?"

"Hm, not sure I can manage that. The helicopters that I fly are owned by the government."

"Oh," Jamal said, clearly disappointed.

"Hey, Jamal," Janet said, "come here." She whispered into his ear and he perked up right away, nodding his head enthusiastically. She pointed to a door and Jamal hurried to take his post.

Meanwhile, the female guests were gathering on the dance floor; it was time for Janet to throw her bouquet. It did not go unnoticed that she aimed for Aimee, who caught it effortlessly.

Janet's father then took the microphone and, in his shaky voice, announced that the newlyweds were about to make their departure. Everyone stood, champagne glasses in hand, and the room erupted with cheers as Jake and Janet waved and blew kisses. Janet borrowed the microphone from her father and said, "Thank you, everyone, for coming! We love you all! Please take a party favor on your way out!"

And then, without further ado, they were gone.

Jamal stood proudly at the exit door holding a decorative wicker basket full of scratch-off lottery tickets. As the guests filed past he made sure that they each took one.

"What's this?" one man asked.

"It's a lottery ticket," Jamal replied. "Maybe you'll win some money!"

"Thanks," the man replied, inspecting the ticket. "This is nice, but I never win anything." He tucked the ticket into his coat pocket, nodded and went on his way.

Jamal watched him go and muttered, "Well, mister, you're going to win this time."

ALSO BY LYNN RICHARDSON:

The Big Tickle
Steel Bridge Road
Uncle Wilson
The Far Side of the Orchard
Lucky Old Coot

www.amazon.com

Made in the USA
Coppell, TX
18 July 2020

31272029R00146